For Alora and Erienne

John Rabe is a retired South African legal, litigation and bankruptcy specialist who has been a car nut since he was a toddler! He has written many motor related articles for various publications and is an enthusiastic model car collector and builder. Armchair activities include watching cricket and rugby. He is married to Brenda and has a daughter and two grandchildren in New Zealand.

John Rabé

SWITCHED FORTUNES

AUSTIN MACAULEY
PUBLISHERS LTD.

A CIP catalogue record for this title is available from the British Library.

ISBN 9781785547638 (paperback)
ISBN 9781785547645 (hardback)
ISBN 9781785547652 (eBook)

www.austinmacauley.com

First Published (2016)
Austin Macauley Publishers Ltd.
25 Canada Square
Canary Wharf
London
E14 5LQ

Chapter 1

He was fast approaching the hump towards the end of Mulsanne Straight. Glancing in his mirrors he was sure that the white Porsche had narrowed the gap. The blazing headlamps appeared closer.

The headphones in his helmet crackled.

"How are things going Kevin?"

"The engine feels healthy enough, but the loss of those five hundred revs is hurting, Werner is definitely gaining."

"Hang in there Kev, you're halfway to the pits. Don't worry, Werner is due in at any time as well. We'll sort your electrics, you won't lose much time... you'll easily catch him later."

He glanced in the mirror again. The blazing headlamps of the German car were metres away. The chicane was coming...

***

"Wakey, wakey, Dad, no more sleeping. Time to get up, you promised to swim with me today!"

Kevin Richardson woke with a start. His attractive honey-blonde haired wife Ann and daughter Tracey were leaning over the foot of the bed grinning. Tracey had lifted the corner of the duvet and was tickling his foot. He involuntary pulled it away as the electrical sensation surged through his befuddled mind. He turned to look at the clock radio on the side pedestal. The digital letters read 7:00.

"Hey what's this, can't you leave a guy in peace on a Sunday morning? I was dreaming of my race at Le Mans!"

"Too bad, Kev. You've relived that race hundreds of times over. You'll soon have another chance to do even better. Besides, I need some milk and fruit juice for breakfast. Won't you pleeease fetch some?" Ann's eyes were trying to register mock regret that she had rudely interrupted his dream, but the creases at the corner of her mouth and dimples in her cheeks told another story.

"That's what I call pathetic planning. How do you run out of these basic commodities over a weekend?" His weak attempt at trying to sound really annoyed lacked conviction.

***

Johannesburg, South Africa

Kevin parked the gunmetal BMW some twenty metres into the driveway alongside the east wall of his home and clambered out. Holding the remote, he looked towards the still closing automated steel-barred gates. A silver Audi with distinctive alloy wheels idled past the gate along the road beyond the sidewalk. The male passenger stared at him while talking animatedly on a cell phone held to his right ear. Kevin noted the driver's curiosity as he craned his neck around his passenger to see down the driveway as well. Although the front window had been wound down, the car was too far away for Kevin to distinguish any features.

"What nosey buggers!" Richardson muttered as he turned on his heel. Something about the car bothered him for a few moments. Where had he seen it before? Had it been at the supermarket, or had he hooted at it the day before? He dismissed the subject from his mind and carried the groceries into the house.

***

The purring became a roar, the roar a howl, as the 200 plus horsepower threatened to rip through the alligator-shaped bonnet. The garage walls stopped reverberating as the needle of the rev-counter swung back and settled at a steady idle. It was just as well neighbours Eric and June were away for the weekend. Their Sunday morning sleep would otherwise have been shattered. The perpetrator of the noise looked at his watch. Only half past nine, but what a glorious day! How could people sleep late during weather like this?

Kevin Richardson was smiling as he switched off the ignition and the twin exhausts stopped burbling. He loved the "Big Cats" – the four-wheeled kind, designed by Bill Lyons – Jaguars to be precise. His acquisition of the XK 140 Roadster six months before had been the fulfilment of a boyhood dream. The sleek British Racing Green machine had made a bigger hole in his pocket than he cared to divulge to Ann, but had in any event been paid for out of his second place earnings from last year's Le Mans 24 Hours endurance race. Purists argued that the XK 120 was the ultimate XK, as it was lighter and purer of style. Kevin had however, managed to acquire an immaculate condition factory built "Special Equipment" version of the XK 140 Roadster which had been fitted with a more powerful engine at the factory. This more than compensated for the weight brought about by the improved creature comforts.

Success in motor racing had come relatively late in life to Richardson, who at thirty-eight was a freelance car designer. At just under six foot, he was a trim one hundred and fifty pounds. His blond hair of but a few years before, had turned light brown, but he was becoming increasingly dismayed by the relentless "salt 'n pepper" takeover and greying sideburns. Yesterday's trip to Armando the local Italian hairdresser had resulted in it being cropped quite short with the back just over the collar. Irregular visits resulted in a much denser head of hair but displayed more grey than he liked. His light bronze tanned face and arms were the result of time spent on the cricket field and tennis court in summer. Winter saw him playing as much "Action Cricket" as could be fitted in between business trips. He also enjoyed hiking but was finding less and less time to get out into the wide open spaces. Although not classically handsome, he was not bad looking. Green eyes and a slightly aquiline nose gave his face character.

Until five years ago his track exploits had been confined to club racing where a tight budget and no sponsorship had restricted his natural ability following several expensive shunts. This had still not prevented him and the 1967 Renault Gordini 1300 from showing a clean pair of rear wheels to often much bigger-engined opposition in consecutive Historic Saloon Car racing championships.

A last-minute withdrawal from the annual Kyalami Nine Hours endurance race by the South African Champion in November had given Kevin his big break. He and privateer entrant and co-driver Jeremy Barker had brought home the latter's ageing and ailing Porsche into third place overall against all odds, out-driving several "Big Names" in the process. A trial for the works Jaguar team which had won at Le Mans in June 1988 for the first time since 1957, had followed at Silverstone in January. This had culminated in a regular drive for the marque in World-Championship events for several seasons before their withdrawal from sports car racing a few years later.

A number of good results as well as Richardson's enthusiasm and willingness to get his hands dirty, had not been lost on other Team Bosses. His background in car design had been a bonus. Several of his ideas for improving the sports racing cars' aerodynamics had been adopted by his former team and had improved their pace. One of his designs for a revolutionary road going sports coupe was already taking shape in another motor manufacturer's design studios. He had not previously envisaged moving from South Africa, but pressure from the factory, career prospects and the time he was being forced to spend away from home and loved ones, had already made up his mind.

He was also looking forward to testing Honda's latest car at the Le Mans trials in a fortnight.

***

"Breakfast is almost ready Dad," Tracey, his pretty blonde-haired ten year old daughter's call cut into his daydreaming. "Thanks Trace, tell Mommy I'll be in as soon as I've washed my hands." He brushed his hand lightly over the red leather upholstery, swung his legs over the sill, straightened and palmed the door closed with a solid clunk. The XK had badly needed that tune up…

Chapter 2

"Are you coming for a swim, Dad?" Tracey looked at him expectantly. The blue water beckoned. It certainly looked inviting.

Richardson took another sip of the Cabernet Sauvignon – Merlot blend and replaced the tulip-shaped wineglass on the low coffee table. "Maybe later, once Mommy's delicious lunch has settled." He let out his belt a notch, stretched his legs and leant back contentedly against the recliner. Ann looked up from where she lay on the paved pool surround and smiled. Her look then turned reproachful.

"Now, Dad, don't forget you promised Trace you'd play with her in the pool this weekend. You've been away so much, she's beginning to wonder whether she still has a father." She glanced at Tracey, winked and turned back to her novel.

They had celebrated their eleventh wedding anniversary three weeks before. Ann had worn very well, or for that matter, not at all, for her thirty-five years. Kevin felt proud and on occasion, even a bit jealous when colleagues looked at her appraisingly. She really did not look a day over twenty-five. She was very attractive, her oval face framed by cheek length honey-blonde hair. Her piercing blue eyes seemed to look right through you. Her perfectly proportioned figure was another reason Kevin was glad to have beaten the queue of potential suitors all those years before. Ann's golden brown tan was a legacy of hours spent on the tennis court and reading beside the pool. She had certain other business interests of her own, was bright, but in Kevin's opinion, was wasting her substantial talent. On the other hand, Tracey had benefited by having a full time mother.

"Daddy, will you please fix my watch, the strap has broken?" She handed him the watch she had been given for her third birthday. "Sure Trace, I'll see what I can do after I've had a little nap." He slipped the digital watch into the breast pocket of his shirt and lay back, closing his eyes.

Kevin dozed, dreaming of the Aston Martin he hoped to add to his collection. It was a DB 2/4 Hard Top – One of a handful built in the mid 1950's. A tip-off by Jeremy Barker and a chance visit to a garage in London three months before had unearthed the classic which was complete, but in need of a ground-up restoration. He had left a substantial deposit with the coachbuilders, enough for them to start the long process of rebuilding, but he would have to come up with the balance by the end of the year.

Hopefully the Honda's reliability and a fair slice of luck in the forthcoming endurance races would boost the sponsors' bonuses enabling him to complete the restoration and take delivery of the Aston.

"Mommy, please may I have some orange juice?"

"Sure darling, there's a jug in the fridge."

Tracey disappeared indoors as a sudden whirring whistling noise woke Kevin with a start. He rose to his feet as a large helicopter appeared over the roof and prepared to land between the house and the pool. Kevin almost lost his balance from the buffeting of the rotor's downdraught which plucked at his clothes threatening to burst the buttons of his shirt. He struggled to focus on the blue and silver machine, but was forced to turn his head away from the bombardment of stinging dust particles whipped up by the blades. He ducked involuntarily although the spinning rotor blades were metres above his head. He blinked and rubbed his eyes. It was as if a tornado had struck. Dust and grit stung his bare skin. Just before it touched down, Kevin saw Ann roll onto her left side, her scream lost in the din, the novel went flying and she disappeared into the pool.

The door of the helicopter opened, two men waving automatic weapons of a make not immediately recognizable to Kevin jumped to the ground. The pilot stayed put. The two wore black masks of the 'Superman' style – a figure of 8 shape covering their foreheads to midway along the bridge of their noses. Green and brown camouflage battle dress and matching caps completed the picture. Although he only caught a three-quarter glimpse of the pilot from the back, he noted subconsciously from the bare forearms that he was black rather than brown – probably of East African, rather than local origin.

"Now will you come quietly and nobody will get hurt?" It was a command rather than an inquiry from the larger of the two men as he advanced towards Richardson. The accent was that of a typically well-schooled English speaking South African. Although not wanting to do anything that would endanger Ann, Richardson involuntarily pulled away as the man gripped him roughly above the right elbow. Then everything went black and he sank to the ground.

Chapter 3

They were already airborne when Richardson came to. Voices and the noise of the engine had awakened him. It took a few seconds for him to realize what had happened. He opened his eyelids a few millimetres to get his bearings. He had been trussed hand and foot and lay at the back of the cabin. Ann lay in a spreading pool of water a few feet in front of him. Rivulets had formed a web across the floor. His temple throbbed where the smaller of the two men had clubbed him with the butt of his rifle whilst he had wrestled with the other. A stinging, burning sensation from his lower forearm caused Kevin to peer downwards. Two angry red welts ran on the inside of his wrist to the heel of his hand. They must have ripped off his watch when they bundled him into the chopper.

"We'd better give the guy a shot as well before he wakes up." The larger of the two raised his voice above the cacophony in the cabin as he arose from where they had been kneeling alongside Ann's still form. Richardson saw the hypodermic syringe in his hand and feigned unconsciousness as they glanced in his direction.

"Good idea. How long to the airstrip Kingwill? The pilot who had half turned in his seat, lip read correctly in the din. He raised his right hand and clenched and unclenched his fingers and thumb twice.

"Ten minutes – okay." The smaller man had removed his mask and soft peaked cap. His thick accent was without doubt that of an Afrikaner. Through slit eyes Kevin noted the short cropped dark brown hair, neat clipped moustache with longish curled ends and tanned athletic figure beneath the battle dress uniform. The man was a clone of the S.A.D.F. permanent force officers Richardson had encountered during his national service. He moved towards him and Kevin had difficulty in continuing the pretence as his sleeve was rolled up. He was unable to stifle an involuntary shudder as the inexpertly wielded needle found its target. Whatever it was, the drug was potent and within seconds Richardson felt drowsy. He drifted into sleep hoping Tracey had remained indoors and was safe.

***

He awoke with a start. It was pitch dark and it took him several seconds to shake the cobwebs from his fuzzy brain. Then he remembered! He tentatively tried to probe the darkness with his right hand but realized it was tied to the other. His feet were bound as well and his right leg throbbed. He rolled over onto his back to allow circulation to resume. Kevin's lower left leg and foot felt as if they were being bombarded by hundreds of tiny pricking needles as sensation started returning as blood again flowed through the blocked artery and capillaries.

"Ann, are you alright?" he called softly. "Ann, where are you?" His concerned voice was drowned by the cacophony in the confined space. The droning told him that he was no longer in the helicopter, but a propeller engined aircraft. 'It's a transport plane of some sort' he thought. There were no visible portholes in the fuselage or they had been covered. His rolling exploration had revealed a hard floor and no seats. He had however, encountered what appeared to be several wooden crates in the three metre wide hold. He had not found Ann. He was desperately concerned about his life partner, his lover and mother of their lovely, oh so bright daughter.

Why had they been kidnapped? What do they want? Who are they? Is Ann alright? Richardson's brain was in turmoil. Did the kidnappers want to prevent him from competing at Le Mans? Were they hoping to get a ransom from Honda? Richardson almost laughed aloud. How ridiculous – there were a few dozen other sports car racing drivers who were better known and hotter property than he was at this stage of his career.

The aircraft banked suddenly and Kevin rolled across the smooth floor, his head thudding into one of the crates. He stifled a cry as the corner of the wooden box again homed in on his still sore temple. A low moan came to him from beyond the boxes. "Ann is that you? Can you hear me?" His voice was barely above a whisper. He tried to gather and swallow saliva to lubricate his parched throat. There was no reply from the enveloping blackness.

"Ann, where are you? Are you okay?" He managed to raise his voice, but it was hopeless against the aircraft's thrumming engines. He rolled forward as the nose of the aircraft dipped sharply. He wondered whether they were preparing to land. The plane levelled out and the gradual descent continued for what seemed to be several minutes. Kevin realized they were going down, as the pilot throttled back. The plane suddenly banked and Kevin could not stop himself from taking another blow to the kidneys from the corner of another crate.

He found himself wedged against the forward wall of the compartment by the g-forces and could not roll away. The aircraft levelled out and then they were down. His breath was again knocked from him as they bumped down, rebounded, touched again and settled into an undulating deceleration as the wheels followed every crater and pothole on the runway.

By his estimate, at least ten minutes passed before a scraping sound from beyond the skin of the fuselage told him he was about to have visitors. Muffled voices carried to him through the hatch. "I wonder how our passengers enjoyed the flight?" It was the voice of the Afrikaner military man. He laughed.

"Sleeping like babies, I'm sure," the cultured English-speaking South African replied. "That stuff we gave them is good for at least sixteen hours."

Suddenly the hatch swung open. The dim oval silhouette of the doorway told him it was still night outside. Richardson decided that as he was supposed to be unconscious, it was best he played along, at least until he was reunited with Ann and had established the reason for their abduction.

Two men wearing battledress climbed aboard the plane. One grabbed his legs and the other found purchase under his armpits. Richardson was carried to a waiting three ton army truck with a canvas tarpaulin over the load area. He noted through slit eyes that it carried South African Defence Force plates. He was dumped unceremoniously in the back and was propelled towards the back of the cabin. The men loaded several crates near the tailgate and some minutes later they laid Ann about a metre from him on the corrugated metal floor. She was unconscious and her face looked pale in the moonlight that shafted through the rectangular gap above the tailgate. Ann appeared to be wearing a loose- fitting army overall.

"Whew Steve, that was a close shave we had at Waterkloof! For a moment I thought that nosey M.P. was going to ask his troops to inspect the 'plane." It was the voice of the Afrikaner from the helicopter. Richardson knew Waterkloof well. It was one of South Africa's main air force bases near Pretoria. Had they flown there first in the chopper?

"You can say that again Jan. If that mad Alsatian had not run across the airfield at that precise moment and diverted that military cop's attention, our entire operation would have been buggered. Don't know how we would have explained these bodies and guns amongst the medical supplies." Richardson recognized the voice of the other thug who had administered the drug. They were standing on the corrugated metal edge of the load area.

"Well Steve, we'd better get a move on if we're flying back to Pretoria tonight."

"Right, Jan. By the way, do you know that these two will have company? Apparently Sergeant Smith from Fifteen S&T got nosey and asked too many questions. He was picked up at the pub and is being taken to the hospital where Dave will arrange for him to disappear. The CO of Fifteen Supply and Transport has been told that Smith has been granted compassionate leave to fly to Jo'burg to visit his brother who was pretty messed up in a motor accident."

In the dim light Kevin noted that Steve was a full head taller than Jan, probably over six feet. Longish, possibly blond hair, curled over his collar.

"Ja well, Steve, we must be careful. We can't let things slip now." The Afrikaner was thoughtfully twirling the handlebars of his moustache. The sound of approaching army boots crunching on gravel reached him.

"Privates Trevor Ryan and Mike Miller reporting for duty, sir."

"At ease, chaps. Are you the relief drivers for this vehicle?" The question came from Steve. The deference to rank intrigued Richardson. None of the abductors had carried any visible rank in the chopper and in the poor light he could not discern whether Jan or Steve wore any insignia.

"Yes Sir."

"Have you been briefed?"

"Yes Major. We got in last night. We're staying at the base in Ondangwa. They think we're on a routine military camp."

"Well, you'd better get your kit transferred to our local camp, as all your duties will be performed here. Your direct reporting line is to Captain Van Den Berg."

"Right-o sir!"

Is Steve a senior officer in the S A Defence Force? What the hell are they involved in without the knowledge of the local military? Kevin wondered.

One of the soldiers closed the tailgate and clambered over it. He sat down just inside the tailgate on the left hand wooden slatted bench that ran the length of the load area and leaned his elbow on the flange of the rear flap. His right thumb and forefinger encircled the barrel of what appeared to be an R1 automatic rifle while its butt rested on the floor alongside his right boot.

The Bedford's engine churned, coughed, then reluctantly barked into life. The driver blipped the throttle several times to clear the misfire, let out the clutch and they were off. After several minutes during which they appeared to make little headway, turning this way and that and on occasion coming to a virtual stop, the driver turned left, accelerated through the gears and engaged top. Kevin examined his surroundings. The soldier placed his rifle on the bench alongside, took a packet of cigarettes from his breast pocket, stuck his hand into his right trouser pocket and extracted a box of matches. He lit the cigarette. The flame briefly illuminated his face and particularly, his prominent nose as he inhaled deeply. Richardson saw the young pimply face of a dark haired boy still in his teens.

By the light of the match he also saw that Ann was lying with her back towards him on some sacks about two metres closer to the guard. During the initial part of their journey, the sacks had obviously slid on the smooth metal surface beneath, carrying her further away from him, but her bound feet had caught behind a steel spar supporting the bench running along the right hand side of the vehicle's load area. Kevin knew Bedfords like the back of his hand. He had spent half of his National Service being tossed about in the back of them while on military manoeuvres.

Several subsequent army camps had fortunately been spent at their controls.

Kevin suddenly tensed as he recalled his military service. Those bench stays had long been a weak point of the Bedfords' passenger carrying abilities. They snapped frequently leaving a jagged spar under the seat. This did not necessarily render the seat unusable as there were several supports under each section. He edged towards the right hand side of the truck. The guard hadn't moved for some time and was possibly dozing. He could not see the glow of his cigarette. Richardson drew a blank with the first two stays spaced about half a metre apart. Then he struck gold! A stay had broken a few centimetres from the floor. About five minutes and double as many lacerations later, the thin rope gave way and his wrists were free. His ankles seemed to take longer as his blood-starved fingers fumbled to untie the knots.

An obscenity came from the cabin as the driver swerved too late and they hit a pothole. The guard's gun clattered to the floor and something solid smashed into Richardson's right ankle seconds later. He only just managed to bite off the scream of pain that met his sharp intake of breath, willing his clenched teeth and tightly compressed lips to open. The guard clawed at the side of the vehicle as he almost followed his weapon. Kevin lay still for what seemed like several minutes while the guard, after glancing around the dark interior settled back and resumed his dozing.

Richardson sat up and explored the darkness behind. His probing fingers felt something soft. It was a body. He recalled the conversation between Steve and Jan at the landing strip. The man's breathing was shallow and although the moon seemed to have disappeared behind a cloud he was positive that the body was not wearing military uniform. A quick search failed to produce anything from the man's pockets and he switched his attention to the guard.

It would be a piece of cake to overpower him and toss him over the tailgate, but where were they and how long had they been in the clutches of these madmen, whoever they were? Was Tracey alright? Had anyone been alerted and had they managed to pick up the trail of these bastards?

Tracey's watch! Richardson patted his breast pocket. Its slim profile had eluded the thugs in the helicopter. The green digital display glowed in his hand. 02:19 – It was almost twelve hours since they had been abducted!

He rose to his feet and crept silently towards the guard but nearly lost his footing as the driver slowed, made a ninety-degree right turn and braked, the big tyres skidding several feet before the lumbering giant came to a rest. Just in time Kevin managed to grab hold of a vertical roof support stopping his frame from catapulting into the guard who in his comatose state grabbed hold of the tailgate just stopping himself from pitching headfirst out of the vehicle. Richardson gingerly stepped back several paces and crouched in the shadows. The guard resumed his dozing.

In the pale moonlight Richardson discerned that they had passed through an open gate. What appeared to be diamond mesh fencing, topped by several strands of barbed wire stretched to the left and right of the opening, but he could see little else other than about fifty metres of the snaking dusty track along which they had come. His vision was further blurred by the still settling cloud of dust thrown up by the truck's wheels and sucked under the tarpaulin. It took a supreme effort to stop the cough that threatened to purge his air passages of the choking particles. The vehicle shivered slightly as the engine was cut. The driver's door creaked and the gravel crunched beneath his boots as he jumped down.

"Identify yourself!"

"Private Ryan! I've come to collect some medical supplies for Seven Field Regiment, Private Miller is in the back."

"Right. We've been expecting you. You'll find your stuff at the guardroom. Lieutenant Botha is on duty tonight."

"Thank you Corporal." Ryan's crunching boots approached the Bedford. Richardson heard the cabin door slam shut. The engine fired at the second attempt and they crawled forward slowly. Miller had not moved since they had entered the compound. His head appeared to have become wedged in a fold in the canvas tarpaulin. To Richardson he appeared to be in a deep sleep. Was that a snore? Richardson discerned several vehicles on either side of the gravel pathway. Large shadowy objects were possibly tents or bungalows. Ryan stopped the Bedford about fifty metres along the road, jumped down and approached the tailgate.

"We'd better take these two to Casualty and report to the guard room before those guards at the gate get suspicious. There was no reply. "Hey, is anyone home?" Ryan's voice sounded irritated.

Miller awoke with a start, nearly sliding onto the steel floor of the load area. He took a full five seconds to get his bearings before replying.

"Sure...um... sure thing, Trev." Miller tried to sound alert and unsurprised as he got to his feet, grabbing at the top flange of the tailgate to steady himself. He still felt groggy. With an effort he climbed over the flap and jumped down nearly losing his footing as he landed on the gravel below. Richardson heard the sharp protest of the cold unlubricated left metal catch as Miller started opening the transversely hinged tailgate. The right hand lever also let out a yelp.

He moved back into the dark depths of the interior and lay down hoping that his still form would not attract the attention of the soldiers whose eyes would probably take a while to adjust to the blackness. Ryan and Miller climbed into the truck and between them manoeuvred Ann's leaden form towards the edge of the load area. They jumped down, picked up the apparently lifeless body and carried her to the left beyond Richardson's line of vision.

Kevin crept towards the tailgate and was about to jump down as well, when he heard their voices approaching. "Two!" They had said they were going to take the 'two' of them to Casualty. Instinctively he rolled the unconscious form of Sergeant Smith to a position midway along the load area of the truck. Grabbing one of the sacks, he crept under the transverse bench behind the cab as far as he could and pulled the foul-smelling bag over the length of his body.

The soldiers clambered aboard, rolled Smith towards the rear of the vehicle and repeated their previous procedure, closing the tailgate before carrying the limp form away. As soon as they were beyond earshot, Richardson crept to the tailgate and peered out. They were in a large enclosed yard. Some distance away, what appeared to be a three metre high security fence stretched as far as he could see in the still dim light.

Beyond the fence, lamps on even taller poles spaced at about twenty metre intervals, cast a path of light along the perimeter. The open gate through which they had come lay to the north and was surprisingly, in virtual darkness. In a cubicle to the right he noted the shadowy silhouette of the guard who had challenged the Bedford's entry. To Richardson's left and about twenty metres away, a long, low, rectangular building lay dimly outlined in the moonless night. Faint, possibly lamp light, emanated from several of the small square windows. The "guard house" he presumed.

Richardson was about to climb over the tailgate when a glint from the floor caught his eye. 'The rifle!' Miller had

26

not yet missed it. He picked up the weapon unclipping the magazine without thinking. From its weight and his memory of using the weapon many, many times during military service, it felt full. He would check the tell tale holes in the side of the metal casing in daylight to confirm his assumption. He put his right arm though the heavy-duty woven sling and hoisted it to his shoulder. Memories of countless parades and drill exercises threatened to hijack his thoughts and he had to consciously concentrate on his immediate situation.

The night beyond and within the camp was eerily quiet although a gentle breeze had risen since Kevin had left the confines of the truck. He jumped down lightly and crept towards a group of stationary vehicles parked to the right of the gate. Some fifty metres to the west of the Bedford lay a large double storey building fronted by an irregular row of tall trees. Here and there faint light flickered between the foliage. In the darkness it resembled a rather dilapidated block of flats.

He reached his objective, which from a distance had appeared to be a vehicle park, without being challenged. There were three rows of vehicles, possibly fifteen or sixteen. In the dim light he made out four short wheelbase Land Rovers with SADF plates, a couple of Bedford forward control troop carriers, similarly marked, as well as several other unfamiliar rugged looking utility vehicles. Russian? He wondered. A sudden crunching sound from beneath his shoe broke the silence. Kevin's other foot froze inches above the ground as he surveyed the darkness balancing on one leg like a heron. The car park had been covered with a thick layer of crushed stone on which the vehicles stood. Nothing stirred. He could not see the front of the gate cubicle. The Bedford still stood unattended outside the guardroom.

Alongside the open parking area were several open sided carports with corrugated iron roofing. In the pale moonlight Richardson discerned half a dozen or so civilian cars. The oval headlights of a dark hued current Subaru Impreza saloon – a personal favourite performance car, caught his attention. To its left a sorry looking ancient VW Golf was bedded down on soft tyres. To the right a modern lighter coloured Volvo awaited its driver. Beyond the Volvo, a recent BMW 5 Series saloon with wide rims looked potent. From reflections on its curved body panels it was possibly dark blue. With slow, deliberate and measured steps, Kevin eased forward and gently tried the driver's door of the Subaru. No luck, it was locked.

He was creeping past an early 1980s Audi 5E when he stopped in his tracks and retraced a step. A glint below and behind the steering wheel in the vehicle's interior had caught his eye. Kevin cupped his hand alongside his cheek to block the reflection on the side window glass and peered into the inky blackness of the interior. He inched along the window straining his eyes, but other than a faint glow from the dashboard instruments, he could discern nothing else. The driver's window had not been fully closed and a gap of several centimetres beckoned at the top of the side screen. He could have sworn he had seen a key in the ignition but doubt now gnawed at his initial anticipation.

No tell-tale light warned of the vehicle being fitted with an alarm or movement sensor. Richardson's fingers, then his hand, probed the gap above the window glass. All hell did not break loose. Reassured, he inched his right arm through the opening. It was a tight fit and at the first attempt he was unable to penetrate beyond the middle of his forearm. He withdrew it, moving forward, closer to the downward curve of the glass. Crouching, using both hands and progressively taking his weight off of his feet, he exerted downward pressure on the glass. It would not budge! In a final attempt he lifted his feet and pulled down hard.

Without warning, the glass soundlessly dropped a further precious centimetre. This time he tried his left arm. He managed to probe several centimetres deeper and down into the interior, but the thin hard edge of the glass was cutting off the blood supply below his elbow.

His arm ached and he was starting to lose sensation in his fingers. He could not quite reach the steering wheel and his elbow would have to pass through the gap as he had no leverage to reach the door catch mounted on top of the door trim. He had to reach the ignition switch! He would probably have to break the window...

Richardson straightened his frame and turned his head through a 180 degree arc. There was no sign of movement at the gate or guardhouse. The breeze had however, picked up further and the flickering lights behind the trees in the distance were now winking more intensely.

Changing his line of attack, Kevin withdrew his arm and moved closer to the centre pillar of the car. He massaged his arm and rapidly opened and clenched his fist several times to get rid of the pins and needles that numbed his fingers as blood circulation returned. Using his right arm, his fingers gently probed along the car's roof lining above the driver's seat. He found what he was looking for! The interior courtesy light switch! Some of these cars had switches located above the driver's safety belt mounting rather than in the centre of the roof.

Left or right? Which way was 'off?' He had owned one of these cars more than a decade ago, but most certainly had no memory of such an infrequently used control. Hold on...most cars had three-position switches! One kept the light on, another illuminated the interior when a door was opened, the other kept the light off. The switch felt as if it was in the middle of its arc. Surely that would make sense for the 'off position?

He gripped the top of the glass with both hands and pulled downwards with all the force he could muster. It did not budge. Renewing his efforts, he jerked the window towards the ground, again lifting his knees in an attempt to bring his bodyweight to bear on the window mechanism.

Something gave. For a fraction of a second he thought the window glass was going to buckle and shatter, but the screen suddenly slipped down a further three centimetres in its frame before finding purchase and locking solid. The dull thud probably sounded louder than it had actually been, but Richardson nevertheless sank to his knees. After what seemed to have been an age, but in reality had probably only been thirty seconds, he slowly arose and did a 360 degree survey of his surroundings. No one had stirred. A faint rustling sound close by appeared to be the branch of a tree scraping against one of the vehicles.

Kevin felt for and pulled up the knob at the base of the window. A dull click told him that the door was now unlocked. Withdrawing his arm from the interior, gingerly and with bated breath his fingers gently levered the door handle. He allowed an audible sigh to escape his lips as the light stayed off and the silence was not shattered by the strident tone of an alarm. 'Alarms were not fitted as standard equipment on these anyway.' he thought. "Should not have got my guts in a tangle!"

His heart sank. There were no keys in the ignition! Kevin collapsed against the backrest of the driver's bucket seat and closed his eyes. He felt dizzy and light-headed. What a waste of effort! He must sleep. With a supreme effort he reached forward and felt behind the driver's sun visor. There was a metallic tinkling sound and something bounced off the steering wheel before hitting his right knee and coming to rest in the foot well.

In a flash the keys were in his pocket. He closed the door gently, not daring to push it fully home in case any noise drew unwelcome attention.

Chapter 4

"Get going you lazy buggers! Do you want those Cubans to fill your asses with AK 47 lead?"

Kevin woke with a start and lifted his head from the steering wheel. He turned his head to the right – the Sergeant-Major's bellow had come from only a metre away. His eardrum was ringing, foul smelling diesel fumes caught at his throat through the Bedford's open cabin window. All hell had broken loose. Powerful engines were being gunned and the huge treads of the four wheel drive monsters were throwing billowing clouds of thick dust into the night air. They and scurrying soldiers' outlines were eerily silhouetted in the dust and smoke blanket lit by the vehicles' headlights.

Kevin struggled to focus. Lack of sleep had taken its toll as the regiment had moved camp forty-two times in the past sixty days. On some days they had moved three or four times when Angolan spotter planes had circled overhead.

He glanced at the luminous hands of his old fashioned chronometer. Five past twelve. They had only stopped at the ruins of the once upon a time southern Angolan town, an hour before, to heed the callings of nature and refuel the armoured column. Intelligence reports at that stage had placed the Angolan Government's Cuban forces some two hundred and fifty kilometres behind. The pro-Unita South African forces had probed to within forty kilometres of Luanda – the Angolan capital, before the West had asked them to withdraw. Unconfirmed rumours indicated that the order had come from the US.

The trees and world beyond the Bedford's windscreen were spinning – Kevin desperately tried to focus. He had been in a deep sleep such as he had not enjoyed for months. The trustworthy old motor grumbled to life. He switched on the headlights and depressed the clutch pedal. His hand reluctantly responded to the impulses sent by his befuddled brain. It pulled the walking stick of a gearlever towards him and engaged second gear with a crunching protest. Grumbling, the ungainly-looking forward control vehicle lumbered towards the column of mixed armoured and support vehicles that was fast disappearing from the clearing into a break in the forest to the north.

Kevin slotted the five ton truck into a gap between a short wheelbase Land Rover and another Bedford. The description "road" flattered the track ahead. Twin parallel ruts cut across the soft desert-like sand. They had been eroded by countless military vehicle wheels during the ongoing war and when wet would no doubt pose a challenge to even the most sophisticated four-wheel drive systems. The raised centre caused by ever deepening ruts threatened to 'beach' vehicles lacking in ground clearance.

His head dropped towards the steering wheel. The four-wheeled matt military green elephant lumbered towards a massive tree on the left verge of the track. Kevin opened his eyes just in time and hauled the large diameter wheel towards the right. The beast seemed reluctant to respond but missed the hundred-year old pine by the thickness of its bark. He started as a loud ripping sound was added to the cacophony of the vehicles ahead and behind. A thick branch had pierced the rear canvas canopy just behind the cabin and had torn a jagged rent along its entire length. The back of the Bedford weaved drunkenly to the left and right as the vehicle struggled for traction in the loose sand and its tyres rebounded off the sheer-sided ruts. The yawing stopped as the heavy-duty rubber regained grip.

He glanced in the rear-view mirror and noticed that the Bedford behind had stopped in a cloud of steam. Another vehicle had stopped alongside to render assistance.

Kevin's eyelids struggled to counter the relentless load being applied to them. His chin dropped to his chest and his foot slipped from the accelerator pedal. The mammoth slowed. Kevin awoke and sat bolt upright on the seat as a searing pain shot through his forehead. He had hit his head on the rim of the steering wheel. His left foot found the clutch pedal and the rumbling engine grasped at the new lease of life. His fingers gingerly probed the throbbing lump that had already started to form.

Almost immediately the track dropped sharply and the Bedford started to pick up momentum. Kevin's right foot patted the brake pedal instinctively seeking to counter the acceleration. The tail lights of the vehicles ahead were receding into the distance. He felt for the light dipping switch on the dash panel. His fingers brushed against something which made a clicking sound. Immediately everything was plunged into pitch darkness. He was now wide-awake. "I've hit the bloody blackout switch!" he thought. His fingers scrabbled frantically for the switch stalk as he slowed the vehicle.

Another noise became audible above the engine note. The cabin was suddenly filled with the sound of gushing water. As Kevin found the light switch and the dark abyss was illuminated, the right-hand side of the vehicle tipped slightly. Before him the swift-flowing murky waters of a river beckoned! In the darkness the Bedford's wheels had missed the low-level bridge by about a metre and landed on the right-hand bank of the river. The headlamps turned the ripples silver and the water's unwelcome attraction was relentless and magnetic...

Kevin's right foot stabbed at the brake pedal imploring the mammoth to stop its slide. The locked tyres valiantly tried to reverse its forward momentum but the front ones slid along and down the muddy bank. Kevin's heart fluttered as the Bedford came to a virtual standstill and for a fleeting moment he thought he had won. The sheer weight of the truck and the steeply angled bank were too much. His heart sank as the locked front wheels slid relentlessly towards and into the water.

After what seemed to be an age, the vehicle came to rest. The nose was a good half-a-metre lower than the rear which was perched precariously on the riverbank. His feet suddenly felt cold. He moved them and heard the splash of water. The black liquid was trickling in around the unsealed edges of the door bottoms at a steady rate. As he watched mesmerized, the sound seemed to intensify and he felt the cold liquid moving up around his ankles. The floorboards had not been designed for an amphibious vehicle and the foot wells were rapidly filling.

The engine had stalled during his efforts to stop the truck, but started immediately on the button – he had to get out before the electrics got wet! He engaged reverse gear and four wheel drive but the old warrior's wheels – without the aid of a limited-slip differential – spun uselessly in the mud. The metal monster seemed to be digging its watery grave deeper...

He forced the Bedford's right hand door open against the pressure of the fast-flowing torrent. The water level had already virtually equalised inside and out of the cabin but the strength of the in-flowing current threatened to completely swamp the cockpit. He reached across to the left hand door which burst open, quickly reducing the flow to a trickle over the floor.

Leaving the engine running, he gingerly climbed out of the right hand door and down using the footrests alongside and on the centre of the wheel rim. Upon reaching the latter, he crouched, probing the depths with his left foot. He shivered involuntary. The glistening black liquid was icy and still seemed to be beckoning...

His exploring boot found what felt like several large rocks the size of footballs. Using his arms to take his entire 160 pounds weight, he gently settled first his left and then right boots on the stones. His footholds appeared secure but the icy water extracted a further series of shivers as it penetrated his khaki overall to the waist. He probed his way to the rear of the vehicle. From the glow of the taillights he noted that the rear wheels had dug themselves into the muddy bank.

He clambered to the top of the bank. Some 500 metres back along the track, the convoy seemed to have regained some semblance of order. The overheating Bedford appeared to have been pushed to the side and rest of the vehicles headlights were snaking across the veld towards him.

Kevin clambered over the tailgate and was glad when his groping fingers found a shovel in the dark damp depths of the load area. Although standard kit, shovels were in demand when nature called and once they had served their purpose were often not put back where they had been found!

The grumbling sound of the approaching column suddenly became a cacophony and they started to cross the low level bridge. "Hey Troopie, where did you get your licence – in Cuba? You should rather have gone on a submariner's course!" Kevin glanced up from his digging to see the Commander atop the turret of the Panhard-based Eland 90mm armoured car which had come to a halt on the approach to the bridge.

"Sir, is there a recovery vehicle back there?" Kevin enquired.

"Should be, but of course we stick to the beaten track and in any case this beauty can go anywhere!" A loud hooting cut the exchange, the Bedford behind was getting impatient. Kevin caught a glint of the Eland driver's eyes through the narrow post office box slit before he gunned the engine and the vehicle shot forward spraying mud in all directions.

Kevin looked back along the track. About ten vehicles, mainly Land Rovers were picking their way towards him. He had managed to move most of the soft mud and slush for about a metre behind the back wheels, but the layer below was still spongy. He had also wedged several flat rocks ahead of the rear wheels. He fervently prayed that the tyre treads would be able to obtain purchase. Kevin climbed into the cabin, engaged reverse gear, depressed the accelerator and let out the clutch. The engine revolutions increased as the rear wheels spun freely, the back of the truck moving from side to side – the front wheels seemed to have dug themselves deeper into the mud and silt on the riverbed. He suddenly remembered seeing a torch in the cubby hole. It was still there! "Silly arse!" he mumbled, putting it in his breast pocket.

Leaving the engine running, Kevin jumped from the cabin into the water but lost his footing on the slippery rocks and mud beneath. He felt a twinge in his left ankle but a second later the strongly flowing current swept him around the front of the Bedford towards the middle of the river. His flailing fingers managed to grab hold of the radiator grille bars at the second attempt and he gingerly hauled himself towards the vehicle. His body was suddenly wracked by a series of shivers and he almost lost his grip. Kevin realized that he was freezing from the combination of icy cold water, cool night air and the tension caused by his inability to solve his predicament. Crossing his forearms, he rubbed his upper arms and shoulders vigorously, but the attempted friction was countered by his sopping clothes and sore hands.

He squinted at the luminous hands of his watch. Twenty past one! He had been in the river for the best part of an hour! By the dim glow of the taillights he saw that his hands were cut and abraded from his endeavours. Blood was oozing from a deep cut in the joint of his left thumb. Although his fingers were numb from the cold which dimmed the pain, he winced involuntarily. A sudden searing stab above his eyes reminded him of the bump on his forehead. It was still there! "Don't crack up now!" he thought.

Back at the top of the bank, Kevin realized that no vehicles were to be seen along the track along which he had come. The only sound in the night air was that of the relentlessly gurgling river ahead of the Bedford. "There must be more to come," he mused and turned his attention back to the task at hand.

In the darkness, it took him fifteen minutes to gather about twenty medium sized rocks from the edge of the river and the bank. Some of these he wedged into the sand below the back wheels before he warily waded back into the cool waters. The riverbed into which the front wheels had sunk was almost a metre below the water line. Pushing rocks into the soft slush under the tyres entailed ducking his head under water. Working blind it took rather longer than intended.

Rising from the dark shimmering waters he muttered, "Time to get out of here before..." biting off in mid-sentence almost as if someone was likely to overhear! "Can't take too much more of this..." He thought. A distant rumbling to the south made him turn.

Vehicles were on the move and although he was below the top of the bank and could only see a dim glow from their direction, there seemed to be an urgency about their engine notes. "Maybe the recovery truck is sweeping the withdrawal route." He was starting to talk to himself too often, he thought, as he scrambled to the top of the bank. About a kilometre across the veld to the west, three pairs of headlights in line astern were slowly wending their way along the meandering rutted track. Even at that distance, the rise and fall of their engine revolutions and the erratic movement of their headlight beams from side to side across the grassy plain and up and down – one second into the heavens and the next – onto the path directly ahead, as the drivers guided their wheels, told Kevin they were in a hurry.

More lights illuminated the skyline on the horizon and several more vehicles appeared some distance behind. The front vehicles were closing rapidly on his position and he could see from the close coupled headlight beams that there were three Land Rovers. He patted his back pocket. The torch was still there. It also still worked despite his unintended swim!

He moved towards the centre of the track and started to flag down the leading Rover with his torch. A sudden staccato of machine gun fire came from the second group of vehicles which had closed to within possibly half a kilometre. Bullets whistled past him as the leading Land Rover accelerated across the bridge. At a crouch Kevin moved towards the second vehicle imploring him to stop, but had to jump back to avoid being run down.

The driver of the third one, possibly recognizing him as being on the same side shouted "Get out of here, those Cubans don't take prisoners." Kevin noted a row of bullet holes along the vehicle's aluminium flanks as it hurried into the night, the small circular red taillights disappearing almost immediately in the cloud of dust churned up by the chunky rubber treads.

"Hey, what about me, you bastards?" But their headlights were rapidly receding into the darkness towards the north-east. Kevin spun around. The pursuers had stopped in a hollow, still some several hundred metres down the track, possibly to reconsider their advance as they were potentially vulnerable to counter attack from the ridge over which the Land Rovers had disappeared. Kevin estimated there were possibly six vehicles, but could only discern the glow of their lights from behind the wild indigenous trees and shrubs. He sprinted towards the Bedford, his boots losing their purchase on the slippery slope. Struggling to remain erect, Richardson only just retained his balance. Deciding against holding onto the vehicle, he forged through the water, losing his footing on a rock as he lunged for the grab handle to the left of the cabin door. His chin caught on the step alongside the right front mudguard just before he disappeared beneath the icy waters.

Stunned for several seconds, he surfaced spluttering and gasping for air. He was facing the dimly glowing headlights of the Bedford and realized that he was being drawn towards the middle of the river. "Don't lose it now," he thought as he lunged at the forlorn looking beast. The fingers of his right hand brushed against and closed around a sharp but robust feeling metal girder. The front bumper!

Kevin drew himself towards the Bedford, worked his way around the eyelevel open door and clambered onto the step above the mudguard. The idling of engines and glow to the south appeared no closer. He settled into the driver's seat, turning to his left, he groped behind the seat back. His rifle *was* there! He drew the R1 automatic weapon towards him, cocked it and jammed the butt between the transmission hump and passenger seat. Hopefully he wouldn't need it...

His heart sank. What about his rucksack and spare magazines? Reaching across, his left hand probed the depths of the passenger foot well. The bag had not been washed out. He extracted two dripping magazines from the soggy bag and placed them on the passenger seat. He fervently hoped that he would not have to test claims that the R1, based on the legendary Belgian FN rifle, worked even after being immersed in water!

Despite the coolness of the night, the events of the past few hours had made him forget that his wet state made him a prime candidate for pneumonia. A sudden shudder wracked his frame. He took a deep breath to steady his nerves, but was immediately overcome by the pungent petrol and hot engine oil fumes escaping from the engine cover. Despite the open windows, the cloud of gas seemed to be hanging suspended below the roof of the cabin. He struggled to control the coughing bout that threatened to take over. Shivering, he scooped several handfuls of water from the depths below his knees. The cool liquid mercifully stopped the burning tickling sensation in his throat. His wristwatch told him that three minutes had elapsed since the last remnants of his regiment had left him to engage the enemy.

With a crunch of solid metallic protest, the non-synchromesh reverse gear was rammed home. Kevin gunned the motor and let out the clutch pedal. For a split second it seemed as if the wheels were gaining traction, but suddenly the engine wheezed and with a shudder expired. His heart sank.

"Come on old girl, don't let us down now," Kevin pleaded. He depressed the clutch pedal and pushed the starter button. The headlights dimmed to a brownish glow across the dark waters as the starter motor made a reluctant half – hearted attempt at turning the big pistons. He quickly flicked the light switch off and stabbed a finger at the starter button. The big-hearted little motor hesitantly turned the reluctant engine over for several revolutions. After what seemed to be an age, but was most probably a matter of seconds, it suddenly grumbled and growled to life. Kevin engaged reverse and dug his right foot into the foot well.

The rear tyres scrabbled for grip, the mammoth shuddered, the cab seemed to rise under him like a merry-go-round horse and suddenly they were on the bank He pulled the large diameter steering wheel to the right, allowing the back of the vehicle to move in the same direction at a 45 degree angle to line up the bridge to the east.

A glow from the left made Kevin aware that the moonless night was much lighter than it had been. Through the windowless passenger door he noted that several large vehicles were rapidly making their way up the incline towards his position. Before long, if not already, the Bedford would be silhouetted against the night sky and would be a sitting duck.

He started as consecutive dull thuds followed by a cracking noise were magnified by the confines of the cabin. The back window was a spider's web, but the lamination kept it in one piece. Without thinking, Kevin grabbed his rifle and lined up the nearest vehicle, possibly a hundred metres away through the Bedford's passenger door. Taking aim slightly above the left hand headlight he squeezed the trigger once. Realizing that the gun was not set for automatic firing, he pulled it a second and third time in rapid succession.

Jamming the butt between the seats, he rammed the gearlever into second gear still looking at the approaching convoy. The leading vehicle suddenly swerved to the right. As if in slow motion, the front wheels lifted and seemed to paw at the air for help, before it rolled across the path of the closely following truck, which rammed it amidships. The sound of tortured metal and splintering glass was followed almost immediately by a massive orange ball of flame that turned the night into day. Within seconds the surrounding countryside was alight.

Kevin's stomach churned as agonized screams rent the air. Soldiers milled around and unintelligible orders were barked. He pressed the accelerator and with a snort from its exhaust, the reliable old beast rumbled into the night. He had a lot of catching up to do before he reached safe ground.

Chapter 5

"The President of Zimbabwe, together with a large entourage of Cabinet Ministers, is due to arrive in Johannesburg today for talks with the South African Premier before departing on the first leg of his European tour. Sources close to the President indicated..." The newsreader was cut off in mid-sentence, followed by an intermittent staccato of atmospherics as the listener sought another station.

Richardson awoke with a start. He was sweating. It took several seconds for his eyes to adjust to the darkness and remember where he was – on a ribbed metal floor of a covered vehicle. He must have dozed off! He had not dreamed of that experience from his army days for years...

Peering through a tear in the tarpaulin, he realized what had awoken him. An automatic rifle was leaning against the front mudguard of an early white Volkswagen Beetle and a uniformed guard sitting in the front seat appeared to be fiddling with the controls of the radio in the centre of the dashboard.

"Police Headquarters in Johannesburg report that they have not as yet uncovered any clues as to the motive, identity, or destination of the men who kidnapped South African racing driver Kevin Richardson and his wife from their Sandton home yesterday afternoon. Their ten year old daughter is staying with relatives."

Kevin felt in his trouser pocket for Tracey's watch. It was 6H33. He had dropped off for two hours!

He remembered his dream. It had taken him four hours to locate his regiment which had camped just inside the

Angolan side of the border with Namibia. He had not been reprimanded for not keeping up with the convoy. In fact, no one had even missed him! He had not been impressed by the total lack of concern on the part of the officers for the wellbeing of their citizen force members. A few hours later they had crossed back into South West Africa. An excruciatingly slow, five day train trip through Windhoek and the drier, almost desert-like regions of South Africa had followed. He had felt like kissing the ground on arrival at Park Station in Johannesburg.

***

"A helicopter belonging to a South African hotel chain believed to have been used by the abductors, was recovered in a field near the Waterkloof Air Force base near Pretoria. Police investigations are continuing."

"International singing star..." The newsreader's voice died again, as the guard found a pop music station.

Richardson recalled the events of the early morning hours. After watching Ryan and Miller from the shadows of the car park depart in their Bedford, he had made his way to the entrance of the large building. A sign above the double glass door entrance proclaimed it as being "Ondangwa Hospital." Namibia? Could they possibly be in the former South West Africa, more than two thousand kilometres from Johannesburg? The mere thought of it seemed beyond belief. Then the penny dropped! Why not? He could very well be in the former South African administered country. There had, in retrospect, actually been many clues as to their whereabouts in recent hours.

He recalled several trips that had taken him to this part of Africa during a three-month military camp years before. Taking into account the apparent duration of their flight, notwithstanding that a substantial part of it had been spent in a state of unconsciousness, he realized that the concept of being in South West was not necessarily that far-fetched.

Beyond the double doors, an olive-skinned nurse in a white uniform manned the desk positioned on the left side of the brightly illuminated reception room. Two other doors further along the front of the building had resisted attempts at entry. Whilst contemplating other ways and means of entering the block, he had only just avoided detection by two armed guards patrolling the grounds. One of the guards had sat on the steps leading up to the front door while both of them had lit up and smoked their cigarettes. Kevin sought refuge under one of the carports behind the row of trees, while they conversed in low tones. Finding the rifle a hindrance he had secreted it in a dense shrub behind the Audi. He would collect it later.

After unsuccessfully trying to get around the building which was protected by diamond mesh topped by razor wired security fencing, Kevin clambered aboard an apparently derelict Bedford in the vehicle park to contemplate his next move. Pulling aside the remains of the rear canvas tarpaulin, he noted that the windows set in the building facade were too high to reach and that the rain-gutter down pipes were situated too far from the windows.

Specks and slashes of light poured through countless gashes in the Bedford's canopy. Richardson peered through the glassless back window of the cabin. The front had been blown apart, most probably by a landmine. Nothing but twisted metal remained of the cockpit space designed to accommodate the driver and co-driver. Although the engine had clearly taken the brunt of the blast, the block was intact. Its mountings had given way and the big lump of metal hung forlornly between what remained of the front wheels and suspension.

The floorboards had disintegrated. The dashboard would have been unrecognizable but for the apertures which Kevin recognized as previously having framed the speedometer and other gauges. The roof panel and doors were gone. Kevin shivered involuntarily as he noted the tangled wires that had once been the springs of the front seats. They now resembled fish skeletons...

The guard switched off the radio and made his way across the gravel road to the guardhouse. About ten minutes later a troop carrier arrived with four guards to replace the twelve who had done the night beat. A brief argument ensued and although he could not make out much of what was said, he gathered that the night shift was annoyed about being relieved late. He guessed that only the gate was manned during the day shift and that it was deemed unnecessary to patrol the grounds. From 7:00 private cars started arriving, as well as a Mercedes Benz bus which brought relief nursing staff, leaving a quarter of an hour later with those who had done the evening shift. He noted that all vehicles were stopped and signed in or out. Some were randomly searched.

A small circa 1988 Mercedes 190 Series pulled up alongside his Bedford and a tanned, well-built grey-haired man in his mid-fifties climbed out. Turning his back to the car, he eased the door closed with his buttocks until the catch clicked. Using the key, he removed what appeared to be a doctor's bag from the boot and walked briskly towards the hospital building.

What was of interest to Kevin however, was the folded white garment that lay on the rear parcel shelf of the German car. He looked towards the gate. No one was to be seen. The Bedford was parked between the Mercedes and the gate. He vaulted over the tailgate of the troop carrier wincing as his injured ankle protested and quickly opened the unlocked driver's door.

It was as he had hoped – a white dustcoat of the type commonly worn by doctors. He slipped it on behind the Bedford and was pleased to note that even unbuttoned, it hid the soiled parts of his shirt and most of his slacks, the latter looking rather worse for wear after his ordeal. Half of his handkerchief moistened with water from a puddle helped remove most of the grease and grime from his face. He studied it in the surprisingly intact Bedford's rear-view mirror. It would have to do – his hair virtually covered the ugly welt above his temple and there was nothing he could do about the day's growth of stubble or bloodshot eyes.

Richardson gently closed the door of the Mercedes, hesitated, then, rounding the rear of the truck, he set out briskly for the hospital not daring to look towards the gate. He covered the fifty or so metres in seconds although it felt like minutes. The half-expected challenge did not come. A nurse on duty at reception looked up disinterestedly as he pushed through the spring-loaded doors, but looked away and continued her animated telephone conversation in what Kevin guessed was Portuguese. Another desk beyond hers was unmanned.

Passages led off to the left and right, but Richardson instinctively strode straight ahead past the desk through an archway, finding himself in another deserted corridor. Without thinking, he turned left. Hugging the wall, he crept past several small empty wards on either side. Then he froze. A male voice with a Scottish accent had carried to him from behind a closed door on the right hand side of the passage. He backpedalled several steps, crossed the two metre wide corridor in a stride, crouched and put his ear to the keyhole. Three separate rectangular signs starting at head height mounted one below the other proclaimed **"Operations Room"**, **"Strictly Private"** and **"Keep Out"** in descending order.

The muffled conversation continued on the other side of the door. The next door on the same side was ajar. After carefully satisfying himself that the room was empty, Kevin quietly slipped through the door, closing it silently behind him. His eyes took several seconds to adjust to the gloom within. Pale light came from two squares in the middle of the far wall. A thin sliver of light at floor level indicated that a connecting door linked this with the occupied room next door. He put his eye to the keyhole, but a domed circular shiny metallic orb with a halo around it, immediately told him that it was blocked by a key.

Chapter 6
Namibia

"First these arseholes grab the wrong guy, then they let him get away."

"I wonder if the bugger slipped away back at the airstrip or whether he's lurking around here somewhere?" The second man's voice carried clearly to Richardson through the door which he noted was bolted on his side.

Maybe we should tell fifteen S &T that we don't need their help for a while as we will be able to provide our own security for the next week or two. We can bring in a couple of our chaps by this evening to guard Mrs Richardson and sniff out her husband, in case he's lying low around here."

"Good idea, Jim. I'll write a note to fifteen S&T's C.O. right away if you'll get one of the driver's to take it into town by lunchtime. Do you know the chap's name?

"No, a new Commander took over recently.

"Bloody 'phones! The landline's down again." Kevin heard what was clearly the crash of a telephone handset being dropped or smashed back onto its cradle. There was silence for a few seconds. A further bang was followed by the sound of something dropping and bouncing on the floor. "When are they putting up that mast so that we can get some sort of reliable cell signal coverage? I can't work under these primitive conditions."

"I think we could be in business soon. I saw a low bed truck about ten kms along the road to Ondangwa a couple of days back. It was carrying what appeared to be masts or poles on the back. It was in convoy with a couple of other vehicles."

"What's the plan to get hold of Jensen, Dave?"

"Jan and Steve are working on it in Pretoria. Trouble is, Jensen is due to leave for Singapore again in a week which doesn't leave us much time. He's also gone to ground since the news of Richardson's abduction broke." I doubt that he has made the connection. Dave's voice was the deeper of the two. Richardson guessed that the accent may well have originated from London many years before.

So they *had* been kidnapped by mistake! Who was this chap Jensen? Where was Ann being held? Kevin shook his head in frustration. How is she? She must be dehydrated after the ordeal. His throat was parched. He hadn't even thought about the fact that they had had nothing to eat or drink for over twenty-four hours.

"Where's Kingwill?" David Wilson's question broke the silence.

"He's due any minute. It's 8:55, he should be here in 5 minutes or so."

"Then let's go. He can take over here."

The voices continued from the adjoining room for several minutes, but Kevin did not glean anything more of value. He thought he heard the sound of a printer. He heard the door slam and a second metallic click as if a "Yale" type catch had engaged. They walked past his room, deep in conversation. Keeping their voices down, he could not make out anything of the exchange. He gave them a couple of minutes. There had been no further sound from the room, so he gently slid back the bolt and turned the doorknob. He gently pulled the connecting door towards him. The key had not been turned!

It was an office of about five metres square. Illumination was provided by several recessed blocks of ceiling-mounted fluorescent tubes. Three small rectangular windows were set into the upper part of the wall opposite the corridor. The room was divided by a row of desks upon which stood a number of small screen monitors facing the far wall. He subconsciously counted eight. A large photocopying machine confronted him.

Several upright steel filing cabinets covered another wall. On a desk next to the door through which he had entered, stood a computer and printer. A telephone and a stack of filing trays caught Richardson's eye, or rather, the large envelope in the top tray. It was unsealed and was addressed in bold hand printed lettering to 'The Commanding Officer, fifteen Supply & Transport Depot, Ondangwa.' Kevin withdrew the sheet of paper from the envelope. Printed on an "**Ondangwa Hospital**" letterhead, it read:

"Dear Sir,

As another group of trainee guards has arrived to support our existing force, we will not need you to provide us with any guards for the next few weeks. I'm sure your chaps would like a break.

We will be in contact, but it is unlikely that we will need your assistance until the morning shift on Monday 20th.

Thank you.

Yours sincerely

David Wilson"

He replaced the letter in the envelope, folded it and absent-mindedly pocketed it in one of the deep cavities in the lower regions of the dustcoat. He picked up the handset of the old fashioned telephone but replaced it after the long repeated beep tone confirmed that there was no service. The fact that the receptionist had been using her 'phone fleetingly crossed his mind, but his thoughts were sidetracked.

The top drawer of the desk was ajar. A key protruded from the keyhole and a glint from within caught his eye.

As he bent to investigate, his foot kicked an object on the floor. It slithered along the cement and clattered against the wooden skirting board behind the desk. He froze and listened intently for what seemed to be at least a minute. No sound came from the corridor. Continuing his search, his hand closed on what his fingers immediately recognized as a cell phone. It was a modern compact Nokia and was switched on and fully charged. The signal strength indicator hardly registered on the screen. Leaving it on, it joined the Audi keys in his right hand trouser pocket.

Turning his attention to the drawer, Kevin drew it fully open. The metallic reflection had been from a bunch of keys. A Subaru emblem key fob and car key was of immediate interest. Attached to the ring were two heavy duty keys and three smaller ones. Filing cabinet or desk drawer keys he guessed. Placing the keys on the desk, he examined the contents of the drawer.

Several flat folders bearing hand printed labels of Nigeria, Nicaragua, Columbia, Sri Lanka and other foreign country names were of no obvious interest. From a hurried perusal, they appeared to contain invoices and correspondence relating to medical supplies purchased. A single page list of names and telephone numbers aroused his curiosity. The international dialling codes and foreign individual names intrigued him.

Kevin was about to fold it and find another home in the dustcoat when he remembered and turned to the photostat machine. It was switched on and still warm. "Rather they don't miss it too soon." he thought. He locked the drawer and found place in his other trouser pocket for the Subaru keys. Patting his person, he smiled and thought "Should've brought a kit bag!"

Richardson started to move away from the desk but checked in mid-stride. He retrieved David Wilson's letter, found a pen in another drawer and started writing below Wilson's signature:

DEAR SIR,
MY NAME IS KEVIN RICHARDSON.

MY WIFE ANNE AND I WERE ABDUCTED FROM JOHANNESBURG TWO DAYS AGO BY DAVID WILSON AND HIS ASSOCIATES. I DO NOT KNOW WHAT ILLEGAL ACTIVITIES THEY ARE INVOLVED IN.

ANNE HAS BEEN DRUGGED AND IS BEING HELD CAPTIVE HERE. I MANAGED TO ESCAPE.

THIS STORY HAS BEEN ON THE SABC NEWS.

WE ARE IN DANGER. PLEASE HELP.

THIS IS NOT A JOKE.

THANK YOU.

P.S. MY ATTORNEY IS PAUL KINGSWOOD TEL (011) 435 7565

His haste had resulted in rather a scrawl. "It'll have to do. Please let it be delivered today!" he thought. He folded the letter, inserted it into the envelope and grimaced whilst licking the flap. Richardson slid the rectangular paper lengthwise through his thumb and forefinger to ensure adhesion and placed it back in the "Out" tray.

He was about to cross the room to the monitors when he noticed that a large glossy paper map of Namibia hanging from a nail, had a slight bulge in the middle which caused it to stand slightly proud of the wall. Lifting the side of the map slightly he found what he had half expected – a small safe had been let into the wall behind. Kevin carefully lifted the map from its hook and laid it on the floor. Two keyholes glared at him from the centre of the heavy steel door.

At his first attempt the key fitted into the left hand elongated eye, but would not turn. Switching keys brought success. He turned the cold steel handle through ninety degrees and pulled. The heavy door reluctantly swung open.

Two shelves divided the compartment into three horizontal sections. A key board was mounted on the inside of the door – keys were still swinging to and fro on their individual hooks. Kevin immediately noted a duplicate set of Subaru keys. The four rings of an Audi emblem on a key fob also registered in his subconscious. A brief examination of the middle and lower shelves revealed the contents to be of no particular interest. A number of bundles of cash notes on the top shelf however, were. They were large denomination bundles of US Dollar and S A Rand currency.

Kevin slipped a clip each of one hundred Dollar and two hundred Rand notes into a pocket and replaced the bundles in the safe. He would need the cash if only he could get Ann away from here... He lifted the duplicate set of Subaru keys from their hook and closed and locked the safe. Returning to the desk he replaced the original set of keys in the top drawer leaving it ajar as found.

He crossed to the monitors. The black screens of the first three reflected the overhead lights. One monitored the front gate, but the picture appeared frozen. Another trained on the double door entrance seemed to be functional. Two of the others appeared to be monitoring sections of the perimeter fence.

Kevin's heart skipped a beat! The last screen was trained on a white hospital bed. It was occupied by what appeared to be a white woman lying on her side. The figure's back was to the camera and although the sheet was drawn up above her shoulders, part of a blonde head protruded, the hair spilling onto the pillows and sheet. "Ann! Where are you?"

Chapter 7

The sound of approaching voices startled Richardson. He dropped to his knees looking around for a place to hide.

"Are you coming for a cup of tea Kingwill?" Kevin thought he recognized the Portuguese accent of the receptionist.

"Be along in a couple of minutes. Just want to check on a few things." It was a deep East African accented voice. A key was being inserted in the lock.

Kingwill? Why was that name familiar?

He only just managed to close the inter-leading door, when the door to the just vacated office opened. He silently slid the bolt and turned to survey the room. His eyes took some time to adjust to the gloomy interior. Bookshelves lined three of the walls and Kevin concluded that it was the hospital library. A desk, couch and two easy chairs made up the rest of the inventory. From the unaired musty smell it was clearly seldom used. He pocketed the key protruding from the lock on the inside of the door and continued his exploration of the passage. The room alongside was a lounge-cum-dining room and a printed sign on the right hand of the open doors proclaimed that teatimes commenced at 9H30, 12H30 and 14H30.

Satisfying himself that the room was empty and the passage clear in both directions, he slipped through the open doorway. The coffee machine looked inviting, but he reluctantly decided against the risk of lingering any longer than he had to. He grabbed a paper cup and filled it from an inverted water cooler bottle mounted on a counter. The icy liquid burned his parched throat, but he quickly downed a second cup. Grabbing two handfuls of biscuits from a plate on the counter which joined the miscellany in his coat pockets, he returned to the library, turning the key in the lock.

It was 9H20 and the sign on the door had warned against continuing his search for Ann whilst the corridors were likely to be full of staff heading for the canteen. He waited until 9H45 by which time a noisy hubbub emanated from the room next door. After checking that that the passage was deserted, he slipped past the open doorway of the canteen in two strides.

The corridor made a ninety degree turn to the left and Kevin realized that there was another wing to the building that was not apparent from the front. He passed two elderly African women conversing in Portuguese whom he took to be cleaners, but they did not give him a second glance. A sign hanging from a door handle stopped him in his tracks. In bold letters it proclaimed "**DANGER, DO NOT ENTER, HIGHLY CONTAGIOUS DISEASE.**" The warning was repeated below in smaller letters in what he presumed to be an African language.

Without thinking Richardson tried the handle. It turned and although it did not register immediately, he was not surprised when the door swung inwards. He found himself in a brightly lit small private ward with a single occupied bed against the far wall. The drapes of heavy white curtains covered the window behind.

The occupant was facing the wall and a blanket was drawn up halfway covering the head. His heart fluttered. Could the blonde hair that spilled on the pillow be Ann's? It was!

"Ann darling, wake up." He shook her gently by the shoulder. She moaned softly but showed no signs of wanting to regain consciousness. "Come on darling, we must get out of here!" There was more urgency in his efforts now, but she would not respond.

He turned to survey his surroundings. The white painted room was stark, the only other inanimate occupants being a grey steel cabinet alongside the door and a wooden chair at the foot of the bed. A broom standing in the corner near the head of the bed looked out of place.

Richardson spun around as the door behind him creaked. Too late he saw the electronic eye in the ceiling that had given him away. A burly African man wearing a khaki shirt and similar slacks was pointing a silenced pistol at him. His satin ebony skin was reminiscent of the helicopter pilot. Kevin guessed he weighed around 100 kg and stood nearly two metres tall.

"Don't move." There was menace in the dark brown eyes and a faint smile played around the slightly parted full lips. Several days scruffy looking stubble did not improve the picture.

The man's plate-sized hand seemed to engulf the pistol. Kevin saw his banana-sized finger tightening on the trigger. He lunged at the intruder driving his left fist into the black giant's solar plexus. Glass tinkled behind him as a bullet ricocheted off a side wall. His impetus rather than the blow, knocked the gunman off balance and he staggered against the wall, trying to grab hold of Richardson's dustcoat. Kevin landed on his hands and knees.

Before the Heavyweight Title Pretender could recover, Kevin launched himself upwards and hit him with a left uppercut to the jaw, simultaneously driving his knee into the giant's groin. The pistol clattered across the floor. Pain shot up Kevin's arm and he feared that he had broken his hand. To his surprise, the black giant crumpled to the floor in slow motion, the wall behind supporting his massive frame in a sitting position, the massive head lolling at an awkward angle on his shoulder.

Kevin retrieved the gun from where it had come to rest against the skirting board. Holding it by the silencer, he cracked the butt against the unconscious man's temple to make sure that he had not only been stunned and pocketed the weapon.

Richardson leaned against the wall and took several deep breaths, contemplating his next move. He used the handle of the broom to turn the camera lens through one hundred and eighty degrees and suspected that it was not the first time it had been used for such purposes.

The sound of distant hurrying footsteps approaching along the corridor roused him to action. The steel cabinet, after initially resisting several attempts to move it, left two ugly scratches on the painted cement floor as Kevin manhandled it against the door. Holding the end of the broom handle with both hands, he jumped on the wooden shaft with both feet three quarters of the way down, simultaneously drawing the end upwards. The wooden shaft gave way with a sharp cracking sound, splitting at an acute angle, the pieces still held together by long splinters. Kevin drew the two ends together and rammed the tapered wedge into the 10mm gap below the door, kicking the broom head with the heel of his shoe to drive it deeper into the crevice.

Quickly glancing at Ann and observing no change in her state, he clambered on to the end of the bed. He noted the jagged hole in the otherwise immaculate white curtain as he drew it aside. He kicked out what remained of the shattered glass pane, brushing most of the shards from the sill. Easing his buttocks forward, he jumped to the ground some two metres below. He grimaced with pain as his ankle reminded him that it would not take kindly to much more abuse.

Chapter 8

The three metre security fence towered dauntingly twenty metres away. Its shiny metal mesh blocked all thoughts of escape in either direction as far as he could see. Between Kevin and the fence was a small vegetable garden. The soil appeared to have been freshly dug over. What interested him however, were the pickaxe and other gardening tools stacked on the bed of a wheelbarrow parked next to the wall.

Grabbing the handle of the pickaxe, he ran towards the fence. Using the tapered steel shaft as a lever he set about trying to separate the wire from one of the steel poles. Without warning several strands of the thinner wire snapped catapulting Kevin into the fence. Regaining his footing he pulled the mesh away from the pole. A gap of about 30cm had been left at hip level. He stretched the mesh as far as he could and climbed through the opening tearing his slacks and scratching the skin underneath. Ahead lay knee high grassland. He tossed the pickaxe into the grass and headed for a sparsely populated forest about fifty metres away.

Reaching the wood, Richardson zigzagged behind several of the larger trees, but realized that the saplings would provide little shelter from pursuers. Several shots ricocheted through the trees to his left, but appeared to be more out of warning than threat as he doubted that he had been sighted due to the undulating terrain. A hundred metres further on he was pondering where to go when he found himself in a clearing and confronted by a row of five similar small cottages. He sprinted between the second and third buildings and found himself face to face with a large, dark complexioned woman. She glared at him over the top of the sheet she had just draped across a thick rope which served as a washing line. Shouts in the distance brought him back to reality and he made to continue his flight.

"Wait, you run away from bad men. I help you." The accent was Portuguese. Angolan? The question flashed through Kevin's head. A short, swarthy man of stocky build with dark brown wavy hair had appeared from behind the woman using his arms to deflect the washing. He was a good head shorter than his companion. His black bristling moustache seemed to cover half of his face and although at first glance the picture seemed intimidating, the piercing blue eyes hinted at kindness.

Kevin did not hesitate. His pursuers were close. Without waiting for another invitation he followed the man into the fourth cottage. He noted the poor furnishings as he hustled past consecutive open doorways which appeared to be the kitchen, bathroom and living room. The man stopped in front of a large solid wood double wardrobe. "I, Manuel" the man grinned, then turned and almost ripped the heavy left hand door off its hinges in his urgency to open it. Before he could protest, Richardson was bundled into its cavernous depths, the door slammed and a key turned in the lock.

"Hey!" Kevin started to protest as he realized the obviousness of his hiding place and the inevitability of discovery. For that matter, he had a nagging suspicion that Manuel had neatly duped him into becoming a boxed present for his pursuers.

The stale smell of unaired sweaty clothing caught at his throat and he fought the urge to cough and sneeze. An exploration by touch, of the old cupboard's contents, revealed that it was the best part of half-a-metre deep and probably three times that, in width. He had landed on what felt like a pile of scratchy folded blankets. In the seconds before the door had been banged shut, he had glimpsed that the cupboard was at least three quarters full of mainly dark hued clothing hanging from an overhead transverse rod.

Kevin gingerly manoeuvred his weary frame into a sitting position so that he was right at the back of the cupboard with his back against the right hand side wall. He stretched his legs along the cupboard floor and in the darkness tried to arrange the blankets over his legs without disturbing their shape too much He reached up and gently pulled several items of clothing suspended from the rod towards him to hide as much of his upper body as possible. In the darkness there appeared to be several musty smelling long coats which almost touched the floor.

After what seemed only seconds, he heard several urgent but muffled voices in the distance. Doors slammed and the sound of breaking crockery interspersed with shouted obscenities carried to him through his padded cell. Suddenly the voices were in front of the wardrobe. The heavy old cupboard rocked slightly. "Where's the key you son of a bitch?" Richardson recognized the voice but could not immediately place it. "Open this door now or you'll be very sorry!" A loud bang on the door followed by the sound of an open handed slap and the resultant whimper were hardly muffled by the solid wood.

"This ees my son, Manny, hee's room. He has key – he keep cupboard locked and say 'Stay away from my theengs, old man." Manuel of the ferocious countenance had apparently become as meek as a lamb. In a pleading voice he continued: "I tell you gentlemans, me and Maria no see any strange white mans." The heavy cupboard rocked again. There was a sudden splintering of wood and the left hand door burst open allowing a flood of light to transform the pitch blackness. Kevin drew back into the shadows, not daring to breathe.

A hand appeared and fingers felt for the latch securing the right hand door at the base of the cupboard. The catch was obviously stiff as the fumbling metacarpals, assisted by curses, failed to budge it. The hand's fingers closed around the edge of the door and from a gap between the dangling clothing, Kevin saw the dark wood arch outwards as pressure was applied. It resisted and the hand withdrew.

Several dull thuds sounded around him before Kevin realized that the interior was being probed with a bayoneted rifle. He bit off an exclamation as he felt the skin of his left inner thigh being pinned rather too close for comfort to his family jewels. He was seriously contemplating surrender when he heard the same voice say: "Nothing here!" The dangerous blade was withdrawn and the cupboard door left ajar. Richardson remembered the voice as being that of Private Trevor Ryan, the Bedford driver.

"Come on Mike, let's have a look next door." So Mike Miller, the dozy Private was with him. Kevin wondered how long it had taken the latter to miss his rifle. He heard their voices recede.

Manuel appeared at the opening. "Come out Meester, those men they gone." Richardson scrambled from the cupboard. Maria stood in the middle of the room, beaming.

"Thank you for not turning me in, Manuel." Kevin held out his hand. Manuel's firm handshake was that of an artisan, Kevin felt the scratchy rough skin and calluses from honest work. "Theese is Maria, my wife. She no speak Inglees, but understand a little." Maria had had a change of heart since their encounter outside. The glare had been replaced by a full toothed smile. Kevin had difficulty in suppressing a wince as her huge hand crushed his grazed fingers. She led the way to the kitchen.

Over a meal of sausages, fresh bread and strong coffee Richardson briefly explained his and Ann's abduction, as well as the mystery of their having been mistaken for persons unknown.

"My son Manny Junior is male nurse at hospital. He very clever and learning to be doctor. He tell us about blonde woman who they keep in room and they geeve drugs to make sleep all the time. This is private hospital since last year. Very bad men in charge. There bad stories. Some people say these men sell guns and drugs to regimes in Africa. The nurses and doctors, they are scared. They want to tell army about theengs, but they need jobs..."

Chapter 9

Richardson examined his face in the mirror. The cold shower had made him feel almost like a new man. The shave with Manuel's cutthroat razor had demanded concentration. His fingers gently massaged his temple. The congealed mass of blood and matted hair had gone. Maria's ointment had soothed the former angry red welt which was now hardly noticeable under his combed hair which was also several shades darker.

The parallel scar lines on either side of his wrist were still painful. The locating pin on Tracey's watch strap had fortunately been trapped in the strap end loop and had not been lost. It had taken a click to fix and he now wore it on his right arm. The dark rings under his eyes from lack of sleep were virtually hidden by the olive-coloured lotion, also provided by Maria. On the other hand, they probably contributed to making his new identity more realistic! He had had a couple of hours rest, but could not sleep. Ann dominated his thoughts. He had to get her away from her captors. His whole body was still stiff and sore from his ordeal of the previous days.

Kevin almost smiled as his attention focused on the dense dark brown moustache that now adorned his upper lip. This self-adhesive example had been produced by Manuel who had grinned, but not commented until Kevin had allowed him to do the honours.

"You now look just like José – my brother!" he had beamed. "You look like real handsome Portuguese gentlemans."

Richardson had not raised the subject, but he had no doubt that this Portuguese family had been involved in a number of clandestine repatriations in their time – no doubt all in a good cause!

Manuel had provided the clean but frayed-collar white shirt and charcoal grey slacks. Matching grey socks with holes in the heels had completed the new outfit. "Manny don't wear these no more – you take them." Richardson had expressed his gratitude. His old shirt reeked of perspiration, was spotted with blood and he doubted it would ever come clean again after his stint on the floor of the Bedford.

His old slacks had reflected the same grimy state. Two inches below the crutch in the left trouser leg, were two neat slits where Ryan's bayonet had penetrated and exited and nearly done considerable damage! Manuel had faithfully promised to burn the clothing in case the soldiers paid a return visit. His right ankle was still sore from its contact with Miller's rifle in the Bedford. Depression threatened to replace his buoyant mood as a pain shot up his leg. The angry sensitive red ten centimetre weal served as a reminder of his ordeal. When last had he felt like utterly exhausted like this? Possibly during his initial six week stint of army basic training many years before!

Dusk was approaching. Kevin settled down on a hard divan in a spare room at the back of the cottage to review their plan of action which he had spent the afternoon rehearsing with Manny Senior and Junior. Manuel had warned him about using the route to Ondangwa which was some sixty kilometres away by road, as he was certain that Ann's captors would have set up at least one roadblock to bar his way. The telephone lines were still down and Kevin had been unable to make contact with the CO of fifteen S&T Depot.

Manny Junior had slipped away from work around 12:00 after arranging cover. He was a six inch taller and more muscular version of his father with the same swarthy complexion and wavy brown hair. After initially being suspicious of Richardson, he had been very helpful once Kevin had proved his credentials. He had provided invaluable input in so far as hospital routine covering staff and guard shifts were concerned.

The evening hospital shift was manned by a skeleton staff which comprised two nursing sisters and five nurses. One of the latter manned the switchboard and reception area. Two or three doctors did their rounds between 18H30 and 20H00. Ondangwa Hospital's upper floor housed three large general wards which were currently occupied by about fifty patients from the surrounding territory. Around forty of these were in fact exiles from Angola who had been wounded in the ongoing civil war. Some were soldiers, others innocent civilians who had been unable to get away from the crossfire. Visitors were not encouraged by the current management team!

Manny Junior had drawn a rough map of the hospital layout. The smaller general wards were situated at the front of the building. The kitchen, canteen, the administration offices and a dozen or so private wards were located at the rear of the ground floor. Ann was being held in one of the latter compact rooms.

Due to the proximity of the hospital to the Namibian border with Angola, the local regiment in Ondangwa – fifteen Supply and Transport provided guards around the clock. Although the South African Defence Force had to all intents and purposes been withdrawn from the territory, Richardson wondered why citizen force troops in the guise of guards were still present in Namibia. These troops appeared to regularly relieve the locals as was currently the case.

Manny Junior confirmed that twelve guards would arrive at 18H00 to relieve the night shift and that these would share three eight hour shifts. Two patrolled the inside of the perimeter fence, one manned the gate and another randomly checked the buildings and internal grounds.

Richardson remembered how boring guard duty had been during his stint of National Service and the regular annual three week camps that had followed. Most of his service had been done near Bloemfontein, the capital of the Orange Free State Province of South Africa. That region was not only the butt of many South African jokes due to the flat terrain and the predominantly farming community, but his regiment's superiors had also somehow always contrived to do their annual camps during the winter months when one was lucky not to catch pneumonia from "pushing beat" in sub-zero temperatures.

His memories of sleeping on the ground in poorly insulated tents and shaving in cold water tapped after breaking stalagmite icicles from the spouts, were not fond ones!

The hospital was managed by Dave Wilson who had apparently worked at a military hospital in South Africa before relocating to Namibia the year before. The 'Jim' whose voice Kevin had also heard from the library, was Jim McDonald, a long standing friend of Wilson's whom he had recruited to be his deputy and Administrative Manager. These two were not liked by the hospital staff. Wilson had been ruthless in dismissing staff for petty offences and ruled by fear. Various other business involvements occupied most of his time and he took little interest in the welfare of patients or staff.

Turnover amongst doctors had been high and replacements recruited were of dubious standard, some coming from former 'Iron Curtain' and Middle Eastern countries. The Namibian authorities had thus far turned a blind eye to unconfirmed horror stories emanating from the medical facility. Wilson had promised a substantial capital injection and had even spoken of privatizing the operation.

He wondered what clandestine activities the Scottish born fraudster was involved in and what roles his motley band of recruits played. The hospital provided a perfect cover for their operations, whatever they were. Wilson had money and his lack of financial demands on the Namibian Government kept them willingly at a distance. He was clearly well connected in influential circles, but why had his troops carried out *their* kidnapping?

Kevin dozed dreaming of Ann in his arms...

Chapter 10

Kevin drew back into the shadows of the thorn trees as the Bedford three-tonner rumbled past in a cloud of dust, its brake lights glowing as the driver slowed down and coasted through the open gateway. From his vantage point he saw two rows of black bereted soldiers sitting on either side within the load area of the lumbering vehicle.

The truck drew to a halt inside the hospital grounds. After the sentry from the booth had crossed the front of the vehicle to exchange pleasantries with the driver, it pulled away and stopped some fifty metres beyond in front of the guard hut.

Richardson squinted in the fading light but could only guess that the distant discernable movement represented the replacement guards clambering from the vehicle and carrying their kit into the guardroom. The driver made a U-turn and parked the Bedford on the verge to await the withdrawing sentries. Some ten minutes later the vehicle passed his position in the undergrowth on its way back to base camp, wherever that was.

The walk along the path from Manuel's cottage had only taken a few minutes. Although most of the residents of the settlement were still on duty at the hospital, Manny had led Kevin on a circuitous route around the settlement to escape prying eyes, before joining the pathway which met the main road to the hospital about a hundred metres from the main gate.

He heard and felt the beat of an engine approaching along the gravel track from the south towards the hospital. He drew back into the bushes lining the road. Several

68

seconds later an elderly Mercedes Benz radiator grille came into view trailing its clinging cloak and train of swirling brown particles. Kevin coughed and tried to shield his face with his free hand.

Richardson turned his back on the enveloping dust cloud and waited for most of the choking brown mass to pass and settle before he knelt down and opened the briefcase Manny had provided. He removed, unfolded and pulled on the now sparkling clean dust coat.

On the left breast pocket was pinned an identity card proclaiming him to be 'Doctor Ricardo Texeira''. This had been produced from a cardboard shoebox containing half a dozen similar cards and other identity documents. These had belonged to staff no longer on Ondangwa hospital's payroll. Manny had winked while he pinned the card to the jacket.

Kevin's mouth had started opening, his lips already framing a question. The burly Portuguese had however, turned his back and Kevin bit his tongue as he realized the futility of enquiring about its origin. The passport-sized photograph was unclear and would probably stand up to unsuspicious scrutiny. He had not paid much attention in the in the past to just how many Portuguese men cultivated bristling moustaches!

The bus slowed and drew to a halt some distance in front of the gate. Before the side exit door could open, Richardson had halved the distance between himself and the vehicle, the dust cloud ahead serving as a perfect screen from any inquisitive eyes in the bus or camp ahead. He peered around the back of the circa 1950's coachwork and saw that half-a-dozen people of various hues and sexes had already alighted. Some had already passed through the gate some ten metres beyond.

Animated Portuguese was being spoken by an African nurse and another lighter skinned woman attired in similar white uniforms who were possibly exchanging tales of their past twelve hour's experiences. They were followed by two men in blue overalls. He guessed that the latter were maintenance staff. Two more nurses brought up the rear.

Kevin noted with relief that the door was situated on the left side of the bus and his position and for that matter, all of the disembarking passengers could not be seen from the sentry hut on the other side of the vehicle. He patted his left trouser pocket, gaining reassurance from the cold solid steel feel of the Czechoslovakian made CZ 83 pistol that nestled against his thigh. It had a full magazine of 9mm shells. The loose fit of the pants ensured that there was no visible bulge.

He waited for two more passengers to alight – a well-groomed dark skinned man of about fifty with greying temples, possibly a doctor – dressed very much as himself, in black slacks and a light grey jacket, carrying a doctor's bag, and another nurse. The bus doors closed with a pneumatic hiss and the engine's revolutions rose. Kevin looked over his right shoulder. The driver had turned the power assisted steering sharply to the right and was preparing to make a three-point turn. He rapidly closed the ten metre gap to the woman ahead.

Some of the staff ahead called out greetings as they passed the cubicle, others stared ahead or ignored the guard as they carried on their conversations. An intermittent grunted response carried to Kevin from the confines of the booth. With trepidation he approached the open doorway, ready to make eye contact with the guard if necessary so as not to arouse suspicion. He turned his head to the right and was about to nod when he realized that the guard, a youthful blond-haired soldier of about nineteen, was not even paying attention to the passing pedestrians.

Perched on a stool, he was deeply engrossed in the contents of an open magazine on his lap. An upturned black beret lay on another stool. An automatic rifle dangled ungainly, suspended by its sling from the vertical projecting corner spar of the high-backed chair. Although he would not have put money on it, Kevin could have sworn that he'd seen a flash of naked flesh from a centre spread.

He was about two metres past when the challenge came. Richardson's heart sank and he froze in mid-stride. He was contemplating his options when the guard launched into a prolonged coughing bout. Kevin's lungs released their tension and he allowed an almost audible sigh to escape. An involuntary thought passed through his mind that anyone close behind would have seen him almost jump out of his skin and his shoulders then visibly relax.

The other 'doctor' who had by now opened a gap of about twenty metres over him, glanced around. Kevin averted his gaze and stopped to retie his shoelace. The last thing he wanted was to be engaged in conversation. When he finally looked up, the man ahead appeared to have lost interest and was already close to the main building's doors. Richardson shortened his gait and disinterestedly sauntered past the dimly lit rambling building that served as the guardroom.

Voices carried to him from within, but he could not make out any of the conversation. The twenty metre long building was fronted by a full length open veranda. Small barred windows at head height were set in the wall at two metre intervals. Kevin noted that the light within emanated from several flickering lanterns suspended from roof beams. Three high-backed wooden chairs stood on the veranda's red painted cement floor to the left of the wooden door, which was ajar.

The 'doctor' ahead had passed through the hospital's front door. Kevin glanced around. The guard was still in his cubicle and no one else was in sight. He soundlessly crept up the four stairs of the veranda and put his ear to the centimetre wide crack between the door and frame.

"So who's going to do the ten to two o'clock shift?" Kevin recognized the irritated voice of Corporal Trevor Ryan. "Mike, Geoff and I did it last night and we're not doing the same beat two nights in a row. We'll do tonight's stint until ten but that's it. Heinrich is already at the gate."

"Okay Rob, Pete and I will stand. It's a real crappy shift and a waste of bloody time." The disgruntled spokesman was unknown to Kevin. So Ryan and Miller would be on duty as of now. So what? He thought, those two in any event did not know what he looked like!

***

"Your wife has been moved to another ward further along the same wing, away from inquisitive eyes. Two guards have been posted – one outside the door and another inside the room." Manny Junior's faultless and confident command of English surprised Kevin. He betrayed only a slight Portuguese accent, but Kevin guessed that even this minor blemish could be attributed to his current interaction with colleagues at the hospital and his parents whose mother tongue was that of the former colony's rulers.

According to his father, Manny had spent some five years studying in South Africa. After completing an unrelated degree, he had decided that his future lay in helping the lesser privileged people of his home country – Angola. Studying by correspondence was however, proving more difficult than he had envisaged.

Manny stood up, picked up the kitchen chair upon which he had been sitting and turned it through ninety degrees so that he now faced the headboard of the bed upon which Kevin reclined. He sat down.

How could he gain access, immobilize the two guards and get Ann to safety? Kevin pondered.

"Has she eaten? How is she?" Kevin's mind was in turmoil. He was deeply concerned for the love of his life, his partner and friend, his comforter in times when he felt low. They had shared so many good times together and there were still so many things they looked forward to doing. His eyes glistened. Suddenly he lifted his head from the pillow, raised his upper body and in one motion swung his legs over the side of the bed to face Manny. He sat with his hands on either side of his thighs, his fingernails digging into the edge of the bed, his knuckles white.

"What are the bastards up to? What right do they have to put Ann through this? I'll kill every last one of the swines!

"I'm sure she's okay." Manny responded. "They won't harm her." He reached forward and briefly squeezed Kevin's shoulder.

Manny saw that the emotions of the man sitting across from were balanced on a knife edge. He was going through a stage where he desperately needed some morsel of hope to clutch at. Although he had only known the fit and healthy looking man on the bed for a few hours, he was in no doubt that he would not only survive his current setback, but would do all in his power to exact revenge upon the unscrupulous individuals who had so cruelly placed his wife in danger.

"According to my friend Conchitta – the sister in charge, the dosage of the drug they have been giving Ann is enough to keep her under for about four hours. Only Wilson, McDonald and that Nigerian have been in her ward at meal or medication times. Conchitta is unhappy. Wilson has let it be known that your wife is suffering from terrible abdominal pains and needs to be kept sedated until certain medication arrives and she can be operated on."

"But they know they made a bugger up, they grabbed the wrong guys! Why not let her go?" Kevin stood up and started pacing the room.

"That's all very well, but what do they do about you?" Manny responded. How do they explain why you were kidnapped in the first place? You may well not be able to identify them, but you can certainly lead the police straight here to find out just what is going on..."

Too late Manny realized his mistake. He and his bloody big mouth! Of course Kevin realized the danger he and Ann were in. He did not need reminding.

Kevin turned his back and Manny saw his shoulders rise and fall as he took several deep breaths.

"What can we do? We've got to do something. I can't sit around here while Ann is lying there helpless. Even if she were allowed to regain consciousness or had some lucid moments, she wouldn't know what the hell is going on and would be worried about Tracey ... I'm going back in there and we'll see about ..." Exasperation had been replaced by a steely resolve.

Manny smiled. "That's more like it!" He was pleased that the emotional phase had passed. He would do all he could to help his concerned, frustrated and angry new friend. He was in no doubt that Kevin would do the same for him if their roles and predicaments were reversed.

"I'm sure Conchitta will help us. She's been here for eight years and is dedicated to the hospital. She was due for promotion when Wilson took over. From the outset he has tried his best to find reasons to transfer or get rid of her, but it's almost as if he has resigned himself to having her around, at least for the present. I do, however, have an idea." He leaned forward to continue, but Richardson interrupted.

"What's her present status?"

"She is the ranking sister, but Wilson has removed her from the management team, used lame excuses to shift responsibilities to newly recruited employees and all but ignores her existence. She's biding her time though...There have been so many strange goings on in recent months...she's compiling a dossier...as long as she can hang in there for a while longer."

"Wilson seems to have friends in high places in the SADF and S A A F – there are a couple of youngsters here who were supposedly doing their South African National Service back in that country. Here they are private guards and it seems as if they are working for Wilson and McDonald! You've already encountered Ryan and Miller. There are three or four others as well... Conchitta will definitely help us, she's clever and..."

"Where are they staying?" Richardson cut in. Manny was warming to the subject and Kevin was surprised at the Portuguese nurse's ability to string sentences together with hardly any noticeable pause for breath.

'Who?"

"The guards...all of them."

"They sleep at a camp about five kilometres from here just off the road to Ondangwa. They have turned part of what used to be a rural primary school into barracks. They call it Operation Centre Bravo or Bravo."

"And Wilson and McDonald?"

"They share a dilapidated old house in the hospital grounds. It's on the eastern side, behind the hospital. No one is allowed near it. Wilson holds a lot of meetings there. Various strangers come and go. Hospital business? Who knows? Some of us have our doubts..."

"What about the school kids?"

"The school was shot up during the height of the Angolan civil war. Due to the previous connotation, parents were afraid of their kids remaining in the area due to its isolation. The population is scattered and the few kids whose folks still live around here, have been sent to boarding school."

"Wilson's friends in high places? Kevin's question was repeated in the arch of his eyebrows.

"There are three I know of. You encountered two of them in the chopper. One is a short moustachioed Afrikaner S A Defence Force Captain by the name of Jan Van Den

Berg. He is almost a permanent resident here. He stays in quarters at Bravo but spends a lot of his time in Ondangwa. Kingwill bunks there as well."

"Then there's the guy who seems to be the 'head honcho' from South Africa...S A Air Force Major Steve Harvey. He's a pilot based in Johannesburg and used to arrive for a monthly meeting at the hospital, but we've seen rather more of him lately... I've heard he has a friend in Windhoek with a small private jet which makes his local commuting rather easier."

"Rumour has it that Harvey and Van Den Berg are partners in a pharmaceutical business and are using S A A F transport craft for their own purposes as well.

Something had been bothering Kevin from the time they had landed and he had realized that they were in Namibia. The plane he and Ann had arrived on had clearly been an ancient piston-engined aircraft. He had not seen the outside of the plane, but would not have been surprised to learn that it was an old Douglas DC3 Dakota dating back to WW2 or earlier.

These workhorses had, to his knowledge, still been used by the South African Air Force for transport purposes until recent years. He had no idea as to their fuel range, but had wondered about their ability to still undertake a flight of possibly two thousand kilometres, particularly from a reliability point of view. For all he knew, in their unconscious state, his and Ann's captors could have changed planes several times or landed to take on fuel.

"Are there any landing strips around here?

"There's a small landing strip just beyond Bravo that can take a small private jet. There are a couple of small planes housed in a hangar – probably belonging to local farmers. I know that Wilson has been picked up there on a few occasions. There's quite a large airport at Ondangwa which dates back to South Africa's presence here at the height of the Angolan War. Why do you ask?"

"What types of aircraft are there at Ondangwa?" Richardson had already guessed the answer.

"I've only been there once or twice in recent months – to deliver packages to Jan Van Den Berg, but I saw some old twin-engined passenger jets with Air Namibia markings and one or two old planes. Someone mentioned ...a Dakota and a Viscount? I don't know much about planes. On the other hand, if you want to know the specs of the latest cars...?

"And the third high profile connection?" Richardson interrupted before Manny went off at another unrelated tangent.

"Well...we don't know much at all about him. His name is Dieter. Nobody seems to know his surname. He is a well-built blond chap with a German accent. He turned up a couple of days ago. Even David Wilson seems ready to jump when he speaks. We have heard of him before but he has not been here previously. I think he may well be the owner of the private jet based in Windhoek."

"Is he a South West African of German descent or the real thing from the Fatherland?"

"I have no idea." Manny shrugged.

"Conchitta sounds like a fantastic person." Kevin cut in, changing the subject. "How old is she? Is your interest purely professional?" He winked.

"Um...well, we um..." Manny was momentarily lost for words. His olive brown face had assumed a reddish hue. "I... we, are seeing each other. She is a beautiful woman."

"I can't wait to meet her. Now, about that help you were talking about..."

Chapter 11

Richardson resumed his walk along the brick paved pathway towards the hospital entrance. He was within ten metres of the double doors when they opened and three men emerged, one in military uniform. They were in earnest conversation. Kevin ducked into the shadows of one of the trees alongside the pathway leading to the gate opposite the doors and dropped to his haunches. He doubted he had been seen against the rapidly descending grey cloak of darkness.

Keys tinkled. "We'll use the Volvo." Richardson immediately recognized the cultured voice from the 'plane. What was his name again? Steve? That's it, he thought – the Major. He wondered why and how he had returned from Johannesburg so soon.

"I wonder where Richardson is hiding out?" Kevin recognized the Scottish accent of Jim McDonald. "If he gets to Ondangwa we're in deep shit!"

"He couldn't possibly get through. He has to get past our roadblock first which is impossible." Steve responded. Fortunately the telephone lines are still down. "We'll have to eliminate both of them. The woman hasn't a clue as to what is going on, but we don't know what Richardson has seen or heard."

"What's the latest on Jensen, have you managed to track him...?" McDonald's voice faded as they moved beyond earshot.

Richardson only had a brief glimpse of the third of the trio who had been partially obscured behind McDonald and Harvey. He was tall and wore dark slacks and a pale open necked shirt. From the back his hair appeared to be blond of hue despite the fast fading light.

He rose to his feet and was contemplating his next move when a noisy starter motor under one of the carports close behind, shattered the tranquillity of the early evening. Kevin drew back into the shadows. After what seemed to be prolonged churning, the engine reluctantly fired and Kevin recognized the distinctive bark of an Audi five cylinder engine, albeit a sick sounding one.

The driver revved the engine several times but the misfire persisted. Some half a minute later the vehicle was reversed and set off towards the gate. The headlights had dazzled Kevin as they had been on high beam when the driver switched them on. From his secluded vantage point and squinting to focus, Richardson had not been able to make out anything other than a blurry figure in the driver's seat.

Whilst this was happening, the pale coloured Volvo had also come to life and moved towards the gate in close attendance to the Audi. The guard had initially crossed from the booth to the driver's side of the car and while waiting for it to reach him, had noted the fast approaching Volvo behind. He had waved the Audi through, coming to attention and saluting as the following vehicle had drawn abreast of him.

Not stopping either, the driver of the Volvo had floored the accelerator and within a couple of metres beyond the gate, had overtaken the crawling Audi in a cloud of dust and set off towards the east. Directly above the road, the fiery orange orb of the sun was making a last desperate attempt not to sink into oblivion. A bank of cloud above the horizon was spectacularly tinged a pinkish orange as the provider of light exerted its last influence on the southern hemisphere.

Richardson pondered what he had just witnessed for several seconds before turning his attention to the hospital building. Voices coming along the pathway brought him back to the reality of the task at hand.

Manny had mentioned that visiting hours comprised two sessions: 15:00 to 16:00 and 19:00 to 20:00. Those who bothered, generally arrived for the afternoon visiting period. Due to the poor roads and fear of being stranded if vehicles broke down, very few took the risk after sundown. Nevertheless, three groups of what were obviously visitors had arrived early. They had parked their vehicles in a fenced enclosure inside the main gate obviously designated for that purpose.

Kevin rose and stretched his frame. He left the shelter provided by the dense foliage and moved on to the pathway about ten metres behind the last of the stragglers. Although brightly lit, he could not see much of the reception room beyond the doors. Large sections of the plate glass windows were obscured by a combination of lace curtains and sandblasted squares. He noted through a gap to the left of the doors however, that a different receptionist was on duty.

He grasped the handle of the hydraulically sprung door as it was about to close behind an attractive blonde teenage girl. She held it open for a second longer and flashed him a pretty smile before turning her back. Kevin allowed it to close gently against the spring loaded stay. It squeaked as it covered the last thirty centimetres of its arc and banged closed against the metal frame.

The dark haired, sallow complexioned receptionist was holding a telephone handset to her ear and listening intently. She showed no interest in him. Are the lines up or is it an internal call? Kevin wondered. Don't they ever do anything else? He sauntered past, looking away.

In his haste to avoid being challenged on the previous occasion, Kevin had not had time to properly take in the layout of the room. A large board on the upper part of the wall opposite the entrance displayed a map of the grounds and separate diagrams of the ground and two upper floors. Ward numbers were highlighted in bold red lettering. To the left beyond the second manned desk, a passage led to an ascending staircase. To the right another short passage ended in front of the double doors of an elevator.

The number 'O' suddenly glowed in the centre of the doorframe and the steel doors opened a few seconds later revealing an empty lift beyond.

The group ahead had dispersed, some had taken the stairs and the last members now disappeared into the lift. Richardson turned and found himself confronted by a seated frowning, but very attractive dark haired woman, probably in her early thirties. He noted the particularly well sculptured cheekbones and nose framed by short cropped curls.

Her deep brown eyes burned into him for a few seconds, but sudden recognition appeared to dawn upon her. The wrinkled brow was replaced by smooth blemish free skin, her eyes twinkled and a beautiful smile played around her partially open lips revealing a flawless set of brilliant white teeth.

Richardson noted the maroon uniform with white piping and matching headgear. A small rectangular shiny brass plate with white lettering proclaimed her to be Sister Conchitta Martinez.'

"Good evening Seester." Richardson smiled. He hoped that his effort at a Portuguese accent would have gone some way to disguising his actual roots had he needed to bluff his way past an unsuspecting receptionist.

"Good evening Doctor Texeira." The tone was nicely modulated with a husky timbre, but her origins were clear.

Dropping his gaze, he noted the steaming mug of hot coffee on the desk before her. The tantalizing aroma had wafted up his nose. He realized that several hours had passed since he had left Manuel's cottage and he was thirsty. He made as if to reach for the mug with his left hand, but his thrust was parried by Conchitta cupping a palm over the mug. She stared at him with mock reproach in her eyes, pursed her lips and gently shook her head from side to side.

Her eyes now adopted a steely glint. She unobtrusively moved a finger to her lips and inclined her head towards the central arched doorway through which he had previously located Ann. With her other hand she casually gestured that he should turn to the right and wait for her.

The receptionist still had her back towards them. She was still engrossed in her conversation and seemed to be admiring her reflection in the plate glass window. Her voice was soft and only a muted whisper carried to Kevin.

Conchitta rose from the revolving typists chair and moved towards Kevin's side of the desk.

"Thank you, seester." Kevin turned on his heel and moved towards the doorway. Conchitta followed. He was still about a metre from his immediate objective when a squeak from the door behind announced a new visitor.

Kevin kept moving and turned into the dark passage.

"Oh, Conchitta, before you go..." Richardson recognized the very British accent of David Wilson. "Please ask Kingwill to come and see me at the cottage. There was no reply from the Ops room when I tried to buzz him a few minutes ago."

Kevin heard Conchitta turn around behind him. Just around the corner, a door on the left was ajar. The room beyond was in darkness. He swung his body into the recess. Clinging to the frame he listened for a possible challenge. None came.

"Sure, David."

"Oh yes...before I forget, Kingwill and I will most probably be away for the next few days. Jim will be here to handle anything that crops up."

"Okay, David."

"And please call me Dave...I hate David!" Kevin recognized the barely controlled annoyance in Wilson's voice.

"Right, David...I mean Dave." Conchitta was nervous, but behind the tremor, she had difficulty in hiding her disdain for the man.

Richardson thought he heard a snort from Wilson. The external door squeaked and banged closed. The sound of quick footsteps reached him. Conchitta's head appeared around the jamb of the archway. She looked over her shoulder before gesturing to Kevin to stay put. He stuck out his left hand and raised his thumb. Her head disappeared.

"Hello Kingwill." Her voice carried clearly to Kevin. Even from his remote location he thought that her voice registered surprise. "Dave has been looking for you. Pleeze won't you go and see him at the cottage." There was silence for about ten seconds.

"Yes. Eet sounded urgent. I theenk you should go now." Another period of silence followed.

"I really theenk you should go now. I'm sure eet will be okay if you lock the Ops room."

He heard her replacing the handset in its cradle.

The curly locks appeared around the corner. The bonnet had disappeared. Conchitta closed her eyes and put her hands together as if to whisper a prayer.

Kevin advanced half a pace into the passageway. He smiled, nodded and gave another thumbs up. "Okay, I'll wait." he whispered and withdrew into the room. His eyes took several seconds to adjust to the dim interior. It appeared to be an examination room, its only furnishings comprised a hospital bed, two chairs and several low steel cabinets. A strange contraption next to the bed was possibly a mobile drip apparatus. Various other electronic monitors on the cabinets were presumably diagnostic machines.

Richardson paused. He thought he had heard footsteps coming from the east wing. He peered around the doorframe. Kingwill, dressed in a mottled camouflage green and sand uniform and brown leather belt and boots was approaching at a rapid pace for a man of his bulk. The passage beyond the entrance to reception was bathed in bright fluorescent light. He presumed that the lights in his section had been turned off as the public wards were in the other direction. The darkness also no doubt discouraged visitors from entering restricted areas!

Kingwill made a right turn through the archway with military-like precision.

"Okay, I've locked the Ops room and forwarded calls incoming calls here and to the guard room."

"No problem, Kingwill, we'll hold the fort. I'm sure you won't be long."

The door squeaked. Kevin heard an exchange of female voices and several seconds later Conchitta appeared around the corner. He was about to join her in the passage when she paused as if she had forgotten something. She held up her hand and turned on her heel and disappeared back into the reception area.

Kevin drew back.

Within what seemed to be mere seconds, she re-emerged carrying the mug of coffee and what appeared to be a canister of some sort. Her hands fully occupied, she mouthed what he lip-read to be 'five' and an apology, but the rest of the brief sentence was lost upon him.

Richardson nodded reluctantly and she set off up the passage in the opposite direction. He looked at Tracey's watch in annoyance. "What the hell is she doing now, he wondered? We must get going!"

He leaned against the door jamb listening intently. The click of her heels had receded. He took a deep breath and exhaled slowly. This shit was getting to him. How was Ann holding up? And Tracey...? He closed his eyes and tried to visualize their faces, but the pictures that came to him were blurred. His head throbbed. What is she up to? Kevin felt utterly helpless. He closed his eyes and took a deep breath trying to relax.

The rapid clip clop of a woman's high heels on the tiled floor brought him back to reality. Conchitta came into view around a corner along the passage from the east. She was almost running. He noted that she was still carrying the canister in her right hand. Her left hand was free.

"Kingwill's coffee cold so I give him fresh hot cup." She whispered, smiling.

She turned her head and waved towards the reception area as she passed the entrance. Kevin turned and fell in just behind her as she drew abreast of his hiding place. His inherited pistol had appeared in his left hand.

"We must move." He whispered, trying, but not succeeding, in keeping the annoyance from his voice.

"Don't worry, I don't theenk Kingwill be back very soon – it long walk to Meester Wilson cottage, then maybe he have sleep. Your wife, she okay. You no worry."

Richardson noted that the dim illumination of the passage was coming from night lights spaced at intervals in the ceiling between the now grey and lifeless rectangular fluorescent units.

They passed several rooms on either side before the passage ended in a T-junction. Conchitta turned left and Kevin barely stopped himself from colliding with her when she suddenly stopped and pulled open a door in the left wall. It appeared to be a provisions cupboard. She removed a bottle of what Kevin recognized as instant coffee and replaced it with the canister she had been carrying. It was identical.

"Kingwill, he only drink Kenyan coffee." Conchitta explained matter-of-factly before turning on her heel and entering what Richardson saw was a kitchenette on the opposite side of the passage. He remained in the doorway.

She stopped in front of the sink, unscrewed the lid of the coffee jar and proceeded to flush its contents down the drain. She replaced the lid on the bottle before throwing it into a waste bin.

"I collect it later." She remarked matter-of-factly, clearly not expecting a reply.

Kevin moved from her path as she spun around suddenly and set off down the passage. He was beginning to formulate his own ideas as to the reasons for her strange actions during the past five minutes.

They reached another T-junction. Richardson followed her as she turned left. He started. Over her shoulder ahead, he noted the sprawled awkward shape of a body in khaki uniform. The guard was slumped in a forward leaning seated position on a chair close to the right hand wall. A blue coffee mug lay on the floor at his feet, seemingly intact, its previous contents having formed an irregular pool on the red tiled floor. Streams of the brown liquid had run along the grouting. Splashes of the still wet liquid dotted the corridor wall behind, against which leaned an R1 automatic rifle. Kevin wondered what strange forces had enabled his dead weight to cheat the forces of gravity and had prevented him from pitching onto his face.

Conchitta unlocked and opened a door marked "Dispensary" just beyond the guard. Returning, she gently lowered the body to the floor and dragged it into the dispensary before rolling it onto its stomach. Kevin lingered in the passage listening. His right hand still gripped the briefcase. The knuckles and tendons of his left hand showed white through the skin from the tension as he squeezed the pistol's grip. Conchitta knocked on the door opposite, waited several seconds and knocked again. There was no reply. She depressed the door handle and slowly pushed it open. She turned to Richardson.

"Okay, you do your job and I do mine." She said pushing the door fully open and entering the room.

Kevin followed and dropped to his knees, placing the pistol on the floor. He opened the briefcase drawing out a roll of wide adhesive tape and a pair of scissors provided by Manny. He quickly wound several layers of tape around the soldier's ankles. The wrists were tied behind the limp body's back. He rolled it onto its side and completed the job by winding a double layer of the material across the sleeping soldier's head and mouth. He stood up, pocketed the CZ 83 and crossed the passage, almost colliding with Conchitta as she reversed out of the room opposite dragging another khaki clad body by the boots.

He bent to place the briefcase on the floor but she interjected saying "No, you leave me, I sort them out – you must hurry. He looked past her into the ward.

"Ann darling!"

His blonde wife was sitting on the bed against the far wall, her hands gripping the blanket on either side for support. She was dressed in a white nightgown. Richardson dropped the case and in three strides had her in his arms. On the way, he felt a thud on the toe of his shoe and the sound of something skidding along the floor before clattering against the wall.

"How are you? Are you okay? I've been so worried! Have you eaten? The words tumbled out as he cradled her against his chest.

"Where are we Kev?" She mumbled pulling her head away to get some air. "How's Trace?

"Trace is fine," he consoled. "Some bastards kidnapped us by mistake. We must get out of here."

Footsteps sounded behind him. He turned keeping his left arm around Ann's shoulders.

Conchitta had entered the room. She held a coffee mug in one hand and a large chequered dishcloth was draped over her arm. She bent to retrieve something from the floor alongside the bed. When she stood up, she held several fragments of what appeared to be another blue mug. She dropped them in a side pocket of her tunic. For the first time Kevin noted an upturned chair against the opposite wall. The sister righted the chair and bent down to wipe the floor alongside.

She turned to them, "You must go now, before Kingwill come back." She reached towards a console against the wall and drew a curtain at the head of the bed aside. Richardson noted that a steel door with small cottage type glass window panes was set into the wall. Conchitta withdrew a bunch of keys from her pocket and unlocked the door before allowing the drapes to fall back into place. She opened a cupboard against a side wall and laid a pair of blue denims and a matching blouse on the bed. She dropped a pair of comfortable looking sneakers on the floor.

"These fit me so they also fit you, I much bigger than you."

"Thank you." Ann smiled, clearly battling to keep her eyes open.

"I help your wife dress then lock her in. You go now before they not find me at reception and come here."

Chapter 12
Singapore

Chris Jensen deposited his black slimline briefcase on the low brick wall. Holding the laminated metallic foil shopping bag in his other hand he took several steps up the inclined bridge which crossed the meandering elongated pond. Leaning both elbows on the side rail, he gazed at the multi-coloured fish swimming lazily in the oxygenated bubbling water below.

A smile played around the corners of his mouth and his deep blue eyes sparkled. The tall elegant blond-haired South African of Norwegian extraction was in good spirits despite his lack of sleep. Negotiations in Sri Lanka for the sole agency had gone well. Fernando de Silva had promised to fax the signed agreement to him by Monday in time for Caldwell International's board meeting scheduled for three o'clock the next day.

The flight from Banderanaike International Airport in Colombo to Changi International had only taken an hour and a half, but the ridiculous departure time from Sri Lanka of twenty past one in the morning had threatened to dampen his enthusiasm. He couldn't wait to get back to Jacqui to share the good news and his dreams of the performance bonuses likely to flow from the deal.

He hadn't been able to get hold of her at home or on her cell during his week at the Lanka Oberoi Hotel in Colombo. Both had been on voice mail. A cloud passed over his eyes. He wondered if she had changed her mind... He turned his attention to the crystal clear water below.

Koi fascinated him. He had built his pond only three years before. Professional advice at the time had indicated that the rate of growth of "Nishikigoi" was largely governed by the size of the pond. His collection of fish had however, thrived and they were rapidly outgrowing their habitat.

The water below was populated mainly by Kohaku and Tashio Sanke – the former having white bodies with red patterns on their backs. The latter were tri-coloured with white bodies and both red patterns and black accents on their flanks. A Showa Sanke came into view as it made its leisurely way under the bridge, its black body patterned with red and white markings.

Notwithstanding his limited knowledge of the ornamental fish developed by the Japanese some two hundred years before, his personal favourites were the single metallic-hued silver and gold varieties. He wondered how old some of the magnificent specimens on view were twenty years? Thirty years? He had read somewhere that they had a potential lifespan of sixty to seventy years. An article on the internet had told of a fish that survived for 200 years! He wondered how the life of that particular koi had been documented. Over how many generations had it been bequeathed?

Jensen straightened his six foot frame and stretched. It was too warm. He needed to remove his leather jacket. May as well make my way to the lounge and have a beer, he thought. He had already checked his luggage in for the flight to Johannesburg. He still had a couple of hours to kill. The quality foil bag rustled as he dropped his arm. He was sure she would love the figurine he had bought. He turned and slowly made his way down the ramp.

Reaching the level tiled floor he frowned. Surely he had not left his briefcase that far from the bridge! He picked up the satin black synthetic leather case. It was still locked and looked okay. Oh well, must be the fatigue catching up, he thought and set off for the pub.

***

Jensen was exhausted and he looked it. The flight from Singapore had taken the best part of eighteen hours and he had not slept a wink. Bad weather and a headwind had not helped. He had in any event never been able to sleep on a plane. The Asian chap in the adjoining seat had coughed and spluttered for the duration of the journey. Jensen's head was throbbing, his eyes were sore and was that a nose run? He reached into his pocket for a handkerchief. He hoped his usually cast iron immune system was not going to let him down now.

He probed twice without success in the gloom, then, with an effort, found the horizontal slot into which he fed the parking ticket. He was momentarily taken aback by the reading. "Fortunately not for my account!" he shrugged and proffered his credit card.

The BMW was still in its parking bay on the third floor of the parkade. Not that he had expected it not to be. Although he had thus far not had the misfortune to be hijacked or have a car stolen, several colleagues and family members had experienced such ordeals. Despite the cracking of large syndicates by special branches within the police force, luxury cars and four wheel drives were still regularly stolen to order and shipped over the borders into Africa. Some were reportedly even found in Europe and the former iron curtain countries. Even old jalopies considered by their owners to be "safe and undesirable" were regularly taken at gunpoint for spares.

Without fail he would breathe an involuntary sigh of relief to see the Beemer. Not that he hadn't on occasion forgotten his bay number and spent anxious minutes combing several floors.

Jensen followed the winding exit road from Jan Smuts International Airport and chose the R24 motorway to Johannesburg. The pale orange numbers of the dash mounted clock told him it was 20:15. Despite the interesting destinations he frequently visited, he was always glad to set foot back on home soil. He looked forward to seeing Jacqui, having a soaking hot bath and collapsing unconscious into bed with her in his arms. The way he felt, he doubted he would get beyond the bed. He was struggling to concentrate and the hard drizzle was not making his task any easier.

He reached for the clip at the base of the rear-view mirror and dipped the instrument twice in annoyance. The car behind was driving too close for the weather conditions. The driver was also obviously half blind as the precipitation would merely reflect the bright light and not improve visibility. He wondered if it was an Audi as the bluish glow was reminiscent of the lighting technology the brand currently employed.

20:25. He should be home in another twenty minutes. Jensen moved across to the left into the second lane at the Gilloolys interchange and chose the N3 North link which entailed a two hundred and seventy degree rotation from the westerly direction he had been travelling. As he entered the new motorway at a tangent he noted that the blue tinged headlamps were still close behind. Too close.

Annoyed, he put his foot down. The rear of the car seemed to squat momentarily and then it took off. Jensen looked in the mirror. The other vehicle had been caught unawares and was floundering in his wake several hundred metres behind. A sudden flash of blue light illuminated the Beemer's rear window.

"Shit!" Jensen glanced down at the speedometer, instinctively lifting his foot from the loud pedal. He had been doing over 150 KMH. That meant a heavy fine in view of the 120 limit. The other car was some distance back, no doubt having seen the flash of the speed trap camera. The road ahead was deserted. Even the oncoming traffic was sparse. People were staying indoors in the inclement weather. He throttled back and moved into the extreme left lane. The needle of the speedometer settled at a steady 100.

The rain was now pouring down in what seemed to be solid sheets. The windscreen wipers were hardly coping at their fastest sweep rate. He slowed further. Suddenly bright lights loomed in his rear window and he realized that the other car had moved into the right hand lane and was preparing to overtake. He lifted his foot and the car's momentum slowed even further. He waited for the other vehicle to pass. Despite the glare he was now sure that it was an Audi.

He glanced towards the right hand mirror. Why had the bugger not passed? He was sick and tired of playing cat and mouse in the rain. Jensen did a double take and just stopped himself from swerving. The other car had moved abreast and was keeping pace, less than a metre away, the side mounted rear-view mirrors almost touching. In the centre of the car's front passenger side window the unmistakable menace of a handgun's barrel glinted. Alongside a finger was gesturing for him to pull over.

Without thinking, Jensen floored the accelerator. The BMW took off, the rear wheels spinning and scrabbling for grip on the wet tarmac despite the German vehicle's anti skid technology. The Audi's driver had anticipated Jensen's move and accelerated almost simultaneously, but the BMW managed to gain several significant lengths. In his mirror, Jensen noticed the pale coloured Audi suddenly duck sideways, settling in another lane further to the right. He guessed that it had hit a pool of water and the driver had battled to regain control as the tyres aquaplaned.

Their dice had in the meantime taken a turn to the west as Jensen had chosen the N1 Western Bypass. He wondered how he could shake his pursuers. The rain had eased, visibility was far better, but this nose to tail race had to end. The Audi had stayed in the lane outside and just behind the BMW. He had wondered if the one or two dull thuds he had heard had been bullets ploughing into the back of his car, but dismissed the thought. They obviously wanted his car. A blowout at this speed would mean a written off vehicle which would not bring them any revenue.

A signpost reminded Jensen that they were within 300 metres of the William Nicoll off-ramp. He slowed the BMW slightly, allowing the Audi to almost draw level. Jensen suddenly pulled the steering wheel to the left, leaving the motorway. The Beemer responded without protest, the rear end settling into a controlled drift, and then ran true on its new chosen path. The Audi pilot was caught unawares and responded way too late. From the corner of his eye, Jensen saw the other vehicle's tail lights illuminate. He heard the sound of slithering rubber as the driver battled to bring the car to rest.

Jensen turned left at the red traffic signal without stopping after hastily making sure that no vehicles were crossing. Not a vehicle was in sight. He had gained precious time. It had most probably taken the Audi driver at least a hundred metres to bring the car to a stop. Unless he made a u-turn he would have had to reverse back to the off-ramp. The road was well lit. Jensen switched off his headlamps.

He turned left at the first intersection, accelerated and turned left again into a wooded driveway. He had passed this house on many occasions. The driveway was u-shaped with two entrance/exits and no gates. He had turned into the far leg of the driveway, had coasted slowly to the other end of the u, stopping with the Beemer's nose still just inside and under the protection offered by a row of dense trees.

Several minutes passed slowly by. He had initially contemplated getting out of the car and creeping towards the bushes at the edge of the driveway to see whether the Audi had turned into his road and was lying in wait for the Beemer to appear. He had dismissed the idea when he realized that his would be hijackers were possibly relying on such an action which could very well result in his being cornered away from his only possible means of escape. No one had stirred in the house behind.

Jensen looked at his watch. 21:30. He had been sitting in the car for over half an hour! It had stopped raining. He gently opened his door. He was in the habit of not using the interior lighting so did not check that it was switched off. Leaving it ajar, he crept past the dense shrubs towards the sidewalk. The roadway was poorly lit, the tops of the tall lamp standards largely being encircled by the branches of the tall trees that lined the sidewalk. It was still overcast and the heavens beyond were inky black. Craning his neck, he looked up the road towards the dual carriageway from whence he had turned. Not a soul moved. Gaining in confidence he ventured further out of the shadows. Nothing stirred.

Climbing aboard the Beemer he started the engine and made a gentle three point reverse turn which enabled him to exit via the farthest arm of the driveway. Leaving his lights off he nosed the car gently into the road and turned left. After several hundred metres there was still no sign of pursuit. He turned right and switched on his lights.

Less than five minutes later he stopped and waited for the remote controlled steel gates to open. Although the time clock operated garden lamps were on, the house was in darkness. He wondered if Jacqui was home. A sickening feeling in the pit of his stomach told him it was unlikely – whether she went out at night or not, she always left a couple of interior lights on.

He waited for the garage door to close and climbed the three stairs to the patio. He dropped his overnight bag on the floor. Holding his briefcase in one hand, he stabbed a finger at the doorbell. Without pausing he unlocked the front door. The hallway was in darkness. Jensen switched on several lights. A pilot light from the telephone drew his attention. There was at least one message! In his haste to retrieve it, he dropped the briefcase on to the tiled floor. It teetered briefly before falling flat on to its side with a loud gunshot-like report.

"Hi Chris, I didn't want to spoil your trip, but I guess that this won't be totally unexpected. Although I know you don't agree now, we do need some time apart to focus on what we want from this marriage. I am going away for a while ...Please don't waste time trying to find me...you won't. You have been spending so much time away that we have almost become strangers. We used to be friends as well as lovers, but I don't know what to talk about anymore ...it's as if we are strangers with nothing in common. I will contact you when I am ready which may well be soon..." Her voice was cut off abruptly as the message recording tape ran out of time.

"But I've been working for *our* future Jacqui... please come back, I need you!" Jensen almost shouted aloud in exasperation, tears in his eyes. There were six more messages – one from his best friend Dan about the resumption of their twice-weekly squash games, two from work colleagues and three for Jacqui, but no more from his wife.

He started dialling her mobile number, checked the time and replaced the receiver. She was most probably fast asleep and would not appreciate his waking her.

He retrieved his bag from the patio and slammed the front door. Lifting his arm, he smelled his armpit, wrinkling his nose. "Too bad... I'm knackered ... no one else can smell me." He thought.

Jensen's head was throbbing. He entered their bedroom, kicking off his shoes and switched on the bedside lamp from the remote control at the door. He half hoped he had been having a nightmare and that he would see his beloved's auburn head of hair on her pillow. It was not.

His head was throbbing. He swallowed two aspirin from the bathroom cupboard washing them down with a tumbler of water. Whisky would have been better he thought, but shelved the idea, the combination of alcohol and medicine would not be wise, particularly in his state. He fell face first onto Jacqui's feather pillow. Her smell still lingered. He lost consciousness almost immediately.

Chapter 13

"Chris, I can't go on like this, you eat, dream and sleep work! Our personal and social life has gone to hell. You're constantly preoccupied and not fun to be with anymore. I've had enough!"

"But Jacqui, I told you four months ago that this was the deal of a lifetime. That if you gave me six months and it came off, we would virtually be made for life. So I *have* been staying late at the office and *have* been travelling a lot, but I'm almost there. Just allow me one more trip to Sri Lanka. Da Silva is always cagy, but he is battling to hide his enthusiasm over the latest deal I've put together. I'm ninety-nine percent sure he'll sign. If this deal doesn't work out, I promise that I'll ask Brian to move me to a local portfolio."

"You've said that before Chris. I'm not concerned about more money, I've wanted my husband back for so long that I've almost resigned myself to having to make a life without you. Some of my friends think I'm crazy to sit at home when I could be having fun with them. I'd rather not elaborate on one or two of their ideas of fun 'cause I have never contemplated being unfaithful to you. I've had enough. I'm not sure I'll be here when you get back."

"Jacqui, please..."

The alarm woke Jensen with a start. In his dazed state he battled for several seconds to find the off switch, his flailing arm knocking the bedside lamp to the floor in his confusion. His bleary eyes noted the time – 6.00 am! Why the hell had he not switched it off last night?

What a bloody time to be awoken on a Saturday morning! He thought. His throat was sore, his eyes were gummed up and his nose was running. Thank you Mister Chong, I hope you still feel like shit too!

He lay on his back with his eyes closed. He remembered every word of their one-sided argument. Jacqui had not been prepared to budge. He could hardly blame her, but he *had* at last landed the big one. Da Silva was dead keen after their meeting. Surely there is no way he will pull out now. Or could he still? What if he had been canvassing for competing quotes without him knowing? He may find a cheaper substitute but it will cost him in the long run!

Jensen sat up. What the hell, he was awake now, he may as well get up – he was not likely to get any more sleep. He showered, shaved and dosed himself with three different remedies he found in the medicine cabinet. Well, let's see if they work, he thought. One was for sore throat, another for a runny nose and the last for 'relief for colds and flu.' For a moment he considered checking their expiry dates but the thought passed. What about depression?

Despite his mood, he felt hungry. He had only picked at the light dinner on the plane. He headed for the kitchen. On the way he passed the briefcase lying on the hall floor. He picked it up and carried it to the lounge where he laid it on a coffee table. He would review the agreement after breakfast and see if there were any areas that needed panel-beating. Had he possibly overlooked a sweetener or two which would put the final nail in Da Silva's coffin?

Chris Jensen opened the bread bin. The thought of a simple breakfast consisting of a plateful of bacon, two eggs, three slices of toast and bottomless cups of freshly brewed coffee had started his digestive juices flowing. His stomach rumbled in anticipation. The sight that greeted him made a significant dent in his expectations. A half loaf of white bread had turned a mid shade of green with mould

Oh well, delete the toast he thought and opened the refrigerator door.

The contents totally crushed his mood. The orange juice bottle had about three centimetres left. He opened the milk container and wrinkled his nose. Jacqui must have left immediately after he had departed on his trip. A cracked and warped orange chunk of cheese completed the picture. He closed the door in disgust and checked the freezer compartment. The half dozen or so TV dinners did not appeal.

Oh well, I'll have to go out and stock up...maybe I'll go to Angelo's for one of their 'Man Sized English Breakfasts' he thought. He checked his watch. 7:10. Too early. He filled the kettle. He could still have some coffee with powdered milk!

Then he remembered the previous evening's events! How could he have forgotten? What had those bastards been up to? He passed the hall table and lifted the handset of the telephone. What was the number of the local police station again? He replaced the handset and picked up the telephone number index book. Jacqui kept a loose sheet of paper in the front with emergency numbers as well as others such as the chemist and dry cleaner. His finger stabbed the first three digits before he slammed the instrument down in disgust.

What would he tell them? That two guys in a pale coloured Audi had tried to hijack him. That due to the weather conditions he had not been able to see whether the car even had licence plates? That one of them had pointed a gun at him? No, no one had been injured in the accident and there had been no damage to property. Then he remembered. There *had* been several thudding noises at the back of the Beemer during the chase. He had wondered whether the remote sounds had come from stones and debris from the storm the tyres had thrown up into the wheel wells.

He waited in anticipation while the motorized double wooden garage door disappeared behind the lintel above.

So he *had* been shot at. A round hole to the left of the number plate stared at him. Jensen carefully examined the rear of the vehicle before he sat on his haunches and inspected the underside. Another bullet had penetrated the valence and spare wheel housing lower down.

He opened the boot lid. The upper bullet had gone straight through the double-skinned metal and appeared to have lodged in the squab of the rear seat. He lifted the boot carpet and spare wheel cover and immediately saw the large calibre slug lodged between the tyre and metal panel.

'Aha, at least there is evidence that I was not dreaming", he thought. He left the bullet in situ and checked the back seat from the interior of the car. It had not gone through. More evidence, he thought, relieved that the face of the leather seat face had not been pierced as well. Hopefully the police could dig it out from within the boot without causing further damage.

***

Jensen replaced the receiver. He had telephoned the Vehicle Crime Investigation Unit and had spent several frustrating minutes answering questions that to him at least, had seemed to be totally irrelevant. Only then had he been told that as there had been no injuries, he should make an appointment to see Inspector Tshabalala who in any event would only be available after two o'clock on Monday afternoon.

He dialled Jacqui's number. It was still on voicemail.

"Darling, I'm home and the Sri Lankan deal is in the bag. Please come home. We *can* work this out. I love you..." He gently replaced the handset.

Chapter 14
Namibia

Kevin looked around nervously. Darkness had descended. The picture confronting him depicted a completely different scenario to that which he had encountered hours before when he had jumped from the ward window in broad daylight. The wire fence some twenty metres away stretched as far as he could see in either direction. Illumination of the barrier and a fuzzy narrow strip on either side was provided by yellowish lights on tall steel poles planted at regular intervals. He presumed that a brighter, possibly search light, on an even taller pole to the west, marked the corner of the property near the gate and guard booth.

The wall against which he huddled was in relative shadow. He had removed his jacket in the ward and his dull-hued clothing merged into the background. Black squares in the wall above his head indicated that curtains had either been drawn or office lights switched off, with the onset of darkness. Thick linings helped to limit those lights that were on, to a hardly discernable glow. Further to the west, a bank of lights on the upper floor showed that there was some life after all. Half a dozen small illuminated squares dotted the rest of the wall at random intervals. Probably bathrooms he guessed.

The scenario reminded him of German concentration camps depicted in old World War 2 movies he enjoyed watching occasionally on satellite television channels or from his (and Ann's) personal collection. Personal favourites included "The Great Escape" and "The Wooden

Horse." How he wished that he and his better half were cuddled up now and watching a movie with Tracey, rather than living in one! The latter would generally cuddle up between them, only to fall asleep within minutes contented to be in their company. Richardson's wandering mind returned to the reality at hand.

There were fortunately no sentry-occupied pillar boxes on poles giving uninterrupted three hundred and sixty degree vision and he doubted there were any articulated searchlights. His previous escape had also not uncovered any tripwires!

The hole through which he had previously escaped lay probably fifty metres to the west. It had no doubt been repaired.

He drew a slim cylindrical object from his pocket, placed his hand over the end and with his thumb pressed the button which protruded like a pimple from the centre of the tube. A translucent reddish glow from the thin flesh around the perimeter of his palm told him that the torch was in operating order. Kevin briefly surveyed the inky blackness beyond the fence. The intermediate light in the foreground made it even more difficult for his eyes to make any impression on penetrating the gloom.

Richardson aimed the torch at an imaginary point in the distance.

"Come in, Echo, do you read me!"

Kevin dropped his arm and took a hurried step backwards into the shadows of the wall behind. He winced as his elbow thumped into the brickwork. He was closer to the structure than he thought. Hastily pocketing the torch to free his hand to rub the stinging and protesting bone, he took a deep breath to slow his heartbeat. He had forgotten the guards who had almost crept up on him.

"Roger, O C Charlie... read you loud and clear."

Kevin recognized Trevor Ryan's distinctive deep voice. The two uniformed guards (soldiers!) who had been sauntering along, stopped directly in front of Richardson's position, a mere ten metres away.

Ryan cradled the walkie-talkie to his left ear and turned his back to the hospital building. His companion removed the shoulder strap of his rifle and balanced the weapon against his groin. He lit a cigarette. Despite the low light emitting from the overhead pylons, the flare from the match silhouetted his bereted head and the wire stands of the perimeter fence glinted against the dark background of the undergrowth beyond.

"How're things Trev?

"All's quiet on the Western front, Mike ...surprised you're not catching zeees!"

"Oh, I found me a good book with pictures of birds – the two legged kind." Mike Miller's crackly teenage voice sounded as if it was still breaking. "These youngsters are hardly out of school." Thought Richardson. "How did they get involved with this bunch of crooks?"

"You arsehole! All birds have two legs." mocked Ryan.

"I mean the ones without wings!" Mike Miller sounded sheepish. "How's Geoff?"

"Don't worry, he's here with me. I stopped him from catching a kip in one of the Bedfords. He's polluting the atmosphere and ozone layer with one of those bloody foul-smelling fags of his. I doubt he'll see his twenty-first, if the army doesn't kill him."

"Go to hell! Miller too!" Geoff Simpson responded without enthusiasm. Richardson noticed the reddish glow from the tip of his nose as he inhaled deeply.

"Where are the big brass tonight?" Ryan enquired into the brick-sized handset.

"Oh... Mac, Harvey and Steinmann left together a while back. They and Wilson spent half the day behind closed doors. I think Van is still at Bravo," Miller replied.

"And Wilson?"

"He must be around. He hasn't been past here since six o'clock. Don't be surprised if he pays us a visit."

"Okay Mike, see you later. Enjoy the birds."

"Cheers Trev." Miller replied. The line went dead.

Trevor Ryan clipped the handset to his webbing belt.

Geoff Simpson took a final draw on his cigarette before dropping it on to the gravel next to his boot. Slowly and with measured deliberation, he raised his right knee, then suddenly dropped his heel on the butt as if it were an insect trying to escape. It would have been an uneven contest.

"What's the latest on the blonde lady?"

"They've moved her to another ward. Those two new guys are guarding her under threat of death if they allow any unauthorized visitors. They've tried to spread a story that she must be kept sedated until they can carry out an operation. Wilson has also let it be known to the locals that her husband is a mental case and is likely to harm her if he's allowed in." Ryan responded.

"And her husband?" Geoff Simpson shot back.

"Nobody seems to know. I think Wilson is worried about him getting to the authorities. They don't know what he knows or might have seen. In any case, Van Den Berg is playing dumb. You know that he told us to play deaf and mind our own business if we want to continue getting well paid and not be sent back to an extended stint of basic training. He threatened Mike and me with castration if we tell anyone how those two were brought here." Ryan shuffled his feet and made as if to move on. He was ready to continue their patrol.

"Let's go Geoff.

Simpson shouldered his rifle and reluctantly set off after Ryan who had already taken several steps towards their destination in the east.

***

The sentries had covered at least fifty metres before Kevin slowly pushed his stiff frame away from the cold brick wall. The vertebrae at the base of his neck and between his shoulder blades were sore from the tension of not moving whilst Ryan had conversed with the guard room. He massaged the area and stretched.

He looked at Tracey's watch. The luminous figures glowed 8:15. Where was Manny? He picked up the briefcase.

Richardson crept to the edge of the dimly lit pathway. Ryan and Simpson were now distant specks to the west. He raised the torch, but before his thumb touched the button, two brief stabs of light split the inky blackness beyond the fence. A shadowy figure appeared on the fringe of the light pool beyond.

Three brief pencil thin beams spurted staccato-like from Kevin's torch.

"Manny, is that you?" his whisper was hardly audible.

The figure edged forward so that only a nose and the lower part of a face were visible. The dark slash of the moustache left Richardson in little doubt as to its owner's identity. The dim outline of his body was hardly discernable. Kevin guessed that he had changed into black slacks and shirt.

"Yes. Is everything okay Kevin?"

"Sure. We need to get moving."

Manny darted to the fence and crouched next to a large diameter supporting pole.

Richardson doubted that he would be particularly visible to anyone along the fence at a distance of more than fifty metres. Someone looking out of a hospital window? Well that would be a different story and was something they would have to chance! Kevin wondered whether Manny would try to cut the power cable. Better not, he thought – that would probably draw attention to the darkened area and he might even be electrocuted!

Several consecutive sharp clicking sounds shattered the almost deathly silence. There was a brief pause while Manny waited to see if the noise had alerted anyone else in the vicinity. He used the wire cutters to sever a dozen or so more strands before he pulled the upside-down L-shaped piece of wire mesh free and arched it back towards the intact fencing alongside. He clipped the stiff spring-loaded section leaving a rectangular opening and joined Richardson.

"I have a problem with the Audi, it's got no power – it keeps on stalling. I think the fuel injectors are playing up. You're likely to get stuck..."

Richardson pondered for a few seconds. "Well, I'll just have to take the Subaru. If we put Ann in the Audi, will you make it to the main road? We can transfer her without them even knowing you were involved."

"Oh don't worry about my alibi, I've already been to Camp Bravo to pick up some medical supplies. They're in a bag in the boot. At least I won't have to tell Wilson and Co. that you hijacked the Audi! Let's get Ann."

They found her sitting on the bed in semi-darkness leaning against the wall. Her eyes flickered open as Kevin placed his hand gently over hers and she forced a smile.

"Come, darling we must get out of here."

Kevin and Manny half-carried her between them to the gap in the fence, the former battling to hold his briefcase at the same time. There was no sign of the guards. Once through the hole, Manny led them to the Audi which had been reversed up an incline some fifty metres beyond, just off a track which joined the main road four hundred metres away to the north.

They helped her into the back of the car and she lay down on the bench seat. Kevin placed the briefcase on the floor.

"Darling, rather don't lie down, I'll be back soon and you'll have to get into another car. Please try to stay awake."

She struggled into a sitting position. "Okay, Kev. Sorry, but I'm so-ooo tired."

"I think I'll be able to coast most of the way to the main road." Manny clambered into the driver's seat and turned on the ignition to free the steering lock, leaving the headlamps switched off.

"Give us a push."

Kevin positioned the heels of his hands on the vertical panel of the boot lid. His unstressed fingers rested lightly at right angles on the top of the panel. He anchored his feet in the spongy earth before he exerted forward pressure. His first attempt made no impression at all and for a moment he wondered whether the hand brake was still engaged. No, he remembered seeing and hearing Manny release the lever.

He crouched low against the back of the vehicle and with an almighty effort straightened his legs again. He felt the resistance of the Audi's tyres in the soft sand wavering. Another powerful shove saw the wheels break free and the car started rolling down the slope. Kevin maintained the propulsion for a good twenty metres by which time the car had gained substantial momentum, before he pulled up breathing heavily. Manny waved and the Audi's brake lights flickered briefly as he rounded a bend and disappeared.

He headed back up the slope.

Crouching in the shadows at the edge of the cleared pathway parallel to the fence, he surveyed the length of the barrier. There was no sign of Ryan and Simpson. He looked at Tracey's watch. Half an hour had passed. They were due to make their return patrol.

Keeping low, Kevin made a dash for the fence, unclipping the square flap of mesh as he reached his immediate destination. The steel wire sprang back into position behind him leaving no visible sign of the breach, as he sprinted for the sanctuary of the shadows against the hospital wall. There was still no sign of the guards.

He edged along the wall towards the corner of the building some fifty metres away in the direction of the hospital gate. His immediate objectives, a large tree and the diamond mesh fence beyond, were reached without incident. This razor wire topped barrier which had previously prevented him from reaching the rear of the building, stretched at ninety degrees to the perimeter fence twenty metres away. Patrolling sentries gained access through a well illuminated padlocked gate at the junction of the fences.

From the shadows of the tree Kevin could see the guard hut and gate to the west, although they were curiously, not well lit. In between, the guardhouse nestled in relative shadow, intermittent flickering light from suspended lanterns illuminating small rectangular windows.

To the north, between the hospital building and guardhouse, the vehicle park also lay in darkness beyond the pathway leading to reception.

Kevin removed the Subaru's ignition key from his trouser pocket and pressed the 'unlock' button. In the distance a single brief flash from the headlamps announced that the high performance saloon was present and ready to serve. He waited with bated breath for what appeared to be several minutes but was in reality probably no more than thirty seconds. Nobody appeared to have noticed. All creatures of the night had either died or scuttled into their burrows where they were not daring to breathe. Not even a lonely cricket made a sound.

Reaching into his other pocket, he withdrew Manny's wire cutters and cut a strand of the mesh where it had been secured against the wall. To Kevin's ears, the sharp click seemed to shatter the night. He waited a few seconds, but nothing or no one stirred. He rapidly snipped six more strands. Somewhere in the distance to the east a low howling sound gradually intensified.

Chapter 15

Chris Jensen deposited several bags of groceries on the kitchen counter. He unpacked the perishable items and placed them in the refrigerator and freezer compartments. The rest he pushed aside to sort out later.

He had made himself an enjoyable breakfast and despite the effects of the influenza, he was in reasonably good spirits. Surely Jacqui would be back soon. He was certain there was not another man in her life. He *had* neglected her in recent months, but his potential substantial increase in income, the additional time they would be able to spend together and the likely future improvement in their lifestyle, would surely enable her to realize it had been in both of their interests. She would have to forgive him!

On his way to the lounge he passed the hall table and checked the answering machine for messages. There were none. He tried to focus on other positive issues to counter the feeling of depression that threatened to take hold. He would send an e-mail to Da Silva to thank him for his hospitality and anticipated extension of their business relationship. He retrieved his briefcase from the lounge and made his way to the study.

"That's strange, why won't it open?" he thought. The case had a double locking system comprised of both key and combination locks. The key had refused to turn and had jammed in the keyhole as a result of the force applied in frustration. The metal was close to shearing off. The combination lock was also reluctant to respond to his pre-chosen numerical sequence.

After half an hour of wasted effort, Jensen's anger was difficult to contain. He could not wait until Monday to consult a locksmith and in any event, his attempts to prise open the case had damaged it so badly cosmetically that he would be embarrassed to carry it in future. The screwdriver had slipped countless times scratching the gunmetal-hued locks and had gouged the black leather leaving nasty cuts all along the top.

On two occasions his forefinger had been on the receiving end of slips, the last time the screwdriver had penetrated the thin flesh on the side of the second joint causing him to cry aloud from pain. He had flung the tool against the wall and rushed to the bathroom where he had held the injured digit under the cold water tap for several minutes.

He looked at his left hand. The finger still throbbed and blood had soaked through the layers of toilet paper wound around it. Jensen hung his hand and allowed the red and white ribbon to unravel. The blood had virtually stopped oozing. He gingerly applied a self adhesive plaster but could not help flinching as he carefully secured the end.

As a result of his failed attempts to open the case, strong doubts had started forming as to whether it was in fact his. In his eagerness to review the agreement with Da Silva, he had started to find reasons for the failure of the briefcase to open. Maybe it had been damaged during his trip causing the locks to move out of alignment. He knew that he was clutching at straws and remembered his surprise at finding the case several metres away from where he had placed it in the shopping mall at Lanka Oberoi Airport.

Jensen walked to the garage and returned with a hammer and chisel. "Now we'll see who jerks who around." He thought. Two swift strategically-placed blows smashed the latches and the case fell open.

It *was not* his case. The shallow compartment contained a slim zipped plastic toilet bag, a pair of skimpy blue sleeping shorts, a white hand towel and an empty spectacle case. Strange, he thought, the bag was not as deep as his. He compared the internal depth to the outer dimensions. Something was definitely fishy. There must be another compartment. He felt around the perimeter of the floor of the case. His probing fingers found a small metal clip which would most probably have escaped notice had he not been looking for it. He prodded it with no result. With difficulty he gripped the thin wire with his fingernails and pulled.

Something gave way and Jensen noticed that the thin fibre panel which had covered the entire bottom of the case had loosened. He lifted the panel and did a double take. The case was full of neatly packed bundles of one hundred and larger denomination US Dollar bills. Jensen picked up one of the bundles. The notes were brand new. Two of the bundles stood slightly proud of the others. He lifted them. Below was a bulging rectangular plastic bag containing what appeared to be a fine white powder.

***

"Hello, may I please speak to a senior member of the Crime Intelligence Unit?"

"I'm afraid no senior members are available on a Sunday. May I have your details and I will get one of the investigators to call you." Why am I not surprised, he almost questioned aloud.

"Thank you. Could a senior detective contact me urgently? I cannot give details over the phone." Jensen provided his cell number. After the events of last night he was reluctant to give his address to anyone. In a way he was glad that Jacqui was not around. He presumed that the dealers had switched briefcases with the intention of reversing the swop once he had passed through customs at Johannesburg International. Their plans had obviously gone awry and they had been prevented from intercepting him before he left the airport car park.

Jensen dialled the "lost baggage" number in the directory. The enquiries clerk was very helpful. She had in fact taken a call from a man who had phoned in to report that his briefcase had been accidentally switched. He had given the name "Omar" and a cell number. Jensen's curiosity was pricked. He realized that a call to the number would record his own number and would no doubt enable the unscrupulous thugs to trace him. "Omar's" number, whether via a call centre or not, would at least provide the authorities with a starting point for their investigations.

***

The sound of the front gate buzzer shattered the silence. Jensen opened and closed his eyes. He settled back in the armchair happy to continue his dream.

The buzzing was repeated. Consecutive staccato rings conveyed the increasing impatience of the ringer. Jensen awoke with a start. He took a few seconds to get his bearings and looked at his watch. It was 9:05. He abruptly sat bolt upright before coming to his feet, grabbing at the arm of the chair to steady himself.

"Shit, must have dozed off". He took five wobbling steps to the hall and lifted the intercom receiver.

"Hello!" Through the glass panel alongside the front door, he noted that a white Toyota sedan had drawn up beyond the gate. The African driver had opened his window and stuck his head out to get closer to the microphone. Even from a distance of 30 metres, Jensen could see that he was dwarfed by the white giant in the passenger seat alongside.

"Um, Mr Jensen, I'm Detective Inspector Themba. Inspector Brown is with me. We spoke yesterday."

"Sure, um...sorry to keep you waiting. I'm opening the gate. Park next to the house and I'll meet you outside."

Jensen waited for the car to pass through the gate before he closed it with the remote control. He unlocked the front door and walked to meet his plain-clothed guests who had already alighted from their vehicle. Themba was a slightly built man with a limp handshake.

"Good morning, Mr Jensen, I'm Tony Themba and this is Graham Brown." Themba appeared midget-like next to Brown who Jensen guessed tipped the scales at around 105 kilograms and stood close to two metres in his enormous elasticized casual brown shoes. He consciously dug his hand deep into Brown's massive mitt to prevent him gaining leverage, but barely managed to avoid it being crushed.

"Morning Mr Jensen, nice place you have here – always loved thatched roofing. Nice and quiet here, away from the traffic. Gee, how big is this stand, it must be at least 4000 square metres?"

"Please call me Chris. This way... um, can I offer you gentleman something to drink?" Gingerly flexing the fingers of his right hand out of Brown's view, Jensen turned on his heel and led the way back to the house.

Over the next thirty minutes Jensen recounted his experiences from the time he had noticed his briefcase had been moved in the Singapore air terminal to his eventual giving of the slip to his pursuers in the Audi on Friday evening. Themba had taken possession of the briefcase and its contents which he had placed in the Toyota's boot, before they followed Chris to access the garaged BMW.

Inspector Brown had taken several photographs of the bullet holes in the Beemer and had used a pen knife to extract the slug from the back seat. Jensen had been happy that they had not taken his car away, as he had read many horror stories about vehicles impounded by the authorities that had suffered parts pilfering and other damage whilst in custody.

"Please do not have the damage repaired just yet." Themba had advised.

"We have leads on a syndicate that has operatives in Nigeria, Singapore, the U K and South America and are currently investigating their contacts closer to home." Themba had volunteered. "Do you and your family have somewhere else to stay? It may be a good idea to lay low for a while. These guys are most probably moving heaven and earth to find you."

"I'll sort out something. Maybe I can stay with my brother for a while. I'll get hold of my wife and tell her not to come back here until she hears from me – she's away at the moment."

"Please don't tell her any of the finer details about this, or at least just tell her some suspicious thugs have been loitering. We'll post a car on twenty-four hour patrol with a guard on your premises from today." Brown was in his element and clearly enjoyed taking charge.

Behind Brown, Themba had visibly shrugged and given Jensen a look which had clearly conveyed "Humour him, I'm running things here."

"Thank you Graham. I really appreciate your help. It's frustrating though to have to go to ground and not be able to stay in your own home." The Police Inspector had shrugged. Jensen had contemplated enquiring whether the juggernaut had played rugby, but the thought passed. "Their having my briefcase also doesn't help, as there are notes which will tell them that I planned to go back to Singapore in a week's time and where I intended to stay."

"Hopefully our forensic guys will get some prints off the items in the case which our colleagues in Singapore will be able to tie up to their current suspects." The black officer did not sound convinced.

Themba and Brown had given him further contact numbers and after exchanging pleasantries had gone on their way.

***

Back at the offices of Caldwell International, Jensen sent a brief e-mail to Fernando da Silva in Sri Lanka thanking him for his hospitality and asking for a copy of the agreement after briefly explaining that his briefcase had been lost.

Then he dialled Jackie's cell number. Expecting her voice mail to be switched on, he was surprised when she answered.

"Hello Chris, how was your trip to Sri Lanka?" Jensen was caught unawares. Was that indifference in her voice or was she possibly just a teeny bit interested in his welfare?

"Hi Darling, where are you, I've been trying to get hold of you for ages?"

"Oh, don't worry about me, I'm fine, I think we should meet soon to discuss our future if there is one..."

"What do you mean Darling, of course there's a future... a long, happy one." An uncomfortable silence followed. Before Jackie could respond, he continued. "Jackie, we have a bit of a problem ..." He briefly told her that he had unwittingly become aware of the dealings of a gang of thugs who possibly thought that he knew more about their activities than he actually did.

"They switched briefcases with me at the airport. The police have suggested that we don't stay at home for the time being. These crooks may well tap into our 'phone at home, so don't ring or go there till I let you know otherwise. Are you close by, if so can we meet at our

117

favourite Indian restaurant at seven tonight? I love you so much and can't wait to see you."

"Okay Chris, I'll be there. Bye." The line went dead.

Jensen gently replaced the handset.

Chapter 16

Richardson hurriedly pressed his body through the gap in the wire mesh. He ran towards the vehicle park clinging to the shadows of the west wall of the hospital building. At the corner he hesitated. A bright spotlight had vastly improved visibility around the main gate. Three soldiers armed with automatic rifles emerged from the guard hut and ran past his hiding place in the direction of the hospital reception area.

He was confused. Manny's earlier snipping of the perimeter fence had apparently not triggered an alarm. Why would they only have attached a warning signal to the side connecting fence? Too bad, the alarm had been raised and he had to get moving. Maybe he had not triggered any alarm. Maybe Kingwill or someone else had discovered Ann's escape.

All activity seemed to be centred around the hospital building entrance to the east. From the shadows Kevin carefully checked for any potential observers before crossing the pathway, beyond which lay the unlit vehicle park. Reaching the dark hued high performance saloon he pulled the driver's door handle. His heart sank. Too late he realized that the interior courtesy light might have been switched on. Almost simultaneously he breathed a sigh of relief. It was not!

He was about to climb into the Subaru when a nearby bush caught his attention. The rifle was still where he had hidden it days before. The magazine was still in situ. He released the safety catch. Climbing aboard, he secured the rifle butt between the passenger seat and the central console with the barrel facing into the foot well. He stuck the CZ 83 pistol into his right trouser pocket. He hoped that he would not need to use either.

The Subaru's engine started immediately, the uneven beat of the horizontally opposed flat four cylinder engine was music to his ears. Using as few revs as possible to maintain the car's momentum and leaving its headlights switched off, Richardson edged the vehicle forward from the crushed stone parking area onto the gravel roadway and slowly approached the gate.

A young uniformed trooper wearing a beret and carrying an automatic rifle rushed from the cubicle. He waved at Kevin to stop and approached the passenger side window indicating with a circular motion of his hand for him to lower the glass. Kevin continued to edge forward, gesticulating several times with his left hand jabbing his thumb back towards the hospital buildings, his right hand resting on the pistol. The soldier hesitated, confused.

As a result of the Subaru's ongoing forward momentum, the trooper was now at the left rear corner of the car. Richardson crouched low in the bucket seat. The soldier's lips moved and he took a pace towards the car. For the first time Kevin realized that the car had been fitted with tinted glass all around and he doubted whether the trooper would be able to discern who was in the driver's seat of the vehicle without coming right up to the passenger window.

He suddenly gunned the engine and released the clutch. The four tyres momentarily scrabbled for grip, but then the car took off like a projectile. In the few seconds before the dense cloud of dust engulfed the rear window, he saw the undecided soldier run into the booth. The expected shots did not come. He switched on the main beams thankful that the road had been straight and that he had not gone careering into the dense undergrowth that lined the dusty track.

Three hundred metres from the gate the road curved to the left. Kevin switched off the lights and coasted to a halt alongside the Audi which faced the way he had come. Manny had left the Audi's spluttering engine running fearful that he would not be able to restart it. Ann was leaning against the car. She greeted Kevin with a smile and threw her arms around him as he opened the passenger door for her.

"Hi darling, so nice to see you're feeling better. Come on, let's get going. They can't be far behind." Manny handed him the briefcase.

"Thanks for everything Manny. Hope you don't run into trouble back at the hospital."

"Good luck Kev. Don't worry about me." He smiled and lifted the Audi's bonnet. "I've been stuck here for some time!"

Kevin floored the accelerator pedal and the Subaru took off in another cloud of dust. In his rear-view mirror he momentarily glimpsed Manny climbing aboard the Audi and closing the driver's door waiting for any pursuers from the hospital, before its tail lights disappeared in the dust wake and inky blackness of the night. He glanced at Ann and saw that her eyes were closed.

"Recline your seat a bit but try not to sleep, darling. We may have to get past a roadblock in the next thirty minutes or so. That's if they haven't contacted someone ahead who's already waiting to intercept us."

The gravel road ahead would not have been too difficult to navigate during daylight, but Kevin found that it took all of his concentration to keep the vehicle on the slippery surface whilst still maintaining a reasonable speed. The Subaru's headlights cut a white swathe through the darkness, but even its all wheel drive train was challenged by the deep layer of soft sand that covered the track causing the car to continually snake from side to side. He glanced at Ann.

"Are you sleeping love?"

Her eyelids flickered. "Trying not to..." her voice faltered. Then with an effort "There's so much I want to know, but I'm oh so tired..." She appeared to be drifting into sleep, but her eyes flickered open. "How's our darling Trace? It seems like ages since I saw her. She must be so concerned."

"Don't worry baby, she's fine." Kevin winked, silently praying that their daughter had not been traumatized by their abduction. He was sure that Ann's sister Diane was doing her best to take Tracey's mind off of the events. Fortunately she was very fond of her aunt and had in the past spent a lot of time with her at her own request.

Ann's lips framed another question, but the Subaru's steering wheel suddenly bucked in Kevin's hands as the right front wheel hit a small rock hidden beneath the thick sand. The experienced racing driver's hands countered the skid almost before the car started to slew, the reliable controls of the champion rally-bred car responding instantly to his input.

He glanced at Ann. The seat belt had held her firmly while she braced her elbow against the door. She smiled at him. "You're due to practice at Le Mans soon, aren't you?"

Kevin nodded. "Sure, but that's hardly been on my mind for a while!"

Ann seemed to be more alert now. To maintain her interest and keep her awake, Kevin briefly recounted the events of the past few days.

Some twenty minutes had elapsed when Richardson noticed a faint glow behind the dense dust cloud thrown up by the Subaru's wheels. On some straight stretches he had managed to get the Subaru up to around 140 km/h, but his average speed had been drastically reduced in places by deep ruts eroded by rainwater running both across and parallel along the middle of the track. Several low level bridges and sharp bends had also required careful navigation. Progress would also have been much more rapid had he known the route and its impediments. Ann's presence and safety had also put a damper on the challenge posed.

The glow grew brighter and Kevin realized that the looming silhouette was that of a large powerful SUV with additional driving lamps fitted. The car enthusiast in him wondered what make it was. How the vehicle had managed to close the gap in the Subaru's dense brown wake was a mystery. He thought that he had been making good time under the prevailing conditions!

Richardson's brow furrowed in concentration as his eyes probed the road surface ahead, one eye in the rear-view mirror on the ever looming goliath that threatened to reduce the Subaru from a three box design to a hatchback, the other on the rally-like conditions ahead. He would really be enjoying himself were it not for the unknown menace posed by the vehicle behind.

They crested a rise, the Impreza's wheels losing contact with the road surface, before the body settled on its suspension as the track dipped sharply. He could hear the monster's powerful deep grunt three metres behind. Its pilot was now driving "blind" using the Subaru's lights as a guide, probably hoping that Kevin would slacken off allowing the mammoth to punt it into the veld.

Kevin noted with alarm that 300 metres ahead, the road appeared to jack knife sharply to the right into a hairpin bend, the track dropping out of view of the wide spread of the Impreza's powerful head and driving lamps. He floored the accelerator, significantly opening the gap to the pursuing SUV. The dazzling bright yellow roundels in the back window were reduced to a distant glowing brown blanket.

Despite his concentration on the undulating road surface and the danger behind, Kevin had managed to sneak several glances at Ann in the passenger seat. She was now wide awake and had wedged herself between the door pillar and the centre console. From her profile and the visible curve of her mouth in the tailing vehicle's lights, he had no doubt that she was enjoying the race.

"Hold on tight baby."

"Don't worry about me, I'm fine Kev." The whispered reply barely reached him above the cacophony of the car's motor.

The bend was fast approaching. The road had recently been graded, a high bank of sand having been left in the apex of the bend directly across his path. Kevin's right foot suddenly hit the brake pedal. The g-forces threatened to catapult the occupants through the windscreen as the big ABS-assisted callipers intermittently bit into the brake discs rapidly retarding the Subaru's forward momentum. In the rear-view mirror he saw that the leviathan had closed the gap and was about to mount the Impreza.

Almost immediately, he released the pedal, engaged second, simultaneously giving the steering wheel a sharp tug to the right. A split second later he jerked it in the opposite direction as he caught the car's tail allowing it to drift through almost 180 degrees in the loose sand. He felt the four tyres momentarily scrabbling for grip as he floored the accelerator, before the tail swept into line and the car hared off into the night.

In his rear-view mirror he momentarily had a clear view of the SUV. A strong tailwind had blown the Subaru's brown dust cloud to the south. Too late the following driver had seen the looming embankment. Kevin saw the big wheels stop revolving as the driver desperately speared his right foot at the brake pedal. The massive vehicle snaked, but the pilot had the peace of mind not to swerve, as the forward momentum would no doubt have seen it barrel roll many times into the tall grass and bushes beyond.

Kevin heard the SUV's revs rise as the driver frantically engaged lower gears at point blank range. There was a dull thud and brief tinkling of glass as the front bumper hit the bank. A vertical explosion of dust erupted as the vehicle visibly but almost reluctantly slowed. Its front wheels seemed to paw the air before its sheer bulk and momentum carried it onward into the veld.

The red glow from the SUV's tail lights disappeared to the south, as the Subaru hurried towards the west. Richardson doubted that the SUV's driver had lost further control and that the sturdy vehicle had actually rolled out of sight beyond the bank. The solid sand barrier had undoubtedly re-aligned if not deranged the front suspension. Trees beyond would also have assisted in bringing it to a halt. At best, the SUV's off road adventure would buy them a couple of minutes. The road surface had improved. Grading had removed most of the loose soil and Kevin upped the pace. There was no sign of the pursuing vehicle.

A sudden spasm in his upper thigh made Kevin jerk the steering wheel. The Scooby momentarily slewed towards the left verge before Richardson regained control. "What the..?" he thought, before he remembered. The cell phone! It was still in his trouser pocket and had been set on mute/vibration mode.

He slowed the car whilst he dug the phone out of his pocket. Ann stared quizzically at him in the gloom of the cockpit. Kevin pressed the green button with his thumb, still contemplating his answer, if needed.

"Hello, Doctor Wilson? This is Captain Henry Wagner of fifteen Supply & Transport. I've been away and I've only just found your letter. I wanted to make sure you don't need assistance from us. Er... sorry to 'phone you so late." The voice, whilst clearly that of a well-educated African, also had a curious German tone about it.

"Um...glad to hear from you Captain. This is actually Kevin Richardson. My wife Ann is with me. We've managed to get away from the hospital, but need help. I don't know just how far behind Wilson and his partners in crime are."

"Mr Richardson, so good to hear from you too! Is your wife alright? The South African Police are here. They traced your kidnappers to Namibia. Where are you?"

"Ann is fine, but exhausted. We must be close to Camp Bravo. Expect we will be faced with a roadblock there. Not sure about our progress beyond..."

"Don't worry Mr Richardson, we are at Camp Bravo. All of the birds except Jan Van Den Berg seem to have flown. He's not singing yet. David Wilson has a private jet. We've alerted Windhoek and South Africa."

"David Wilson and a big Nigerian named Kingwill are probably close behind us in a four wheel drive. They went off the road some way back, but may have got going again."

Kevin glanced at Ann. Her eyes were closed. His hand found her knee and squeezed it. "We're nearly there darling." By the faint glow of the instrument panel he saw her smile, but she did not open her eyes. He longed to take her in his arms. Hopefully they would be home soon to be reunited with Tracey.

"...if they are following, carry on past the Camp Bravo sign on the left and turn into the narrow track on the right. We'll wait for you there." Captain Wagner's well-modulated tone cut into Richardson's drifting thoughts.

"Right, look forward to meeting you..." A dull cracking sound from the back interrupted the conversation and a fraction of a second later, a metallic object rattled against the windscreen, coming to rest atop the dashboard. Kevin glanced in the rear-view mirror. The back window had turned into a fine mesh of shattered glass held together by the centre flexible layer of lamination.

From his side mirror he saw that the mammoth had closed the gap to possibly fifty metres whilst he had been speaking to Wagner. "Must go, they're shooting at us." Kevin switched off the cell and floored the accelerator. The Subaru's rear seemed to squat lower for a fraction of a second before it took off like a projectile. His left arm probed for Ann's lap. Her hands found and closed around the phone before she again drew her buttocks lower into the bucket seat and braced her legs.

The dust cloud from the Subaru's wheels reduced the presence of the SUV to a faint glow. The road ahead seemed to be in good order, but a sudden stretch of corrugations followed by a hump-backed rise seemingly had Kevin's lower internal organs alternately bouncing against his lungs and then seemingly dumped around his intestines as the car's suspension bottomed before all four wheels left the road surface. Ann's pursed lips allowed an audible groan to escape.

"Sorry darling, help must be near…"

It crossed his mind that he had not mentioned the Subaru to Wagner. "Too bad," he thought. "Hopefully they'll realize we're in the car!"

There was no sign of the SUV. Kevin mouthed a silent prayer, fervently hoping that the last road obstacle had further weakened the pursuing vehicle's suspension

Rounding a left hand bend, the Subaru's headlamps suddenly picked out a crudely painted arrowed sign attached to a sapling on the right hand verge. In differing sized red lettering it proclaimed "Camp Bravo" as being situated somewhere ahead along the opposite side of the road.

Kevin slowed the car. The glint of several vehicles in the undergrowth and trees caught the corner of his eye. His peripheral vision also registered the stealthy movement of a number of darkly clad figures who had withdrawn into the shadows. Then he was past.

He briefly noticed a gathering of pyramid shapes silhouetted some distance to the south – no doubt the tented camp. Two flickering lights about a hundred metres ahead on the right hand verge caught his attention. As he neared a uniformed and plain-clothed figure on the bank, the former holding what appeared to be a walkie-talkie radio, waved him down. Kevin slowed.

A break in the underbrush appeared on the opposite side of the road. One of the men, who Kevin now saw was of African origin, moved to the driver's side and motioned him in. He lip read the man's urgent instruction to douse the Subaru's lights and complied as the vehicle came to rest two metres behind a khaki hued Toyota Cressida. They were in a dense forest.

Two men approached the Subaru from the rear.

"Well darling, I hope they're friendly, but if they're not, we're in deep shit!" Kevin squeezed Ann's hand before unlocking the doors. She smiled back. Both front doors were suddenly wrenched open from the outside. Kevin's head instinctively spun to the passenger side. By the torchlight he saw a light brown handsome face of mixed parentage smiling down at Ann. From her profile he saw that she had responded in kind, but she stayed put.

"Mr Richardson. So glad to meet you at last! I'm Inspector Themba ...um... Tony, from South Africa." Kevin turned towards the deeply African accented voice. "Our investigations led us to Namibia, but your note to Captain Wagner confirmed our suspicions." Kevin was still clambering from the car when Themba continued – "Are your pursuers close behind?" Without waiting for a response, the slightly built African extended his hand and continued. "Mrs Richardson, please stay here where you will be safe. Mr Richardson, you should also wait until we sort out your followers."

Kevin took the proffered hand and pulled himself from the bucket seat. "Likewise, Tony, we're so thankful to get here in one piece. They were close behind in a four wheel drive, but hit a few obstacles along the way..." Richardson noticed that Wagner was issuing instructions into the walkie-talkie. The sturdily built policeman motioned to Themba and the two set off towards the main road. A rutted track snaked through a narrow clearing and disappeared into the distance beyond the Toyota.

"Sit tight, I'll be back in a minute." Kevin whispered to Ann, motioning her to depress the central locking button. On second thoughts, he also gestured for her to withdraw the ignition keys from the steering column. Without an invitation he followed the military and police officials.

Themba looked back at Richardson as they approached the T-junction. He hesitated and seemed to be on the verge of motioning him to go back to the Subaru, but apparently thought better of it. Instead he gestured to him to stay behind them. Wagner was still speaking softly but animatedly into the handset.

The sound of a powerful motor reached them. Richardson put his arms around the slender trunks of two saplings near the verge of the track along which they had just come and hanging forward, peered towards the roadblock of fuel drums and poles which had miraculously since been set up near the road sign.

A dull glow to the south-east was steadily growing brighter. The throbbing of the motor diminished as the beast's driver de-accelerated before the corner. The approaching glow from beyond the bend seemed to be shimmering and shaking.

The cacophony suddenly reached fever pitch as the grunting leviathan rounded the bend in a flood of light. Kevin guessed that the off road excursion had damaged the exhaust system as the standard silencers were clearly no longer in place. Two of the vehicle's lights, possibly the aftermarket fitments on the front bumper, had been deranged during the impact with the earthen bank. One was now shining towards the heavens at a forty-five degree angle, while the other, clearly hanging by a mere thread, was lighting the roadway beneath the front wheels.

Although the vehicle seemed to be making good progress, this seemed to be erratic and its forward momentum appeared crablike. As it got closer and Kevin's eye's adjusted to the glare of the spot lights on high beam, he saw that the offside front wheel was bent at a jaunty angle.

To his left, Wagner suddenly barked an order into the handset. A powerful searchlight lit up the road ahead of the SUV as if by remote control. Five or six armed uniformed figures emerged from the undergrowth behind and to the right of the drums, one of which proceeded to wave down the vehicle. The 4 x 4 appeared to accelerate and the men had to take evasive action, diving back from whence they had come. It swerved to avoid one of the drums, but a solid thump sent it rolling down the road. A brief staccato burst of gunfire erupted from the verge of the road causing the vehicle to veer sharply to its left, away from the men. It crashed head on into a solid tree trunk with a sound of tortured metal and tinkling glass.

The soldiers or policemen – from his vantage point Kevin was uncertain – approached the SUV, the remaining lights of which still illuminated the forest to the north. After what seemed an age, the vehicle's engine was cut. From his remote position, Richardson could not follow much of the proceedings, most of which were taking place on the far side of the vehicle.

"Please return to your wife Mr Richardson, we will be back as soon as we can." Wagner's instruction was polite but firm. In the gloom Kevin thought he discerned a smile from Themba before he turned and set off after the Namibian soldier.

Chapter 17

"Long distance motor racing enthusiasts the world over are no doubt eagerly awaiting the outcome of this coming weekend's first Le Mans trials. Previous successful campaigners Porsche and Ferrari will be unveiling their latest contenders for the June race, whilst a dark horse will be the new Honda. ..." The broadcaster's voice was rudely cut off as the ring tone of the "hands free" cell phone jangled.

"Hello, is that Kevin Richardson?"

"Um... no, I'm afraid you have the wrong number..." Kevin hesitated as the voice at the other end was unfamiliar. He did not recognize the cell number on the screen either. Both he and Ann were still considered to be in danger, as Wilson and several of his known partners in crime remained at large. For security reasons he had obtained a second phone, which number was known only to a few select people. He reached to cut off the call.

"Please don't hang up, your number was given to me by a police detective. My name is Chris Jensen. I'm sure it will be familiar to you."

"Sure Chris, sorry about that, um, glad to hear from you. One can't be too careful in our prevailing circumstances. We should meet sometime to exchange some rather harrowing stories!"

"That's actually my reason for 'phoning you Kevin. I have to fly to Singapore tomorrow night and was hoping we could meet this evening. We and our families have to be vigilant for the foreseeable future and ..."

"What a co-incidence, I'm flying to London later this week en route to Le Mans. Sure we can meet. I believe you have a home in Bryanston, Chris?"

"Yes, quite close to yours – twenty-five Bell Crescent. What about the new Indian restaurant that opened recently at the Square – I think it's called "Faizels" or something like that. How about 7:30?"

"Sounds great! I know it. I would leave wives or partners out of this?"

"Probably best at present..."

After exchanging final pleasantries, Richardson hung up.

He looked at his watch. Half-past-five! Ann would not be happy about his unscheduled meeting, as they had planned to have dinner out as a family before he left for France. Tracey had settled nicely following their being reunited. Although Ann would otherwise have accompanied him to Le Mans, they had mutually agreed it best not to leave her with Ann's sister again so soon after their ordeal. The whole family nevertheless intended travelling to France for the race in two months' time.

On his way home, Kevin turned into Bell Crescent which ran parallel to their street, two blocks to the north. He slowly cruised the BMW along the narrow suburban road. The uneven numbers were on the passenger side of the car. He passed twenty-three and slowed as he approached the next house. The two metre high brick wall was broken by steel gates to the east. He drew the car to a halt in front of them. Beyond and to the west of the driveway an immaculate thatched-roofed home stood in the late afternoon shadows. It appeared to be a carbon copy of theirs – from the outside at least!

"Well, well, some things are beginning to fall into place!" he thought "Surely the authorities have put two and two together by now, but why haven't they said anything?"

He was slightly annoyed that the architect and builder who had promised them a 'unique" residence some years before, had obviously been involved in the construction of both. Although he and Ann had driven along the road, mostly in an easterly direction, many times, the high wall shielded the roofing material from the road. There had certainly been no reason to stop in front of the driveway before!

After an extended scrutiny of the house and grounds from the interior of his car, he headed home.

***

Some ninety minutes later Kevin turned into the apparently full parking lot alongside "Faizel's North Indian Restaurant." A gap twenty metres along the row of cars caught his attention.

"Seems I'm in luck!" he thought and headed for the bay. He hated parking the Beemer in the street. A dust coated parking attendant sauntered towards him. He turned into the gap and did a double take as he drew to a stop. A clone of his BMW stood in the bay ahead. Even the number plate appeared the same, until he realized it was 146 instead of his car's 145.

"Twins!" The baritone remark cut into his thoughts from behind. Kevin spun around – it was the parking guard. "Nice cars you have there sir!"

"Thank you, but I don't know the owner of the other one. Please watch both of them – I'll sort you out when I come back."

"Sure, um, no problem sir." The attendant withdrew to greet another cruising vehicle.

"Good evening sir, nice to see you again – do you have a reservation?" Kevin was met at the door by a tall, robed, elegantly handsome Indian wearing a cream coloured turban. He recalled the bronze-skinned giant with piercing grey eyes from a previous visit to the restaurant.

"Hi Imraan – I'm not sure..., I've arranged to meet Chris Jensen here, but I doubt he had time to book..."

"No problem sir, we are not busy tonight. He has already arrived. I trust you will find the table suitable. Please follow me." Imraan picked up two menus and a wine list from the desk and turned on his heel.

As they approached a secluded table at the back of the restaurant, a tall, good looking, well-proportioned blond adonis of apparent Arian or Scandinavian origin rose and extended his hand. Reaching across the table, Kevin was struck by his penetrating blue eyes, even in the subdued light of the room.

"Hi Kevin, nice to meet you at last. What will you have to drink?"

An attractive brunette at an adjacent table turned her head to see the originator of the well-modulated voice. Her head stayed visibly craned at an uncomfortable angle for several long seconds. There was no doubt in Kevin's mind that the handsome man opposite had a similar effect on many members of the opposite sex. The handshake was firm.

"Likewise, Chris – a Heineken would be great, thanks." Imraan nodded and withdrew.

Richardson sat down noting that Jensen had already made a significant impression on the level of the golden brown liquid in his own glass.

"Um, before I forget..." Kevin opened. "What a coincidence ... there's a Be-Em just like mine parked outside. It's an exact clone – down to the number plate which differs by one digit!'

"What colour? Not deep metallic blue by any chance?" Jensen enquired.

"Yes – an M5!" responded Richardson.

"It's mine. I took delivery through the local branch of Burtons about eighteen months ago."

"Well, well, suddenly the scrambled jigsaw puzzle is starting to fall into place." Richardson rejoined. "I drove past your house earlier this afternoon and it looks like we have the same taste in architecture as well... What did you do to those thugs to cause them to kidnap Ann and myself and put us through that horrible ordeal?" Kevin's tone was not particularly friendly as his eyes bored into those of the man across the table.

"Please don't blame me, Kevin. It was all a horrible mistake. Those bastards stuffed up..." Jensen was clearly unhappy and at pains to divert the blame. "You will understand as soon as I explain – my um – briefcase was..."

He was interrupted by the arrival of Richardson's beer. Imraan filled the tall glass and withdrew.

"I sincerely hope so!" Kevin's eyes still glistened with a chilling intensity, but the amber liquid visible through the rivulets of condensation that were already beginning to trickle down the frosted glass was tempting. "Cheers... may those buggers spend a long time behind bars." Richardson raised his glass and dropped the meniscus of the refreshing contents by a quarter of the vessel, in one long satisfying draw.

Jensen nodded his agreement, adding: "If and when they catch the ones that count." He went on to brief Richardson on his encounters with the drug smugglers. Kevin in turn, briefly recounted his and Ann's ordeal in Namibia.

"Inspector Tony Themba believes that your Mr Wilson from Ondanwa Hospital has set up shop in Nigeria for the time being. Another ex-S.A. Airforce Colonel ...um... Steve somebody has been seen in Singapore."

"Harvey...Major Steve Harvey," added Richardson. "He was one of our kidnappers."

"Themba says that Interpol have been monitoring the movements of the drug ring for six months and had been close to rounding up several of the leaders when my briefcase episode and your kidnapping drove them underground."

The exchange was interrupted by the buzzing of Kevin's cell phone.

"Sorry Chris, I'd better take this." The number on the screen was not familiar. Richardson had started to rise but abruptly sat down again. "Speak of the devil!"

"Hello Mr Richardson, it's Tony Themba, I've been wanting to get hold of you for the past week, but so much has happened..." The Detective Inspector's voice sounded genuinely apologetic. "Could we please meet at my office tomorrow morning...how about Ten o'clock?"

"Sure Tony...you've certainly left it late, I'm due to fly out in two days' time. Chris Jensen and I have just been discussing you!"

"Oh, so you two have met. I'm sorry, Mr Richardson, I hope you've also had some nice things to say."

"Well, I'm not so sure about that!" Kevin laughed. We decided to have a bite to eat to compare notes. By the way, please call me Kevin."

"Thank you Kevin. Then I won't interrupt your meal any longer." Themba's tone had lightened up. "See you tomorrow then."

"Cheers Tony." Kevin hung up and faced a smiling Chris Jensen.

"They've organized a plain clothes detective to take the same flight to Singapore and to shadow my every move there, as they hope some members of the dope smuggling gang will show themselves. I must admit that although my involvement has been rather exciting, I'm not so sure that I should be the bait in this showdown! I have to go there urgently to sort out a contract that could mean a lot to me financially, otherwise I would be having second and third thoughts about this trip." The twinkle in Jensen's eyes faded and his tone became serious.

"Well, I'm certainly interested to hear what ideas they have for my trip! Let's try to forget this business for an hour or so and order something to eat. I don't know about you, but I haven't had anything since breakfast."

Imraan had been hovering in the shadows waiting for a signal. Kevin caught his eye. He appeared to glide across the floor and reached their table in one seamless movement. He placed the ornamental carafe he had been carrying in the centre of the table. "Mineral water with the compliments of the house."

Kevin half expected the distinguished looking man to utter, "Gentlemen, I'm your genie and you may have three wishes," and was momentarily taken aback when Imraan asked, "Are you ready to order sir?"

Richardson ordered a Chicken Madras, Jensen a Mutton Korma. Two side salads, two Butter Naan breads and a refill of beers sent Imraan gliding his way to the kitchen as if on roller bearings.

***

Some ninety minutes later Jensen showed Kevin the neat round hole in the Be-em's boot. After exchanging enthusiastic praise for their chosen marque and tipping the car guard, they followed each other out of the car park.

Neither noticed the old Ford Cortina which pulled away from the kerb and followed at a respectful distance.

Chapter 18
London

Kevin glanced at his mirrors. The ever present white works Porsche driven by Peter Werner was still glued to his car's tail. So close in fact that all he could see were the following car's roof-mounted identification lights. Mulsanne corner was only a hundred metres away. Werner darted to the inside hoping to pass Richardson's ailing car under braking, but Kevin was alert to the intended manoeuvre and closed the gate just in time.

The bend was negotiated safely and while accelerating towards the kink before Indianapolis, he noticed that Werner had dropped back significantly and appeared to be in the process of regaining the track. A tell-tale cloud of dust in the distance behind, hinted that the German had overdone his late braking strategy and had had to take to the infield.

Arnage and the Porsche curves were negotiated safely. One more series of corners to go and the finish line will be in sight. The misfiring engine sounded really sick. Their chief mechanic's excited voice suddenly cut in.

"Come on Kev. You're almost home. A podium finish at your first attempt! Jerry's bitten his nails to the quick. You can't allow your hard work to be in vain!"

Richardson's racing thoughts hardly absorbed any of the monologue in his headphones. The German's car behind was fast closing the gap. The finish line and chequered flag waver loomed ever larger just ahead. As the nose of his blue Porsche drew level with the flag-waving official, the silver car of Werner flashed past on the inside.

"I've gone and lost it, what if it's a dead heat?" Richardson's heart sank, his mind flashing back to the famous 1966 race when Ford had tried to stage a publicity photo-finish with their three leading cars crossing the line abreast. On that occasion the expected winning car driven by Miles/Hulme had had to settle for second place as officialdom had separated the cars by ruling that the car driven by Bruce McLaren and Chris Amon had started eight metres further back on the grid and had thus covered a greater distance.

"You've done it Kev. Fantastic!" Jerry Barker's animated voice cut into his thoughts. "It was only inches but you did it..."

***

"Ladies and gentlemen, we are commencing our approach. Flight Number 535 from Johannesburg will be landing at Heathrow Airport shortly. Please fasten your seatbelts and ensure that your seats are set in the upright position. Please ensure that your hand luggage ..."

Richardson awoke with a start, his dream shattered by the sound of the multiple chiming gong and the cabin controller's urgent attention-seeking tone.

He closed his eyes again, a smile creasing the corners of his mouth and eyes. He would never forget that race. After twelve hours, privateer Jeremy (Jerry to his friends) Barker's Porsche co-driven by himself had held a strong second place two laps behind one of the works-entered Porsches. That car had clearly been sent out to be the hare with the strategy of setting a pace to break the opposition enabling the other two factory Porsches to fill the podium positions.

During practice at Le Mans several months earlier, Barker had been some five seconds a lap slower than Kevin who had impressed the established teams with his smooth but rapid driving style. His efforts had secured a second place starting position on the grid, ahead of the other two works Porsches as well as other well-known racing marques.

In the race itself, Jeremy who started, had driven a conservative, but steady race, losing ground to all three Porsche Prototypes and a McLaren Coupé. During his two-hourly stints at the wheel, Richardson, helped by efficient pit work, had managed to claw his way back to second position.

At half-distance a fuel starvation problem had cost them time in the pits dropping their car to fifth place overall. Kevin had again driven the rims off of their car and helped by the leaders also encountering problems, had again worked his way up to third. Two laps from the end, the misfiring had started again and he had only just managed to keep Werner at bay.

The white winged cigar dipped suddenly, bumped lightly on the tarmac and they were down. The aircraft's tyres chirped as the pilot applied brakes and the nose did its best to dig into the runway as the opposing forces of the tiny braking wheels, reverse thrusting engines and upright ailerons countered with their combined efforts to bring the massive bird to a standstill.

"Ladies and Gentlemen, welcome to Heathrow. We hope you had a pleasant flight. Please do not..."

Kevin opened his eyes, the race forgotten. There were a number of more important current issues to think about. He yawned. The flight from Johannesburg International Airport had been pleasant. Although he flew frequently, Kevin had never been able to sleep soundly or for any length of time on long flights. His childhood concern of dozing on the train and missing his stop had been carried over into adulthood and flying.

***

After passing through customs Richardson sorted his luggage and was about to set off for the Underground Line when he found his way barred by a burly dark-haired giant of a man wearing a charcoal suit some two sizes too small. Kevin would not have hazarded a guess at the size of the boat-like shiny toe-capped black shoes. While contemplating the best way to circumnavigate the obstacle, a broad smile creased the latter's friendly face. A huge hand was proffered which Kevin was not able to accept due to his hands being full.

"Er... sorry to bother you sir, but it's Mr Richardson isn't it?'

"Umm, I think you have the wrong person, please allow me to pass, I have a train to catch..." Kevin frowned and was ready to club the man blocking his path with his overnight bag if necessary.

"Sorry sir, but I'm DI Pete Smith of Scotland Yard." He shoved a blurred photograph of Kevin printed on a creased sheet of A4 paper towards the latter. "Tony Themba of Jo'burg e-mailed this to us. Could we have a chat? I won't keep you long. Inspector Brown is also expected any day from South Africa."

"Sure Detective. My apologies, but I was not expecting to be met. Shall we grab something to drink at that restaurant?" He nodded towards a coffee shop behind the policeman and continued. "I had breakfast on the plane not too long ago, but you're welcome to have something to eat."

Richardson ordered coffee. The plainclothes policeman chose a Coke and apologetically took up his offer, ordering a double hamburger and chips, explaining that he had worked the previous night and had not yet been home have a shower and a meal.

"Mr Richardson we..."

"Please call me Kevin."

"Thanks, um...Kevin, we have reason to believe that the Wilson gang are as active as ever in Europe, Nigeria and Singapore although they have gone to ground in South Africa. They are no doubt still smarting at your escape from Namibia and don't know exactly what you found out there. You are also possibly able to identify several of their operatives..."

"Pete, I can't believe what has happened and how disjointed my family's life has become over the past couple of weeks – through absolutely no fault of ours at all! My wife and daughter are basically being guarded or their movements monitored day and night by the SAPS. Now you're telling me that it wouldn't even be safe to immigrate!"

Their drinks arrived and after taking a long draw of his Coke, D I Smith continued. "We had a conference call with your force in South Africa last night and we all believe it best to shadow your movements over here as well as your time on the other side of the Channel – not only for your own safety's sake, but we may very well be lucky and catch one or two of the bastar... er... blighters! We have also been in contact with the French Police who are very willing to assist. Please could you keep me closely informed of your movements while you are over here?" He handed Kevin a slip of paper.

The DI's food arrived and he ravenously took a huge bite of the burger before continuing after a good half minute. Richardson studied the unshaven man sitting across from him. He estimated the burly policeman to be about twenty-eight. If anything he was bigger than Tony Themba's sidekick – Inspector Graham Brown, who for no one particular reason, Kevin had taken a dislike to. Smith had kindly green eyes with an underlying steely edge and Kevin had no doubt that he could and did, become ruthless if circumstances dictated the upholding of the law. The DI's relatively nimble movements belied his bulk.

"Kevin, we realize it is an imposition, but my office and cell numbers are there. My landline will be manned whether I'm in the office or not. DC James Broad and DC Paul Collins will be my back-up. Their contact numbers are there as well."

"Thanks Pete, I'm sorry for sounding negative just now, but I've looked forward to this trip for months. My wife was to have accompanied me, but had to stay at home with my daughter who is still edgy after our disappearance last time! This bloody business has taken its toll on my whole family."

Richardson removed the Detective Inspector's slip of paper from his wallet, folded it and tore a strip from the bottom. Accepting the proffered pen and referring to his cell, he wrote down a list of places he intended visiting before motoring to the French circuit.

"Those times are only approximate and have been arranged by my friend Jeremy Barker. I've given you his numbers as well."

"Not to worry Kevin, you'll be discreetly tailed. There are three of us taking turns. Those details are just in case you give us the slip! Please let one of us know if there is a substantial deviation from your plans. I believe that Tony Themba arranged a new cell phone for you as there was concern that they may have tapped into your previous number."

A few minutes later Kevin had settled the bill and was about to excuse himself when Smith leant over the table and whispered. "We rarely do this, but the circumstances are special." Removing a paper serviette from the table holder, he unfolded it across his left hand. He discreetly removed a large calibre pistol from a holster under his armpit.

Although they were the only patrons, Smith kept the firearm covered and passed it to Richardson under the corner of the table away from the line of sight of the restaurant counter. The latter carefully pocketed the weapon leaving a sizeable, but comforting bulge next to his groin.

"Please sign this receipt – I trust you won't have to use it! Your police force knows about this. We can't afford to take Wilson and his cronies lightly. You'll have to give it back to me before you cross the channel. We'll see what we do on the other side – this issue has already been raised with the French police."

"As reluctant as I am to take it Pete, I'm under no illusions that Wilson and the group that kidnapped us could get very rough!" He handed the slip of paper back to Smith and continued "I am so glad that Ann didn't come – I hope and pray that Tony Themba's team look after her and Tracey."

Their business over for the time being, they parted with a handshake. Kevin looked at his watch. It was 9:15. He picked up his luggage and headed for the Underground platform. Jerry Barker was due to pick him up at his hotel at 12:30 for a bite of lunch and an afternoon trip to the restoration firm to check progress on his Aston Martin.

He was looking forward to that trip even more than seeing the new Honda. The new Le Mans contender had been upgraded since his last visit to the UK three months earlier as a result of his aerodynamic input. Several hundred hours of testing had followed. They and an as yet unnamed Japanese co-driver nominated by the Japanese factory, would be testing the new car in anger against formidable opposition for the first time during practice at Le Sarthe in a couple of days' time. Although Jerry was not an aggressive driver, his style was generally not that far off the pace set by the fastest drivers. He conserved his cars which helped over the course of twenty-four hours, particularly if the other two were driving closer to ten tenths.

"Thanks Guv," The black Austin Taxi accelerated back into the stream of traffic as only London 'cabbies' know how, without disrupting the flow. Richardson had enjoyed his trip from the station and had purposely hailed the old circa 1954 Austin FX3. All of his recent trips in and around the capital had been in the FX4 version or later, more comfortable replacement series. The cabby had been only too happy to bend Kevin's ear with a comprehensive history of his vintage taxi as well as the whole range of London cabs.

Austin had entered the cab market in 1929 and had had immediate success easily outselling rival makes. The FX3 model commenced production in 1948, being built by both Carbodies and the Austin Motor Company and soon dominated the market. Its replacement, the FX4 had first seen the light of day in 1958. This much improved taxicab, although being subjected to ongoing upgrades had continued to be produced into the 1990s by which time more than 50,000 had been built. No visit to London was complete without a trip in a black cab.

The cabby had been grateful for Kevin's generous tip. He had handed Richardson a card with his telephone number and had volunteered, "Please call me anytime Guv, I'm always in the area or only minutes away."

An elegant, smart maroon and gold uniformed, grey-haired porter standing on the sidewalk saluted and came towards Richardson and extended a hearty welcome. Kevin returned the greeting. Without further ado, the porter picked up Kevin's compact overnight bag, turned the heavier, wheeled suitcase towards the hotel's double doors and set off.

Richardson had heard a car pull up behind him in the space recently vacated by his cab. He was about to follow the porter when an uncanny feeling that he was being closely observed, crawled up and down his spine. Kevin spun around. A modern burgundy-hued TX series cab was idling a few feet away against the verge. He bent slightly to get a better view into the depths of the cab's interior. The driver smiled and then gave him a quizzical look when he did not avert his gaze. The burly rear passenger, a dark haired man wearing what appeared to be a dark hued jacket and pale coloured open-necked shirt, had turned through nearly ninety degrees to look towards the opposite side of the street.

Kevin stared for a few seconds longer, but the passenger seemed engrossed in whatever had caught his attention and showed no signs of turning around in the foreseeable future. Richardson shrugged, smiled at the now frowning cabby and turned towards the hotel.

"Good morning sir. Do you have a reservation?" The broad accent was that of an Edinburgh born and bred Scottish lass.

"Uh, yes, for two nights in the name of Richardson."

Five minutes later, formalities completed, the porter hauled Richardson's bags towards the plush walnut panelled doors of the lift.

While he followed, Richardson reflected on the dark haired beauty's change in attitude towards him from her initial friendly greeting until, he presumed, her discovery upon presentation of his passport, that he was a South African citizen. He concluded that she was unaware of the radical political changes that had recently and still were, taking place in the Republic.

"Too bad," Richardson muttered and dismissed the subject from his thoughts as the lift doors closed.

"Beg your pardon sir?" The porter turned towards Kevin.

"Oh, sorry, its nothing. Just thinking aloud."

The elderly porter nodded absently, pressed the button for the fourth floor before switching his gaze to the durable ribbed burgundy carpet ahead of his size fourteen shoes.

"And they have the cheek to think that *I* have Alzheimer's," he thought.

***

After unpacking a fresh change of clothing and his toiletries, Kevin dialled Ann's cell number. "Hi darling, how are things at home? I'm missing you. So sorry you couldn't come along."

"So am I Kev. These cops, although well meaning, are a pain in the butt! They insist on posting a guard on the premises twenty-four hours around the clock until you return and also have an unmarked car in the street at all times. It's not always the same car so they are at least *trying* not to stick out like sore thumbs. I am not allowed to even go shopping in my car unless I contact them in advance and give them a full itinerary of my intended trip. I am afraid that I have been rather rude to some of the guys although they *have* taken my criticism in their stride!"

"I'm sorry love, but they have a job to do and are at least taking things seriously. Please play along till I get back. I'd hate anything to happen to either of you while I'm away. I'm also being shadowed since I arrived over here. I actually believe that I met one of the Scotland Yard detectives in a taxi downstairs when I was dropped off, although he did his best to appear otherwise engaged and disinterested in me."

"Enough of that – how is Trace?"

"Oh she's fine. I'll have to think up something creative to explain the presence of the police when I collect her from school this afternoon."

After exchanging pleasantries for a few more minutes the conversation terminated.

Richardson showered, dressed and was about to flop down on the duvet-covered double bed when he remembered having seen a newspaper stand downstairs in reception. He put on a pair of elasticised leather moccasins and after locking the door, headed for the stairs. His daily exercise regimen back home included not using a lift either up or down within reason, if he could help it.

A few steps from the ground floor, the hushed but distinctive brogue of the receptionist carried to him from the desk to the left of the staircase. An indistinct but authoritative male voice responded. As he stepped lightly on to the beige coloured marble tiled floor, the elegant opulence of the hotel struck him for the first time. His mind had obviously been on the taxi occupant when he arrived.

"Just as well Honda is picking up the tab!" he thought as he set out for the white painted metal newspaper stand across the room. Richardson glanced to his left, noting that a well-built dark haired man with close cropped hair leaning on the reception counter, was deeply engrossed in conversation with the receptionist. From side-on he appeared to be cultivating a moustache. A pale cream open-necked, long sleeved shirt and dark blue slacks completed the picture. A similarly hued folded jacket lay over the tiered desk.

Reaching his objective Kevin grabbed and folded the last "Times" left on the top rack. He turned and set off on a parabolic route towards the staircase which took him closer to the reception desk.

The attractive auburn-haired beauty started as she became aware of his presence while he was still some five metres away. She forced a smile as she visibly attempted to regain her composure.

"Please add this to my bill." Richardson called as he was about to straighten his approach towards the staircase. "She's jumpy?" he thought.

"Not to worry, Mr Richardson, morning and evening papers are on the house. Sorry you had such a poor selection, but you checked in after most had gone. I'll keep you a couple of the evening editions if you'd like." The words tumbled out in a continuous nervous stream.

Out of the corner of his eye Kevin saw the well-built dark haired man slowly come erect and deliberately turn towards him. Richardson's glance took in a pair of dark glasses dangling from the breast pocket of his shirt. He felt the man's eyes burning into him and turned his head slightly to meet his gaze.

Kevin's heart almost stopped. He knew the other man! He held the stare blankly for what he believed was long enough before turning back towards the receptionist. He patted his trouser pocket, remembering that he had put the pistol beneath a pillow on the bed before he showered not thinking that he would need it. "How stupid," he thought.

"Thank you very much. I'll collect them this evening." Richardson responded.

The other man suddenly averted his gaze and turned away. He abruptly replaced his dark glasses and after a terse whisper to the woman, picked up his jacket and strode towards the exit.

It took a supreme effort on Richardson's part not to run the last few metres to the stairs. "That was Steve Harvey!" realization suddenly dawned. The South African Air Force pilot had cropped and dyed his hair, and had made good progress in growing foliage beneath his nose. But Kevin was in no doubt whatsoever, the good looking airman could not hide his well chiselled features and piercing blue eyes. The authoritative voice, although muted, was definitely that of the team leader on the helicopter and which he had also heard more than once in Namibia.

Kevin reached his floor in record time and was about to unlock the door when his cell rang, shattering the silence in the corridor.

"Hello."

"Hi Mr Richardson, its Tony Themba here ... from South Africa." He added almost as an afterthought.

"Oh, hi Tony, just the man I need to speak to. Please give me a second." Kevin opened the door and made sure it was locked behind him, before kicking off his shoes and sitting on the bed.

Hi Tony. Sorry about that, I'm now in my room and we should be able to speak without being overheard." Richardson's right hand probed under the pillow behind and his fingers found the comforting cold steel of the pistol. He withdrew it and placed it on the bed next to his thigh.

"Thanks um... Kevin, I've just spoken to Pete Smith. He filled me in on your meeting. He's a very professional policeman. I'm in no doubt whatsoever that you're in good hands."

"Tony, I must tell you..."

"By the way," Themba interjected, "Pete told me that he had mentioned that his team was to be supplemented by Inspector Brown. Unfortunately Graham had a death in the family and has taken a week's compassionate leave. I'm sorry..."

"That's fine Tony. I'm sure I'm in good hands here, but I've just seen Captain Steve Harvey of the S A Air Force downstairs!" Richardson was pleased to finally get a word in.

"What?" The normally composed Inspector on the other end of the line was clearly shaken. "But we had tracked him to Pretoria and had him under surveillance as recently as yesterday."

"Well, he's in London now and was in my hotel a few minutes ago. He's cut and dyed his hair and I have no doubt he's tracking my every movement. For that matter who says I'm not to be eliminated? He was probably on my flight."

"Are you sure?" Themba's tone was still sceptical.

"I don't have the slightest doubt. Although to his knowledge, I have not been conscious in his presence, he must wonder what I saw and got up to in Namibia. I'm sure that I showed no signs of recognition just now in reception."

"I'll get hold of Pete Smith right away. Don't you think it would be wise to call off your trip?"

"You must be joking! I've looked forward to this opportunity for the past year, if not ten! I can't pull out now. If Honda replace me with another driver, I may never get another chance." Richardson paused before continuing.

"In any case what do I tell my wife – must we go into hiding until all of these crooks have been rounded up? Sure, she didn't want me to make this trip, but if they are after me, isn't it better that I divide their resources? Ann cannot be allowed to think our family is actually still in danger!"

"Well Kevin, as I said, we are all doing our best, but Wilson and his connections have shown in the past that they will do anything, and I mean anything, to protect their interests." Tony Themba's voice wavered. "I certainly wouldn't want anything to happen to you or your family."

"By the way," the inspector continued. "We have placed guards both inside and outside of your daughter's school. They are unobtrusive, but I haven't informed your wife and the school authorities think that we are conducting an experimental exercise"

"Thank you Tony. Please don't speak to Ann about this unless it's absolutely necessary. I don't want her worrying for no reason ..." His voice faltered.

"I suggest that you contact D I Smith as soon as you hang up and I will do likewise in a few minutes. Lock your door and don't leave your room before Scotland Yard have swept the hotel."

"I can't be kept prisoner here, I've got things to do." Kevin could not keep the exasperation from his voice. There was a sigh from the other end of the line. He closed his eyes and took a deep breath. Realising that Themba's hands were tied thousands of kilometres away, he continued. "I'm sorry, Tony, but this business is getting to me."

"No problem Kevin, I fully understand your feelings. We *will* catch them soon and put them away for a long, long time. Let's make contact with Scotland Yard and get things moving. Speak to you soon." The line went dead before Richardson could respond.

He was in the process of placing the cell phone on the bedside pedestal when the hotel's internal phone alongside it jangled shrilly in the soundless room. Kevin, who had always prided himself on being unruffled and cool in the most unexpected circumstances, nearly jumped out of his skin, only just managing not to drop the phone.

"Hello Mr Richardson, I have a Mr Barker here for you. Shall I send him up?"

Taking a deep breath to regain his composure, Kevin cleared his throat and responded.

"Thank you, but please may I speak to him first?"

"Hello old chap, good to have you back in civilization. Are you ready to go?"

"Hi Jerry, please listen carefully and don't say anything that may make the receptionist suspicious. Please, I am serious, this is not a joke. Is she close by?"

"Roger, old boy, I'm listening."

"I am being shadowed by someone connected to our abduction in South Africa. I saw him in reception just now and have made contact with the police. For all I know, this 'phone may be tapped, but if that's the case, it's too late now. Come up to the fourth floor and make sure you're not followed by anyone suspicious. It's 402 and er...if anyone else is waiting for the lift, rather wait for it to come down again so that you're alone."

"Fine Kev, understood. See you in just a tick." The line went dead.

Holding the pistol in his left hand, Richardson crept to the door, put his ear to it and listened intently. No sound came from the other side. "Stop being so jumpy," he mentally reprimanded himself, realizing that the thick wood and carpeting would in any event, cushion any sound from the passage beyond, never mind someone who intentionally took care not to be heard.

He gently turned the doorknob and slowly pulled the door inwards. It swung open soundlessly. Putting his cheek to the doorframe, he slowly edged forward until his right eye could see along the passageway to the left. The corridor was deserted and the lift doors some ten metres away were closed. He drew back into the doorway. Relaxing slightly, but keeping most of his body within the protection afforded by the room entrance, he slowly turned through one hundred and eighty degrees to survey the passage in the opposite direction. He exhaled. He was alone, or certainly appeared to be.

Seconds later a chime and simultaneous glowing red light above the lift doors announced the elevator's arrival. They opened with a dull thud and after a few seconds, Jerry Barker took a hesitant step into the corridor. He stood in the middle of the passage and looked to his right away from Kevin. Noting the numbered arrows midway up the wall he turned and saw Richardson who had advanced into the passage. The lift doors closed.

"Hi Jerry, come in for a few minutes, I need to make a call."

Barker looked quizzically at the gun in Richardson's hand and raised his eyebrows, his eyes twinkling.

"I say old boy, have you become Kevin Richardson 008 the long distance racing driver secret agent?" he enquired, a broad grin on his jolly sun-tanned face.

"Come in and shut up you shit!" Richardson good-naturedly retorted, smiling and extending his hand. "Make yourself useful and get us a couple of beers from the bar fridge. I'll be with you in a minute. I just need to make a quick call." He continued, reversing into the room. He sat back on the bed and placed the CZ on the duvet next to his thigh.

Barker advanced into the room and set off in search of the fridge.

Chapter 19

"D I Smith's line, D I O'Driscoll speaking, can I help you?" It was a well-modulated, unmistakeable broad Irish accent.

"Hi Detective ... I was hoping to get hold of D I Smith, but your name was also given to me by Pete. It's Kevin Richardson from South Africa..."

"Oh, hi Mr Richardson, I know all about you. Pete is out with Constable Venables just now, most probably in your area, possibly in the hotel. How may I assist?"

Kevin briefly explained his almost encounter with Steve Harvey and gave a description of the much changed SAAF Captain.

"I think that the receptionist may somehow be connected with Harvey." Richardson continued. "They were in earnest conversation and she certainly appeared nervous when she saw me."

"We'll discreetly try to check her out through the hotel's personnel department." O'Driscoll responded. "I'll get hold of Pete Smith right away. It's probably a good idea for you to stay in your room and lock the door for the time being until we locate Harvey."

"Not you as well!" Richardson responded, but he immediately regretted his outburst. He realized that O'Driscoll was only doing his job and had his welfare at heart. "Sorry, but I have a friend arriving to collect me shortly, and we'll be out for the rest of the day."

"I understand Mr Richardson. I really do, but you're a foreign national and we'd be in very hot water if something happened to you, particularly as we have advance knowledge of potential danger. Please make sure that your visitor is who he says he is and entertain him in your room until we advise you to the contrary. Shall we escort him to your room?"

"Don't worry, he's already with me. Our visit this afternoon has been planned for months!"

"Righto, Mr Richardson. Let me get hold of D I Smith. One of us will come back to you shortly as soon as we verify the Yard's presence in the hotel." O'Driscoll rang off.

Kevin had just replaced the handset when his cell rang.

"Hello Kevin, its Pete Smith here, just to let you know that we are in the area of your hotel."

"Hi Pete, I've just put the 'phone down after chatting to your colleague D I O'Donnell..."

"You mean Dave O'Driscoll." Smith interjected.

"Um yes... I mean D I O'Driscoll. Sorry, but I've met or spoken to so many detectives recently that I'm getting confused remembering just who is who in the zoo! Sorry again, no offence intended."

"Not to worry Mr Richardson. We have a vantage point facing the street on the second floor of the cream building opposite your room. Constable Venables is in an unmarked white Rover diagonally across from the entrance. If you move the curtain and look out, I'll wave."

"That's fine Pete, but O'Driscoll must be trying to get hold of you. I saw one of our kidnappers downstairs about twenty minutes ago."

"Shit!" Pete Smith responded from the other side, clearly taken aback.

"It was Steve Harvey the SAAF Captain, but he looks rather different." Kevin gave him a brief description.

"I'll get hold of Constable Venables right away. Please sit tight." The D I hung up before Richardson could respond.

"Looks like we're going to be cooped up here for a while!" Barker broke the uneasy silence handing Kevin an opened bottle of Heineken before backing into the comfortable looking easy chair at the foot of the bed.

Richard gave his teammate a brief rundown of the events since his and Ann's abduction. "I certainly thought that I'd seen the last of those buggers. Hell I want to get on with my life, we can't live like..." He continued, his lament being rudely interrupted by the ring tone of his cell.

"Hello Kevin, it's Pete Smith again. I'm afraid Harvey *has* given us the slip. Constable Venables knew exactly who I was talking about from your description. Apparently Harvey hung about for some time walking up and down the block. He was seen speaking to a chap in a dark blue Nissan, but Venables didn't put two and two together as his description didn't fit anything we were given. He didn't see him leave."

"That's too bad Pete – nobody's to blame. Your chaps could not have guessed what form Harvey's new look would have taken – he could just as well have worn a wig and no one would have been any the wiser!" Richardson responded. "By the way, Jerry and I are leaving for North Hants now and we're stopping for a bite of lunch on the way."

"Is that wise Mr Richardson?" D I Smith's tone changed to being almost reproachful. "We don't want anything to happen to you chaps. We haven't had a run in with them yet, but after speaking to Tony Themba and agents in Singapore, it appears that they don't mess around when it comes to eliminating witnesses..."

"Please Pete..., um Detective Inspector Smith, if you really want to get onto formal terms again...please try to understand my position, I have a life to get on with. I can't be transported around in a bank security van for the rest of my life."

"But Kevin, you *are* our responsibility for the foreseeable future."

"Sorry Pete, you can follow us wherever we go, but we're going under our own steam. In any case, if you chauffer us in a car which all but broadcasts 'Beware there are several Scotland Yard protectors on board, you're hardly going to smoke them out!"

"Well, um ...if you put it like that." Smith stuttered. "But what about your friend, Mr Barker? Surely you don't want to draw him into this?" The tone of Smith's response hinted that as Kevin was ahead on points, he was left with no alternative but to play what he hoped would be a trump card.

"I agree Pete, It would definitely be safer if Jerry here left me to my own devices in London. We can meet up in France." He glanced at Barker knowing the answer in advance. The latter was in the process of downing the last mouthful of his beer. He burped.

"Tell him over my dead body! We army troopers will sort out that that air force shite and his cronies!" Barker retorted loudly enough for the Scotland Yard Detective to hear. He balled his left fist, brandished the empty beer bottle in his right and eyed the pistol on the bed.

"I'm sure you heard that Pete." Kevin winked at Jerry Barker mouthing a thank you.

"Yes I did, but I'm not happy..."

"By the way, Pete will you be following us in the white Rover?"

"Um no, we also have a pale blue Vauxhall at our disposal around the corner. We'll leave D I Venables downstairs in case Harvey makes a reappearance."

"Just hold on a moment Pete." Richardson turned to Barker.

Anticipating Kevin's question, Barker responded, "I brought the Jag Mark 11. It's parked in the street behind the hotel. While he's on the line, find out whether there's another way out of the hotel."

"Pete, Jerry is driving a dark green 1960's Jaguar 3.8 Mark 11 with spoked wheels, similar to Inspector Morsc's, but in rather better condition and without a vinyl roof." He continued presuming that the D I was not familiar with the sixties' high performance saloon which had been widely used by the police force of the time. "He's parked in the street that runs behind the hotel."

"I do know what that vehicle looks like," Smith retorted. "It's hardly an inconspicuous vehicle if you don't want to draw attention!" the D I continued.

"Well, Jerry hardly expected to be tracked by a bunch of international crooks when he set out to collect me this morning. By the way, is there another exit to this hotel?"

"Yes, to the left of the downstairs lift. It's marked 'staff only'. The passage will take you past the kitchen and into Harlequin Road. Give me five minutes and we'll meet and follow you." Smith's response was clipped and terse before he hung up, clearly unhappy that Richardson and Barker were not prepared to stay within the relatively safe confines of the hotel room.

"I say, what about another beer Kev?" Barker enquired, on the point of getting up and heading for the fridge.

"I think not, Jerry. I wouldn't want you being stopped and given a breathalyser on top of our problems with the cops! What about your so called 'health drive' to lose a couple of kilos before the race?" Richardson replied with mock annoyance.

"Have a heart Kev, don't I look slimmer and trimmer since you last saw me?" The genial Barker sounded hurt and collapsed back into the sumptuous cushions of the chair.

"Well, you had me fooled..." Richardson was on the point of standing up when a loud rapping sounded on the door.

"Who's there?' Kevin called, noticing the pistol on the bed and hastily picking it up. Barker moved to the left of the door.

"Excuse me sir, I have another paper for you. Reception asked me to deliver it." Richardson recognized the kindly voice of the porter.

"Are you alone?"

"Um, yes sir." The porter was clearly mystified by Kevin's question.

"Just hang on a minute." He pocketed the weapon and slowly opened the door.

The quizzical porter took a step back. "Here you are sir, um were you expecting someone else?" He handed Kevin a folded paper. Without waiting for a reply, he continued. "This is a spare one that another guest left lying outside his door. He's booked out."

"Oh, thank you Herbert." Richardson replied noticing the red enamelled nameplate above the porter's breast pocket. "Er, not really. You didn't by any chance notice anyone in reception when you came up? I thought another friend might call on me but he did not give me a definite time. ..." Richardson sounded unconvincing but the porter did not appear to notice his hasty change of tack.

"No sir. There was no one in reception two minutes ago when I took the lift. Well thank you, I'll be off now sir." He turned to go on his way.

"Good looking receptionist you have." Kevin offered, trying to prolong the exchange.

"Er, which one sir."

"The dark haired one that was on duty when I checked in."

"Oh, that'll be Moira. She's a temp. She's only been with us since yesterday as Sue, one of our permanent staff, has been booked off sick. If you ask me, she's a bit unfriendly for a receptionist and we have a proud standard to uphold. Her brother who she has not seen for years also

160

turned up today. Strange that, his accent doesn't sound Scots to me."

"She must be happy to see him."

"Oh, I don't know. Moira's not the talkative type. She seems rather aloof and doesn't really talk much. But I agree with you sir, If I was thirty years younger..." He started turning towards the lift.

"Herbert, before you go. Is there another way out to the street behind? My mate Jerry here, parked his car there."

"Oh yes sir. Downstairs, next to the lift. You can't miss it. I'll show you when you come down."

***

The trip to Hampshire had taken just over an hour. D I Smith had kept a discreet distance behind the Jaguar, never allowing more than one car to get between it and the anonymous blue Vauxhall. The Detective Inspector had somehow arranged another car as back up at short notice, the white Ford Mondeo being occupied by two more hefty Scotland Yard detectives.

Jerry had allowed Kevin to drive the newly refurbished Jaguar performance saloon. Although originally of 1965 vintage, a Jaguar specialist had rebuilt and upgraded the engine, fitted the car with modern brakes, improved air conditioning, revised suspension and a new gearbox. While the outside retained the classic lines of the William Lyons era, the handling, performance and interior ambience made the sporting saloon a viable, if expensive, alternative to the modern, often blandly styled Teutonic and Japanese offerings.

Throughout the trip Richardson had been sorely tempted to floor the accelerator pedal to explore its performance potential, but the risk of incurring the wrath of D I Smith who was already unhappy at the number of force members he had had to deploy, tempered his enthusiasm.

He would after all, have to contend with the detective inspector for the foreseeable future

Smith had not been happy at all when Jerry Barker had asked Kevin to make a detour to the local golf club for lunch. The four burly detectives had looked decidedly uncomfortable and edgy at the separate tables they occupied, one within the lounge and the other on the outside patio to give them the best vantage points of the surroundings. They had hardly resembled golfers, but rather like half of the local rugby team's forward pack.

On the way back to their vehicles, Smith had discreetly taken Kevin aside.

"Please Kevin, no more unscheduled deviations from our plan. I take it that our next stop is at the motor workshop."

"I'm sorry Pete, but Jerry did say we would have a bite of lunch on the way. I guess he hadn't decided the actual venue in advance."

"By the way Kevin, I'm afraid we've drawn a blank with the blue Nissan so far. Unfortunately we don't have the registration number and they are rather common."

"And the receptionist?"

"Seems she did come through an agency. We are doing a check on her, but it could take a day or two. The regular receptionist apparently took ill, but we don't know whether it is genuine or was inflicted by someone else. We don't want to take this er... Moira, in for questioning yet, as that could drive Harvey underground. We are also monitoring several other suspected members of the Wilson/Harvey gang who have been active here for the last six months or so."

***

Back in his hotel room that evening Richardson reflected on the day's events. After lunch he had spent two hours at the restorer's workshops in North Hants swooning over the 1955 Aston Martin D B 2/4 Hardtop otherwise also known as a Fixed head Coupé. One of only thirty-four cars of that configuration produced by Tickford coachbuilders who had been acquired by Aston Martin in 1954 to look after their future interests, when the former business had run into financial difficulties and Aston themselves had run into production problems. Resplendent in Aston Martin metallic light green with a silver roof section, Kevin had been allowed to drive the car for several miles. The deep thrum of the three litre straight six cylinder had sent shivers up his spine. Although he had been hoping to run in the motor on the Le Mans practice trip, a few minor quality flaws in the new tan leather upholstery and a couple of insignificant assembly issues, had led to the car not being released.

Despite having a significant classic car collection of his own, Jerry Barker had clearly been envious.

***

After speaking to Ann and Tracey, Kevin had dialled another long distance number.

"Wagner." The well-modulated but authoritative voice had almost sounded accusing. After a busy day who was bothering him at home?

"Hi Henry, its Kevin Richardson. Sorry to bother you at this time of the evening. I hope I'm not interrupting your dinner!"

"Oh, hello Kevin. No not at all. It's good to hear from you. I trust that you and your lovely wife are well."

"Yes, thank you. We both are. I'm actually still in London. Have you heard about my almost encounter over here?"

"With Major Steve Harvey? Yes I have. I had a chat to Inspector Tony Themba earlier this morning. Apparently

163

Harvey's lying low. Although I'm Military, the police have kept me in the loop due to my involvement with Wilson and the hospital."

"What is the incarceration status of the gang members based in Namibia? Ann and I are battling to live a normal life. My wife and daughter have police protection in Johannesburg and I can't even travel without looking over my shoulder every couple of minutes!"

"I *am* sorry about your family's unfortunate involvement Kevin, but I assure you, the Namibian Police are leaving no stone unturned. Interpol currently have operatives on the ground in Sri Lanka, France, the UK and elsewhere, dedicated to cracking this ring. Kingwill, the Nigerian was spotted in his home country two weeks ago, but has also been seen in the UK, possibly to meet up with Harvey."

"And the other members I encountered in Namibia?"

"Well, Captain Van Den Berg is playing dumb. He insists that Harvey was the driving force from the South African side and that David Wilson kept his cards close to his chest, only confiding in McDonald, Harvey and to a lesser extent, Kingwill. The involvement of Inspector Graham Brown is a real turn up for the books!"

"And the German?" Richardson responded.

"Van Den Berg claims to know nothing about the involvement of Dieter Steinmann, the German who even made Wilson nervous. He says that Wilson excluded everyone from his meetings with the alleged ringleader. His private jet was found at Windhoek airport and he is now believed to be directing things from Europe. I have no doubt that Harvey was and still is a kingpin and Kingwill is also a key figure."

Wagner continued. "We really believe that those four young guards – Private Ryan, Miller and the others don't know anything or only what they may have overheard.

They were recruited to add an air of respectability to the hospital security and to be general dogsbodies."

"They certainly knew something illegal was going on." Kevin opined.

"Oh, they know there was a lot of fishy business going on, but they were well paid to shut up and turn a blind eye. We've sent them back to South Africa where they are being monitored and have to report to a Police Station regularly. They also told us about the other body on the plane with you and your wife. They say that Sergeant Smith was still sedated when they carried him off, but we found his body in the hospital morgue, so a case of murder is being investigated."

"Have you heard from Manny and his folks and Conchitta the nursing sister?" Kevin enquired.

"Oh yes, Manny has been very helpful. He did not trust the management as you know. He was discreetly observant while working under Wilson and McDonald and has given us quite a few leads. The hospital has been placed under government jurisdiction as it is crucial to the healthcare of the region. Conchitta is happily running the show at this stage with the assistance of Manny, whose talents are really wasted as a male nurse!"

Chapter 20
Johannesburg

"But Jacqui, you can't be serious. We've known and loved each other for so long and those years and good times together can't just be thrown away as if they never happened!" Chris Jensen's pleading was disbelieving. His emotions were high and he could not control his stammer, "You...you know I ...love you and always have!"

Tears welled around his eyes before gravity dictated that the transparent globules could no longer balance on the edges of his lower eyelids. Before he could wipe them away, two large droplets fell on to the red tablecloth and immediately spread in a darker irregular maroon circle. He brushed away the fresh tears that immediately took their place. He could not believe what he had just heard. Jacqui wanted a divorce!

They had arrived separately at Faizels restaurant. The turban topped Imraan had been his usual elegant, yet respectful and unobtrusive self. He had welcomed Chris with, "Nice to see you again so soon, sir." and had led them to a secluded table at the back of the large room. Jensen momentarily recalled the pleasant evening he had spent with Kevin Richardson just days before. He had chosen the restaurant for its intimate atmosphere aside from the fact that Jacqui enjoyed North Indian cuisine. He had hoped that this night would cement their relationship and that she had agreed to meet him to say that she was coming back.

"Chris, there's no point in trying to stop the inevitable. Sure the early years were good, but we've drifted apart over the past eighteen months. Our needs are different. *My* needs have changed."

His heart and mind in turmoil, Jensen reached for his glass of red wine. His hand was shaking so much that he had to steady it with the other and concentrate on not spilling the contents over his shirtfront as he took a long draught.

After arriving, they had initially made small talk while they waited for their food and had eaten in silence. Then Jacqui had dropped the bombshell.

"Chris, I've met someone who appreciates me for who I am and I would like my freedom sooner than later."

"What do you mean you've met someone else? How? Where? I thought we were just going through a rough patch. All married couples go through a phase – phases, where they feel that they are in a rut and that there must be someone or something better out there."

"I did not go looking for someone else, but I met a guy at the gym while you were pursuing your career overseas."

"How old is this guy?"

"Oh, about two years older than me. As I said, I never went looking, but he kept on asking me to have a meal with him and eventually I thought, 'what the hell' you were not around and I was lonely."

"Oh, and I suppose I was living it up in Sri Lanka while you were languishing back home?" Jensen's response was angry, but he continued in a pleading tone. "Jacqui, you know that I cleared my job intentions with you a year ago and got your buy in. We agreed that the commission on a couple of deals would enable us to be more financially independent. Don't say now that you didn't agree to our mutual goals." Jensen could not help the anger he felt building up again as a result of Jacqui's betrayal.

"Please tell me what I have deprived you of other than company for a maximum of a week at a time? You know I love you and there has never been another woman in my life. I am sure that you have loved me too. Why do you have to do this now? Do you have any idea what my deal in Sri Lanka will mean to us?" He reached for his glass and downed two thirds of the wine in one long gulp. Picking up the bottle of Merlot he moved to top Jacqui's glass but she waved him away. He topped his glass almost to the brim. He was no longer shaking. Anger had given him courage – for the moment at least.

"Look Chris, don't think I haven't spent sleepless nights agonising and thinking this through, but I don't love you anymore. I respect you, but that's not enough. Sure, we have had good times, but there's no spark to our relationship and I can't face another thirty years of this. Graham has made me realize how much I've been missing and I don't want to have that void anymore."

"Oh, Graham is it? Have you moved in with him already? Is he wealthy? Will he be able to provide for your expensive tastes and financial needs?"

"No, I haven't moved in – I would not do that. I'm still staying with Carol. He seems to be doing all right, but that's not the issue – I enjoy his company – he's kind and attentive and I believe that he cares for me."

"And what does Carol say about this? Did she set you up with this Graham?" The red wine had not dulled his senses. As angry as he felt, a feeling of utter loss was beginning to take hold. He did not know where to turn.

"What does he do? Is he married? Does he have kids?" Jensen did not know what to do. He was running out of questions and was beginning to feel that it was futile to pose them.

"Look Chris, let's please leave Carol out of this. She had nothing whatsoever to do with our meeting and for what it's worth, she thinks I'm crazy to even consider letting you go."

"Kids?" Jensen felt compelled to ask the question, as he and Jacqui had initially tried to have a child but after a couple of months had mutually decided to wait for two years before trying again or seeking medical advice.

"Graham is divorced and no, he doesn't have any children and we have not discussed the subject. Chris, you know that has never been an issue in our marriage."

"What does this knight in shining armour do?"

"Oh he has his own business and is involved in a lot of government work."

"Sounds exciting!" Jensen did not even attempt to keep the sarcasm from his response. He still could not grasp the bomb that Jacqui had unexpectedly dumped on him.

He had politely declined the dessert menu, but as Jacqui had ordered a Dom Pedro, he had decided upon a large black filter coffee to counter the effects of the three and a half glasses of red wine.

They had walked to the parking area in silence. He had followed Jacqui to her car as if in a trance and had opened her door. She had climbed in and pulled the door closed while he stood, still dumbstruck. As she had started edging away she had opened her window and stated matter of factly, "Oh Chris, please go and see a lawyer, I already have." She had driven off before he could respond.

***

Jensen glanced through the porthole. The aircraft was already well into its descending flight path for Singapore's Changi Airport. He had a further momentary pang of regret at having actually made the flight, but consciously concentrated on dismissing the thought. He had battled to conceal his feelings of depression from his colleagues at Caldwell International and had fought against negative thoughts since taking off from Johannesburg International.

He had spent hours trying to convince himself that Jacqui would see reason and come back and that future events would vindicate his decision to travel to finalise the deal with Fernando da Silva.

Two of the customs officials on duty greeted him heartily by name. His frequent trips to Sri Lanka via the aviation hub had resulted in him being almost regarded as a prominent local citizen. Travel documents were generally routinely stamped without even a rudimentary check of his baggage.

Over time the almost compulsory extended waiting period for the connecting flight to Sri Lanka had become tiresome. Initial delays had been looked forward to in anticipation as they had enabled him to get to know the island intimately. He had spent hours thoroughly researching the history of Singapore which first records of settlement dated back to the second century AD. As much as he had come to love the island, his reluctance to take this trip due to Jacqui's impending termination of their relationship, made the prospect of the next eight hours of introspection difficult to contemplate.

Chris was unhappy to learn that the airport hotel where in-transit passengers generally booked in to freshen-up and rest, was full. There was no point in booking into a hotel in the city.

He wondered momentarily why the promised reception committee from Singapore Police Force and possibly Interpol, had not been on hand when he had negotiated Customs, but the thought passed.

Jensen left his luggage in a locker suddenly recalling his previous trip and his switched briefcase. What would Customs have done last time, had they found the drugs in his possession? How would he have convinced the authorities that they had been planted? Would he have received life imprisonment or for that matter capital punishment, as allowed for under the law? Amnesty International rated Singapore as having possibly the highest execution rate in the world per capita, while Transparency

International considered the island the least corrupt in Asia as well as being among the ten most free from corruption in the world.

He was heading towards the terminal exit when the thought of planted drugs gave him a sinking feeling. "What if the bastards had seen his trip as another opportunity to use him as a courier?" He made an abrupt about turn and retraced his steps to the locker. He had not got around to replacing the briefcase and had travelled with one smallish suitcase and an overnight bag which he had taken aboard as cabin luggage. The rectangular compartment door opened with a hollow metallic echo in the otherwise empty corridor. Jensen made a 360 degree turn before removing the bags and placing them on the floor. No one was within twenty metres of the bank of lockers or appeared remotely interested in him.

With trembling hands he unlocked and feverishly searched the suitcase, not finding any signs of tampering or unfamiliar extra items. His file for the deal with Da Silva still nestled between two pairs of slacks. Although the overnight bag had to all intents and purposes not been out of his sight, its contents were also subjected to a thorough scrutiny before he replaced both bags in the locker. He took a deep breath and sighed.

"Okay, now get a grip on yourself."

***

As Jensen passed through the electronic glass doors of the airport exit, he noticed a burly white man entering a taxi on the opposite side of the road. Other than the usual rows of Toyota taxis on both sides of the boulevard, there appeared to be surprisingly little activity for that time of the morning. Some of the taxi drivers were exchanging pleasantries, but no other passengers seeking transport were to be seen.

He chose an elderly but pristine yellow Toyota Crown parked against the verge facing the city.

"Where to suh?" The middle-aged driver enquired, as he hobbled around the back of the vehicle to open the left rear door. He was of Indian origin rather than a member of the majority seventy-five percent Chinese populace of the island.

"Orchard Road please." Jensen thought that he would try and kill some time at the popular tourist shopping district.

"Right-o suh." The driver accelerated smoothly from the kerb.

Jensen surveyed the interior of the immaculately maintained vehicle. In Japan and other markets, the Crown had for years been the luxury model in the Toyota range prior to the release of the Soarer and even more upmarket Lexus brand. Taxi versions of the former were however, rather blandly appointed and purpose built for longevity.

"You've looked after this car very well." He opined noting the gaze of the driver in the rear view mirror.

"She been very good to me, suh." He pointed to the odometer. "Just clock five hundred thousand mile with no ploblim." In profile, Jensen saw the driver's left cheek rise and the corner of his eye crease as he grinned with pride.

"That's fantastic, may she travel many more." Jensen responded, shifting his gaze to the opposite lane of oncoming traffic.

The driver had drawn the Toyota to a stop at a traffic light in the right hand lane of Pan Island Expressway heading towards the city, when Jensen noticed a white Lexus just metres away across the island separating the motorway. Rather, he observed the animated antics of a passenger in the back of the car. He was pointing at Jensen's taxi and appeared to be shouting instructions to the driver.

"Turn left here." Jensen shouted without warning.

The cab driver, who was in the process of accelerating away from the intersection, braked and jerked the large diameter steering of the Toyota to the left. The unsporting suspension caused the heavy saloon to wallow, then the car leaned and the tyres protested as over steer took over, before it finally negotiated the ninety degree turn and set off on a straight course.

Jensen looked back. The Lexus had already crossed the intersection and would have to travel a substantial distance before the next, to make a one hundred and eighty degree turn to follow them.

"Is there problem suh?"

Chris turned to look at the driver, for the first time noticing a plaque on the dashboard proclaiming Aravinda Duarte. An Indian of Portuguese extraction thought Jensen, probably from Goa.

"Aravinda, um, I..." Jensen hesitated. He was hardly going to pour out his personal trials and tribulations to this complete stranger. Then he thought better of it. He could be in serious trouble and there was no one else to turn to.

"Not for anything I have done wrong! Some unscrupulous thugs tried to use my luggage to smuggle items to my country the last time I passed through Singapore, but they were unable to do the reverse switch and they are possibly after me. The local police were supposed to meet me at Changi Airport, but I don't know what happened to them."

"Please call me Vindoo, suh. Another taxi following us for long time now."

Chris spun around without thinking. The closest car was a silver Mercedes Benz sedan about four car lengths behind. He could not see what other vehicles tailed the Merc.

"Since when? How do you know he's following us?"

"Oh right from airport, suh. One gentleman in anudda Toyota taxi he took at airport. He turn when we turn and he careful to keep two car behind, but every time I overtake, he overtake."

"Well, then he's definitely not a member of the local police or Interpol! Vindoo, could you drop me at the Bird Park and phone the police for me? Do you have their head office number? Just tell them that Chris Jensen of South Africa wants to know why they did not meet him at the airport and that he maybe needs their help."

The cab driver opened the central ashtray and reached over the seat to pass Jensen a neatly hand printed business card containing his cell phone number and other personal details. Jensen opened his wallet and passed Vindoo his business card and a fifty U S Dollar note. In the rear view mirror Chris noted the cab driver do a double take.

"That too much, suh!"

"Don't worry about that now. How far to Jurong and how far behind is the other taxi?

"Other taxi have to stop at traffic light, so quite far behind now. Bird Park still half mile."

"Well step on it Vindoo. I'm going to try and hide inside until the police arrive. Can you stay around for an hour or so in case I need you?"

"Sure ting, suh."

Vindoo had been cruising along slowly while concentrating on their exchange, but Jensen had to scramble for a hand hold on the smooth vinyl passenger seat back, as the old Toyota suddenly took off under surprisingly rapid acceleration. Without warning, Vindoo braked and hauled the large diameter steering wheel around. The Toyota lurched clockwise through three hundred and sixty degrees of tyre squeal as its centre of gravity was severely challenged. The driver had to physically unwind the wheel and jerk it to the right to bring the staid vehicle into a straight line. The steering mechanism's slow and reluctant self-centring action had most certainly not been designed with any sporting pretensions in mind.

Before the car came to rest alongside the sidewalk, Chris had jumped out. Vindoo's farewell greeting, if one was made, was lost as Jensen slammed the door. The entrance to Jurong beckoned across the sidewalk. He glanced up the road from where they had just come. Another white Toyota loomed in the distance, but was still three or four hundred metres away. Vindoo made a u-turn and parked opposite the entrance.

Jensen found great difficulty in crossing the sidewalk at a normal, but nevertheless brisk walking pace, so as not to let on to the occupant of the approaching taxi that he suspected anything untoward.

As he passed through the entrance and out of sight, he almost ran past the curio shops to the ticket booth. He paid with a Twenty Singapore Dollar note he had extracted from his wallet while still in the taxi. Chris grabbed the ticket and headed for the turnstile entrance. The cashier called after him about his change, but Jensen shouted, "Keep it as a donation," and passed through into the park and hopefully refuge.

Chapter 21
Singapore

The park was surprisingly empty for mid-morning with only a few gardeners and attendants visible in the distance. Jensen set off along the paved pathway almost at a run but not wanting to alert anyone to his distress. He had spent a lot of his spare "in transit" time at Jurong and knew the park like the back of his hand, but he had no particular plan of where to seek concealment.

He glanced over his shoulder. The reception and curio shop buildings had already receded into the distance. No one else had made an appearance from the ticket area. He passed the Panorail track and was approaching the Flamingo Lake which lay to the left of the pathway. He passed a couple of wooden benches and a trellis under construction which lay in shadow a metre from the edge of the walkway.

Just beyond the benches, he suddenly darted to the left into shrubbery behind a large tree close to the water's edge. Sitting on his haunches, he manoeuvred his body into a position behind the tree from which he had a clear view of the last thirty metres of the pathway along which he had come.

Seemingly seconds later Jensen heard the uneven gait of heavy footsteps approaching and a burly figure came into view. He appeared to be scanning the undergrowth on the side Jensen had secreted himself. Across the walkway a large area of open space offered no refuge. In the opposite direction, the children's playground, exotic bird enclosures and the elevated monorail train line were visible.

Something about the rapidly approaching brown haired man seemed vaguely familiar. Tan slacks were topped by a lightweight cream jacket which hid most of a beige golf shirt.

Jensen drew further back into the shaded protection of the foliage and substantial tree trunk. As the man drew nearer recognition suddenly dawned. It was Graham Brown of the South African Police! Jensen had moved away from the tree but was still obscured behind the shrubs when he suddenly stopped dead.

Brown had come to a halt and turned to face the lake. He had carefully removed a pistol from what was probably a holster beneath his right armpit. Holding the gun across his midriff with his left hand away from possible spectators, he had withdrawn what appeared to be a silencer from his right trouser pocket, which he had then proceeded to push fit over the end of the barrel. He had then shoved the gun into his right pocket. It protruded due to its length, so Brown had cupped his hand over the butt and continued his walk.

During this process Jensen had been utterly confused. Why would the South African policeman need to ready his gun and why did he feel the need for a silencer?

Brown passed the tree without an apparent second glance while Jensen agonised over his next move. Suddenly he heard a rustling in the undergrowth behind. He arose, turning towards the sound. From the corner of his eye he glimpsed a lunging movement and ducked, raising both elbows to protect his head. The butt of the pistol in Brown's hand glanced off Jensen's right shoulder, but the impact was enough to land him on his backside in the shrubbery. Brown sluggishly aimed his size eleven shoe at his groin but Jensen was able to roll over, the intended blow deflecting harmlessly off of his side and almost causing the former to lose his balance.

Brown cocked the hammer with his thumb. "Stop right there. I assure you I will lose no sleep over giving you a second arsehole! Now get up and move onto the path as if nothing has happened."

"What the hell are you doing?"

"Shut up! You'll find out soon enough. And if you think you can get away I have back-up outside."

Jensen slowly came erect while Brown did a one hundred and eighty degree survey. No one seemed to have noticed the scuffle, most of which had probably been obscured by the undergrowth.

"Sit on the bench." Jensen felt the barrel pressed hard up against his spine just above his belt.

He sauntered towards the backless wooden slatted seat of the closest bench and slowly sat down. Keeping the now silencer-less pistol in his pocket, Brown moved past and took up a position in the middle of the other, about two metres beyond.

"How's Jacqui?" Brown enquired with a sarcastic sneer.

"What's it to you?"

"Oh well, the last time I saw her at the gym she made it clear that she was going to move the rest of her things out and was having difficulty choosing between several apartments."

"So you're the "Graham" swine she's been seeing!" Jensen stood up, his fists clenched. "What the hell could she have seen in you?"

"Sit down." Brown edged the pistol from his pocket. "Oh I must admit I had to overcome stern resistance. Deep down she probably still cares for you. I wish I could say that I've slept with her, but there's plenty of time for that!"

Jensen took a step forward, but Brown pulled the gun from his pocket and pointed it at his groin, his lips parted in a snarl. His face still flushed with anger, Jensen slowly retreated until the back of his legs touched the bench.

Reluctantly he sat down, his eyes burning into those of the sneering man who sat just a lunge away. His white knuckles ached from tension and the need to smash the face of the now leering bastard in front of him.

"How long have you known Jacqui?" Jensen's voice wavered. He still could not believe that the love of his life had formed an association with the flabby giant.

"Oh long enough to have known in advance about several trips you made to Colombo."

"Are you saying you've used my luggage to smuggle drugs before?" Jensen's tone was incredulous.

"Wouldn't you like to know? Maybe you'll find out if you live much longer!"

"But why have you harassed me, I don't know anything and in any case the police have the heroine and money?"

"That's what you say. Our Singapore operative conveniently disappeared after that bodged job and we believe it's because he left information in the briefcase you passed to Tony Themba without letting on to me. Now shut up and don't move, I need to make a call." Holding the pistol low down in his right hand, still trained on Jensen, Brown withdrew a cell phone from his jacket pocket and pressed the dial button with his left thumb. Pressing the phone to his left ear, seconds later he made contact.

"Where are you guys? I've got Jensen. We need to get the hell out of here!" Brown listened for a few seconds.

"What do you mean the cops are outside?"

Jensen's heart skipped a beat. Was help on the way? Brown lowered his voice and continued his dialogue, an increasingly deeper frown creasing his brow. The man sitting across from him wasn't close enough to hear the other side of the exchange, but Jensen turned his thoughts elsewhere.

When he had originally passed the bench before seeking concealment behind the tree and also when he had later sat down at Brown's command, he had subconsciously noted a half-metre long bamboo plant support leaning against the side of the wooden seat. This had most probably come from one of the potted creepers which dotted the ground to the west of the bench and which remained to be planted at the foot of the still unfinished trellis.

Brown was still in conversation and was clearly distracted. Jensen gently edged his buttocks closer towards the edge of the bench to his right. He had rested his hands on the wooden seat either side of his thighs from the time he had sat down. Watching Brown closely, he slowly edged his right hand behind his back until his fingers touched and closed around the smooth stick. He gently manoeuvred the spar until his hand had firm purchase around one end allowing him maximum leverage. Brown noticed his subtle movement and edged the gun forward indicating with his head and glaring eyes that Jensen should sit still. The captive turned his legs towards Brown and swivelled his buttocks so that he was squarely facing the man ahead who was still engrossed in his dialogue.

He suddenly erupted from his seat, raised the pole and smashed it across Brown's left wrist. His captor opened his mouth and audibly inhaled as the stinging sensation was communicated to his brain within milliseconds. The pistol dropped on the turf at Jensen's feet. The cell phone flew in the opposite direction onto the paved pathway, as the left hand which had held it, sought to comfort its partner.

Jensen dropped the pole and before Brown could rise he drove his left fist into the soft flesh at the base of the big man's ribcage. Brown flew over the back of the bench into the undergrowth and lay winded for several seconds.

A faint smile briefly played around Jensen's mouth. He was proud of the punch, but he grimaced as he gingerly flexed his bruised hand. He had not punched any one in years since a brief appearance for his college boxing team. Although he had showed promise, he had quickly decided it was a mug's game. He retrieved the pistol. Being familiar with handguns he noted that the safety catch was off. A quick check showed that the magazine of the CZ 83 was virtually full.

"Now you get up and sit on the bench. Keep your hands in front of you where I can see them. I don't need an excuse to give you a third nipple!" Brown slowly obliged, his left hand still clutching his stomach, a grimace creasing his features. Jensen sat down slowly, keeping the gun trained on the man ahead.

Jensen heard voices approaching from the direction of the entrance. Two plain clothed men of oriental origin came into view. The leading man drew a pistol when he noticed the gun in Jensen's hand.

"What is going on here?"

Brown turned towards the sound, but Jensen stood up waving the pistol for him to remain seated.

"I'm Chris Jensen from South Africa. Why was I not met at the airport?"

"He's not Jensen, I am. Don't believe him, he's trying to bullshit you into..." Brown started to stand up.

"I'm sorry, but I recognize Mr Jensen from photos sent from South Africa to Interpol. Please sit down both of you." Brown reluctantly obliged.

Jensen remained standing. "Please handcuff this man, he is connected with the drug smuggling ring. This is his gun and believe it or not, he is a South African policeman!"

Holding the pistol by the barrel he held it out towards the leader of the two who took it reluctantly and gingerly, obviously considering the fingerprints that needed to be checked. The second oriental man had by now also drawn his pistol. Quizzically he took a pair of cuffs from a pocket, moved behind the seated man and clicked them into place.

"What do you mean he is a South African policeman?" the leader was speaking again.

"He is Inspector Graham Brown who has been assisting Tony Themba on the case. He followed me from the airport, overpowered me and told me just now that he thought that one of his gang members from Singapore had ratted on them. I have no idea how he infiltrated the S A Police. By the way who are you two chaps?"

"I am sorry Mr Jensen. I'm Inspector Tann of Interpol and this is Detective Lynn of Singapore Police Service."

He placed Brown's pistol in his pocket and stuck out his right hand, while the other man standing a few metres behind bowed sombrely. Jensen shook the limp hand reluctantly.

"Mr Jensen, I am so sorry we could not be at Changi to meet you but a big truck was abandoned across our entrance and we could not get our cars out. I wonder if this gentleman knows something about it?" He looked enquiringly at the seated Brown who continued to stare at the ground at his feet.

"I still don't understand how this man could have infiltrated the force!" Tann shook his head.

"Oh, by the way Inspector Tann, I'm sorry I didn't mention it before, but Brown here had assistants at the gate just before you arrived. He was speaking to them on his cell, but they apparently told him of your arrival."

Detective Lynn removed a cell phone from his trouser pocket and spoke softly.

Jensen remembered Brown's phone. It still lay on the path two metres away. He retrieved it and handed it to Tann. It was still switched on. "You may well find some interesting numbers on this!"

"Our colleagues outside say there no suspicious vehicles at gate, but blue Toyota left in hurry just now." Lynn lowered his voice and continued speaking to Tann in what Jensen presumed was a Chinese dialect, the latter nodding intermittently and making confirmatory noises.

"We should go now. Mr Jensen please accompany us to the Station. We need a statement from you and we must discuss your trip to Sri Lanka." Tann backed towards the pathway.

Lynn moved towards Brown and motioned for the burly figure to rise. Jensen caught a glimpse of the hitherto inscrutable Chinese policeman's face. He could have sworn that the makings of a smile had almost creased his face. He obviously had no time for corrupt police officers.

**

Back at the Park entrance, Detective Lynn bundled Brown into the back of a police car that had parked behind the Lexus he and Tann had arrived in, and climbed in beside the crooked South African policeman. Tann motioned for Jensen to join him in the back of the Lexus and the driver held the door open for him. As he was about to oblige, Jensen noticed Vindoo the cab driver, waving at him from across the road.

He turned towards the police car driver. "Please give me a second." He crossed the road towards the smiling taxi driver who held up the U S Dollar note in his right hand and a fistful of obviously smaller denomination notes in the other.

"Your change suh!"

"No, please keep it Vindoo, you were a great help. I travel through Singapore often and with your card I will certainly 'phone you in the future when I need an expert driver. Hopefully I won't need a racing driver next time!" Jensen smiled and stuck out his right hand.

"Oh thank you, thank you very much suh." Vindoo beamed.

**

Back at the airport hotel room, Jensen lay on the bed and reflected on the day's events. He looked at the telephone on the side pedestal. He was itching to 'phone Jacqui, but did not trust himself not to gloat about the arrest of her corrupt South African would-be suitor.

He switched his gaze to the foot of the bed where a packet containing another figurine for Jacqui lay. He was sure or certainly fervently hoped that she had somehow had a moment of madness and infatuation that had caused her to seek the big policeman's company. He was still confused and while he longed for her, he also had mixed feelings about her coming back to him on the rebound, when she found out about Brown's incarceration.

After completing his statement at Police Headquarters, Inspector Tann had put the Lexus and chauffer at his disposal to kill time and do some shopping. The Interpol agent had informed him that he would join him on the flight to Sri Lanka later that evening and would discretely shadow his movements in the former Ceylon.

On a sudden impulse he picked up his cell phone and dialled a number in South Africa.

"Inspector Themba." The slightly built policeman's voice was surprisingly deep and authoritative.

"Oh, hi Tony, it's Chris Jensen here. Has Inspector Tann of Interpol been in touch, he told me he was going to ring you?"

"He has indeed Mr Jensen and what a story he had to tell! We are all shocked. Brown joined the service several years ago and while not liked by everyone, he didn't do a bad job. He also has connections!"

"Obviously the wrong sort!" Jensen opined sarcastically.

"Well we certainly have egg on our faces. I'm very embarrassed to talk to our counterparts and colleagues overseas!"

After a pregnant silence Themba continued.

"You know Mr Jensen, I called on at his house after he 'phoned in to say a relative had died a few days ago and he wasn't home. He wasn't answering his landline and hadn't replied to messages left on his cell either. We should have suspected something fishy was going on. We've been so busy that we did not follow up. There was no one else to contact – he's not married you know."

"Don't I, the swine..." Jensen decided it was not the right time to elaborate. "By the way Tony, you told me before my trip that I would be shadowed by a detective to Singapore. Was Brown supposed to have been the shadow?"

"Oh no, Mr Jensen um, Chris, I'm sorry, but the detective we had in mind was pulled off the job at the last minute due to a crisis we had. We should have told you. Graham was actually supposed to have followed Kevin Richardson to London, but it looks as if he decided to take over as your escort cum eliminator!"

"Thank you very much!"

"Don't worry, you're in good hands in Singapore now. Inspector Tann is a very experienced Interpol operative. They are closing in on the heads and other members of the drug ring fast."

Chapter 22
London

The morning after their trip to see Richardson's 'work in progress' Aston Martin, Jerry Barker collected Kevin from the hotel at 8:00 and they had set off to meet the Honda team at Silverstone to discuss the forthcoming practice session in France. Although very different to the conditions they would encounter at the Sarthe circuit, the technical team was particularly looking forward to Kevin's input covering any last minute suspension tweaks.

Kevin was itching to get the feel of the spare Le Mans car at a session booked at the British Grand Prix circuit later that morning. Two of the white and red Japanese cars were already on the way to the French circuit and two spares *they* were using, would follow that evening.

Detective Inspector Pete Smith had again been unhappy to see the new car Jerry Barker had chosen from his collection to use for the one hour trip to Silverstone and later that afternoon, for the journey to France via the Channel Tunnel.

"You will insist on sticking out like a sore thumb while we're trying to keep a low profile for Mr Richardson's sake." The policeman had done his best to berate Kevin's genial co-driver, but had been unable to hide his admiration for the beautiful metallic mint green A C Aceca-Bristol coupé.

"Just you wait until we get on the road to Dover this afternoon and travel through France – we'll just be one of dozens of classic cars heading for Le Mans."

Being based in the UK near the Honda works racing factory, Barker had already put hundreds of practice laps in the white and red Japanese car under his belt at the famous British motor racing circuit, while the car was being developed.

It had not taken Kevin long to have the Japanese technicians beaming and patting each other on the back and he had been rather embarrassed when the usually sombre and subdued men from the land of the rising sun had swarmed all over him when he had clambered from the sleek coupe, having just set an unofficial sports car lap record for the test circuit.

"Your design change make big difference and your driving velly good. We have velly good chance now to beat Porsche." Hiro Yamamoto, the Head Engineer who was also wearing the hat of Team Manager from Honda Japan, had enthused.

"Oh, I don't know about that, the basic car you've provided is superbly balanced and the tyres and track conditions were just right. I doubt that I'll be able to match those times again in a hurry."

His times had consistently been some three seconds better than Jerry Barker and the Japanese drivers had managed to set in earlier practice sessions. Barker had barely contained his eagerness to brush the slightly built oriental technicians aside, to be first to congratulate Richardson.

"I say, old boy, you've just consigned me to the scrap heap! You were superb! Gee Kev. Those are some of the smoothest aggressive laps I've witnessed here. You were awesome!"

"Thanks Jerry, but wait until you try the car with the new settings. It just begs to be driven hard."

Richardson had politely deflected the compliments. He knew that Jerry Barker was unlikely to match his times easily, but was looking forward to meeting and assessing the ability of the Japanese drivers who had already left for France with the advance party. While none had driven at the French circuit before, they had already put in many practice laps with a prototype car in Japan. Twenty-four hours of collective intense concentration on their part and reliability from the cars, would be essential if the German marque's dominance was to be dented or broken.

***

Kevin's prediction to D I Smith had proved to be spot on. The journey to the coast had virtually turned into a procession of British enthusiasts in classic saloons and sports cars of not only local manufacture. Triumph TRs, Austin-Healeys, MGs, TVRs and even rarer obsolete marques had shared the roads with exotics from the Ferrari, Alfa Romeo and Lamborghini stables. Their beautiful A C Aceca-Bristol – one of only 169 built, had matched, but had hardly stood out amongst various magnificent cars on view.

As they neared Folkestone, Barker who was driving, noticed D I Smith who had been tailing them, gesticulating in his rear view mirror. He was contemplating stopping on the verge when Richardson's cell phone rang.

"Um, Kevin, I'm afraid the French won't allow you to carry the pistol in their country. I'll have to get it from you before you go through Customs. By the way, I have good news and bad news!"

"The suspense is killing me!"

"We narrowly missed arresting your friend Major Steve Harvey at a hotel in Hyde Park last night. An interesting development is that the Scottish receptionist at your hotel was in fact recruited by another Scot – none other than Jim McDonald of Namibia fame. We now believe that she is entirely innocent – she says that McDonald is an acquaintance from back home who asked her to fill in at your hotel. She claims not to know how or why their regular lady fell ill. She did however, lead us to the hotel where both Harvey and McDonald have been staying. We nicked McDonald in the shower. Unfortunately Harvey booked out an hour before we got there!"

"Oh great!" Richardson responded not knowing how else he was expected or supposed to react, while still trying to process all of the information conveyed by the rambling Police Inspector.

"We have alerted all ports and airports, but these chaps managed to get in without detection, so we can but hope that they are apprehended!"

Richardson had long been intrigued by the Channel Tunnel or Chunnel or Eurotunnel as it is also known. For that matter he was interested in most things engineering. The 50.5 kilometre undersea tunnel which connects Folkestone in Kent to Coquelles near Calais in northern France, is the second longest undersea tunnel in the world after Japan's Seikan Tunnel. The concept of a Link between Britain and the continent had existed since the early 1800s and discussions over some 150 years had only become reality in 1988 when tunnelling commenced. Three bores had been made – two rail tunnels with a service tunnel in between, at an average depth of 45 metres below the seabed.

He had read all he could find on the project. The studies and understanding of the topography and geology required before boring started through the dipping strata layers and faulting between the English coast and France, were mind boggling.

The tunnel which carried high speed passenger and shuttle vehicle transport and freight trains had been used by illegal immigrants and asylum seekers to attempt to enter Britain. Control zones had been implemented on both sides where the officers of the other nation exercised limited customs and law enforcement powers. For most purposes these were at either end of the tunnel, with the French border controls on the UK side of the tunnel and vice versa.

**

Upon disembarking and unloading their car on the French side, Kevin and Jerry noticed a well-dressed but scrawny, brown-suited man with sharp features and deep set dark eyes approaching. His grey-white pallor, hollow pock-marked cheeks, thin eyebrows and matching moustache gave him an almost horror movie character look.

"Shall we run for it, the devil has come for us?" Kevin heard Jerry beside him mutter under his breath.

"Shut up!" Kevin whispered, barely containing a smile while aiming an elbow at the well-padded ribs of his jovial co-driver.

"Mr Richardson?" he enquired in a surprisingly deep voice for such a slight frame. The accent was undoubtedly French. He simultaneously proffered his hand, an almost evil grin wrinkling his face. From close range, Kevin realized that the man before him had had a horrible accident sometime in his past and had undergone extensive reconstructive surgery to his face, which had left him with a rather lopsided look, one ear having been reattached rather higher than the other. "I'm Marc Cheval of Interpol, I believe that Detective Inspector Smith mentioned that I would be your escort while you are in France."

"Oh sure, Marc." Richardson responded, meeting the firm handshake. "Pleased to meet you – hopefully recent developments will see the rest of the gang behind bars soon so that I can get on with my life!" He turned to introduce the Frenchman to Jerry.

The sound of approaching high revving large capacity two stroke motorcycle engines interrupted their conversation.

"Please excuse me for a minute." Cheval bowed slightly before turning to walk several metres to meet two helmeted bikers in black leathers sitting astride of what Kevin recognised as turbocharged Kawasaki racing bikes.

"Does the devil have a horse rather than a motorbike?" Jeremy Barker enquired innocently once Cheval was out of earshot.

"Shut up will you! He seems a perfectly nice chap." Richardson retorted, aiming a good–natured left jab at his grinning overweight co-driver's ribs. The latter surprisingly parried the blow and replied with a telegraphed right hook of his own, which Kevin deftly slipped.

"If you don't lay off of the brew and scotch you won't fit into the car. On second thoughts…"

"Oh, Mr Richardson." Cheval's deep voice saved Jerry from another sarcastic jibe.

Kevin turned towards the Frenchman. He still stood with the bikers who were in the process of dismounting.

"I'd like you to meet Jean-Pierre and Georges."

They walked towards the group and were introduced to the two "Gendarmes on Two Wheels" as described by Marc. Although they had removed their helmets, they had retained their skull caps. Jean-Pierre was a handsome, light skinned giant with piercing blue eyes and excellent front teeth. Wisps of curly blond hair peeped from the balaclava. Kevin had no doubt that he was a hit with the opposite sex.

Georges on the other hand, while also very good looking, was almost the exact opposite. Swarthy of complexion, his dark afternoon shadow hinted at dark brown or black hair. Deep set brown eyes completed Kevin's conclusion that he was of probable Greek extraction.

Richardson noticed that although the two powerful bikes were similar, Jean-Pierre's was black hued, whereas Georges' was a deep metallic blue.

"Gentlemen, we should be on our way." Marc broke the silence after greetings and pleasantries had been exchanged.

"Kevin, could we confirm our route s'il vous plait? Georges will lead zee way – never more zan few hundred metres ahead. I weel follow you in my Alpine-Renault and Jean-Pierre weel bring up zee rear. "We should take the A16 to Calais, Boulogne…"

"Jean-Pierre, Georges – please won't you discuss the way with old Jerry here. He knows your country almost as well as the British Isles. From what I can gather, he comes over here every month to sample your wines. Sample is most probably a euphemism! Marc, now where is this Alpine-Renault you are bragging about? Is it an A106? I have a Gordini with a similar motor. If I could lay my hands on a right hand drive one...they're as scarce as hen's teeth!"

"Qui, it is an A106. Do you think I was going to drive a Citroen 2CV that could not keep up with your British sports car? I parked it just around zee corner. I have 'ad it for ten year and it has only 40,000 kilometres on zee clock."

The unfortunate, strange looking Frenchmen led Kevin to the diminutive French-Blue coupe. For several mutually enthralling minutes they shared experiences and knowledge of the competitive Renault-Gordini engined cars that had won the Monte Carlo Rally and had been virtually unbeatable during the late 1960s and early seventies.

Richardson looked at his watch. "Sorry to hold things up Marc, I suppose we'd better get on the road, but before I leave France I am going to demand a drive in your car."

"That will only be a pleasure Monsieur!"

Kevin returned to the Aceca to find Jerry holding the driver's door open for him.

"There you are sport, you can drive for the first stint, I know you've been itching to."

"Thanks Jerry, I appreciate your gesture, particularly to let me drive your baby, I really do, but I'm not in the mood to tackle the French roads in a right hand drive car today. It's as bad as driving a left-hooker back home. I suppose I'm stupid as I'll be sitting in the suicide seat anyway!"

Chapter 23
France

They had been driving for several hours. Despite Marc's protestations, Jerry had eventually convinced them to take a scenic, rather than the most direct route to Le Mans on the basis that most of the enthusiastic spectators probably wanted to get to their accommodation and a pub where they could settle down with bottles of amber, red or pale yellow liquid as soon as possible.

Many of the other visitors from across the channel had clearly had the same idea or had hoped that there would be fewer speed traps. The route was surprisingly busy, although the convoy had mostly been very well behaved. A couple of Porsche drivers and a really flying Lamborghini pilot had nailed the "loud pedal" at the wrong time and found to their cost that the "Jean Claudes" were as vigilant as ever and took no prisoners, or did they? Locals had as usual, been of great assistance by flashing their headlamps or waving.

Georges had disappeared into the haze ahead, but Marc who was in radio contact with both bikers, kept relatively close company astern, never falling more than two or three cars behind.

In the interests of maintaining the period originality of the A C coupe, Jeremy had fitted a stereo cassette player in the left hand cubby hole of the facia behind the standard wooden lid. Reception from the circa 1959 standard fitment radio was worse than useless. Jerry had brought along a shoebox full of tapes of 1960's British groups which had kept Kevin entertained. He particularly enjoyed the early blues rock of The Pretty Things, Yardbirds and Rolling Stones.

"That's strange!"

Mick Jagger was in the process of chasing trespassers from his cloud, when Jerry's observation cut into Kevin's daydreaming.

"Uh, what's that?"

"Well, it's just that I noticed Jean-Pierre pull out into the fast lane some way back. He passed Marc and I expected him to come rocketing past ages ago probably to reconnoitre with Georges. This car's got terrible blind spots, but..."

Kevin opened his eyes and turned his head to the left just as the front wheel of a motorcycle came into view. It did not pass but kept pace with the front door of the Aceca.

"Well, you were not dreaming, here he is!"

But something was wrong. Within seconds he put his finger on it – the bike was a dark metallic gunmetal grey whereas Jean-Pierre's was black and this was a Suzuki not a Yamaha! He turned his head further to the left and froze. Not more than a metre away, a burly figure sat upright on the bike holding a large calibre pistol pointed at his head.

"Braay – ke." He shouted, simultaneously throwing his head backwards, pulling his shoulders down into the seat and pushing his butt forward towards the foot well to minimise the biker's target.

Both Jerry and the car were equal to the task. The driver dug his right foot into the foot well, the Aceca's long nose visibly dropped as the front disc brakes and screeching tyres clawed the car to a halt on the verge of the road. Kevin thought he had heard at least two reports above the din of the Stones, but the expected imploding of side window glass did not happen.

"What the..? What did I nearly hit?" Jerry's voice shouted above the noise of the cassette.

Kevin pulled his butt back onto the seat and switched off the cacophony. His feet scattered the cassettes on the floor around them, the box having tipped over from the g-forces of the decelerating car. He was shaking and his left knee was sore from the jarring impact against the base of the dashboard. He reluctantly glanced to the left and then at the road ahead. The biker had taken off and was fast disappearing with Jean-Pierre in hot pursuit.

"You nearly had my brains on your lap!" he responded taking several deep breaths to regulate his racing heartbeat. He grimaced as he rubbed his knee and haltingly described his shock at seeing the menacing black-leather suited figure. A dark-tinted full visor had not given any clue to the would-be assassin's identity.

"All I know is that he was a very big bugger!"

"The elusive Major Steve Harvey?"

"I really can't say."

"Mr Richardson, you okay?" They were interrupted by a deeply concerned looking Marc Cheval pulling open Kevin's door. In his haste, he had parked his Alpine-Renault half on the verge and half on the roadway and had left the driver's door open.

"Yes thank you, I'm still in one piece. I don't know about Jerry's car though."

Kevin clambered out. Jerry Barker had already come around to his side and was scrutinising the bodywork. "Well, I don't see any holes Kev, he must have overshot when we slowed and miraculously we're intact. Hang on, what's this?" He reached out and gently rubbed his finger along a two centimetre long feint grey smudge which ran across the centre of the curved windscreen. "You know what, I think that one of the slugs ricocheted off the glass!"

Marc moved closer and leaned over the side of the bonnet to inspect the line. He too touched the mark and inspected a smidgeon of feint grey residue on the tip of his forefinger."

"Gentlemen, I believe Mr Barker, he is correct. This looks like lead, but it will polish out without leaving zee mark on your beautiful car." The ring tone of a cell phone from Cheval's car interrupted the exchange.

"Please excuse me." The Frenchman ran towards his car and clambered in. He released the handbrake with his right hand while his left one dug the cell from a door pocket. The gradient allowed the car to roll out of harm's way without any added leverage. Kevin and Jerry were only able to make out the odd word of guttural French which carried to them from the confines of the Alpine's compact cockpit. The Interpol agent spoke for a good ten minutes before rejoining them.

"I am afraid I have not zee good news. Zee man who tried to shoot you got away because of zee stupid Georges! About three kilometre ahead from here he went off zee road to check zee bridge across ziss road for zee possible persons planning zee ambush. Just before zee bridge, two and half kilometre from here, zay are working on zee road and zere is only one lane open. Zee shooter got through but a truck zen blocked zee road blocking Jean-Pierre. He 'phone Georges, but it too late. Zee shooter was maybe going at 200 kilometres speed under zee bridge. Georges and Jean-Pierre follow but zee shooter get away. He had no number plate and he maybe turn off at next road.

"Well, you can hardly blame Georges." Kevin opined. "He was being pro-active to investigate the flyover. The road works sound suspicious though."

"My sentiments exactement Monsieur. Georges and Jean-Pierre, zey take details of truck and workers and we 'phone local police. Gendermes on zee way to check zere how you say, credentials? I think we go now."

Jerry Barker followed the man from Interpol back onto the road. Passing traffic had not showed too much interest in them as a number of cars had also pulled off along the route to allow bursting bladders to be emptied as a result of the occupants imbibing enormous quantities of beer.

According to Barker this was considered normal amongst many of the enthusiasts from across the channel. Some stocked up on the amber liquid before crossing the channel, but many were realizing that they could just as well buy the local brew due to competitive pricing. Kevin wondered just how much of the qualifying practice due to commence the next morning would actually be witnessed by some of the occupants he had observed.

Two minutes later they arrived at the scene of the "road works" and slowed. An unmarked yellow truck stood on the right hand verge. Four or five white-overalled workers were in the process of loading cone-shaped bollards on to the truck.

Jean-Pierre had been awaiting their arrival. He waved them on, falling in behind the Aceca. Georges remained behind, obviously waiting for the local gendermes who would escort the truck and its occupants to a police station for further interrogation.

***

Later that evening after 'phoning Ann and enjoying a delicious early supper with Jerry, Marc Cheval and the two motorcycle policemen, Kevin settled down in his room to ponder the events of the last few days. He had not mentioned the attack to his spouse.

Georges and Jean-Pierre had been reluctant to join them for a meal, feeling out of place, but Jerry had insisted. An attempt by Georges to apologise for the afternoon's events had quickly been stifled by Richardson who had responded:

"Please Georges, I did not expect an attack and in any case, no one could have predicted what form it would take. We would have needed the whole French Army to have escorted us and checked and secured the entire route beforehand!"

After several glasses of red wine they had all relaxed. Jokes had flowed from Jerry whose command of their language had surprised the Frenchmen. Some of the English ones had ended up rather different and possibly even funnier than intended, after being translated by the Interpol agent for the benefit of the motorcyclists.

Kevin had looked forward to the next day's practice and the forthcoming race for the best part of the past year. Renowned amongst his friends, acquaintances and fellow racing drivers for being cool and unflappable under pressure, the attempt on his and Jerry's life as well, for that matter, had shaken him to the core. He held up his hand and studied it. The faint tremor was becoming less noticeable.

He was still contemplating whether he would read for a while before turning out the light when the ring tone of his cell phone broke the silence. Chris Jensen's name appeared on the screen.

"Hi Chris, where are you in the world?

"Sorry to bother you at this hour Kevin, but I reckoned that if you're in the UK it's about eight o'clock there. I'm in the Departures Lounge at Shanghi Airport in Singapore and its three in the morning – my flight to Sri Lanka should have left two and a half hours ago!"

"Not to worry, Chris, I'm actually at Le Mans where it's about nine but I'm still wide awake. What's up?"

"Oh nothing much I suppose, except that our mutual friend Inspector Graham Brown is securely behind bars on this island and will shortly be deported to good old RSA."

"You must be kidding! What is he doing in Singapore and why has he been taken into custody?"

Chris Jensen briefly recounted the events of the past twenty-four hours. Dumbfounded, Richardson listened without interruption. Jensen did not mention that Jacqui had been misled by the trickster whom neither of them had liked from the outset. He was not ready to face that humiliation yet.

"Well Chris, it still hasn't sunk in. I can't quite match your story, but I was shot at today by an unknown biker as well. The infamous Major Steve Harvey narrowly missed arrest in London, but one of the guys close to David Wilson was grabbed. Hopefully he will sing soon so that they can nail the other kingpins and wrap up this mess so that we can get on with our normal lives." He returned the favour, summarising his experiences since arriving in London.

Richardson heard a chiming sound over the phone followed by an unintelligible announcement in the background.

"Sorry Kevin, I'll have to run, Inspector Tann of Interpol has already headed for the plane. Speak to you soon and good luck tomorrow! Maybe I can come across to watch you race in June."

"That would be great! I'm going to hold you to it."

Chapter 24
Le Mans

Saturday morning, after an early breakfast Richardson and Barker headed for the car park where they found the duo of two-wheeled policemen and the strange-looking but friendly Interpol agent already waiting. Le Mans' famous racing circuit was about twenty minutes' drive from their hotel where many other teams had also booked in due to its close proximity. Kevin had been glad to renew friendships with several opposition drivers the night before, but had been grateful that they had also wanted to turn in early.

They arrived at the circuit just after 8 o'clock and were introduced to their Japanese co-driver – Hoshi Tanaka, a slightly built man with a perpetual smile and dark spiky hair. "His name 'Hoshi' mean Star"- Hiro Yamamoto, the Chief Engineer had enthused – "He very good driver, win Champion races at Suzuka track Japan just last month. We lucky have him in team."

"That's very good to know." Richardson responded. "He will have to be a star for us to stay in touch with those Porsches! By the way, what does 'Hiro' mean in the Japanese culture?" Almost immediately, Kevin regretted his question, not wanting to offend the obviously proud man from the Land of the Rising Sun. What if it had an unusual or strange meaning?

"Oh, my full name Hiroshi, that mean to 'command' and 'fly.'" The confident Japanese was not fazed at all by the enquiry and continued, "Kevin – that mean 'agility' – I think we make very good team."

"Thank you, that's very interesting, you have an intriguing language. I suppose we had better get out onto the track." Jerry Barker had been out of earshot and Kevin had not wanted to enquire into the Japanese equivalent characteristics of his overweight friend's name in case it had a negative connotation which would have given them a grumpy teammate for the rest of the day. As it was, Hiro had looked askance when Jerry had enquired as to the whereabouts of their whisky and beer stocks.

Kevin had laughed at Barker's joke, but the Japanese had not been convinced. The shadow of a smile briefly played around Kevin's eyes and mouth as he pondered the sight of Hiro decapitating Jerry with a large ornate curved samurai sword, as he staggered out of the car smelling of beer.

Within two hours Kevin had put in around twenty laps of the 13.6 kilometre long circuit, half with the designated lead car and the balance with the reserve car. Barker and Tanaka had also circulated, the latter initially rather slowly while getting to know the track. Kevin's best lap had been some five seconds faster than Barker while Richardson estimated that the Japanese driver would most probably need the rest of the day to post a competitive time.

Of concern however, had been the performance of two of the three works Porsche team cars and one of the British driven McLarens. Richardson's best lap had placed him in fifth position on the grid. The second works all-Japanese crewed Honda had been way off of the pace down in provisional tenth place.

Kevin had spent half an hour with the mechanics suggesting and supervising suspension and down-force adjustments to the rear wing before again setting out to attempt to break the superiority of the German cars which had monopolised the front row of the grid.

Since the inaugural race in 1923, the circuit length had been changed on various occasions due to the implementation of innovations and re-profiling to accommodate larger run-off areas in the interests of improving safety for both drivers and spectators. The main outline of the circuit had remained substantially unchanged from the earliest days when country roads had been linked to form the track.

One of the most notable changes occurred in 1990 when the five kilometre long Mulsanne Straight was effectively cut into three with the building of two chicanes to curtail the speeds in excess of 386 Km/h that were being achieved. This change had been much lamented by drivers as they had previously used the straight to "relax" on, if one could relax at that velocity!

Unfortunately the chicanes had led to some 3000 more gear changes being required during a race and had also led to the typical driving squad being increased from two or three, to three or even four drivers. Over 320 Km/h was nevertheless still well within reach of the more powerful prototypes on various points of the track.

On his first circuit following his out lap, Kevin was in the process of decelerating on the approach to the right hand kink at Indianapolis corner just before the sharp left-hander when he noticed what he presumed to be a spectator, seeing that he was not wearing the official marshal's garb, standing just off the left hand verge of the road.

"What the hell are you doing here, you idiot?" he mouthed, braking rather harder than he would otherwise have, his concentration momentarily interrupted. At the speed he had been travelling, he had not discerned much more than a flash of a darkly clad figure lurking close to the kerbing. He radioed his pit and asked them to lambaste race control for not having a marshal on site.

Having written off the lap, he consciously tried to delete the incident from his mind so that he could concentrate on feeling whether the adjustments to suspension and trim had made the Honda coupe smoother to drive.

As he passed the pits two laps later, the headphones in his helmet reverberated.

"Well done Kevin san, you just set pole position!"

"Thank you Hiro, but it's early days yet."

On his very next lap, while still accelerating away from the very sharp hairpin corner known as Arnage, Kevin felt the front of the car momentarily "go light" before the rear-end broke away and it suddenly spun clockwise out of control several times along the way to Porsche Curve.

Miraculously the car stayed on the tar leaving elongated thick black rubber doughnut impressions on the tarmac. Richardson pulled the car to the side and climbed out to investigate. The right front tyre had burst, shattering part of the surrounding glass fibre wheel arch. A large, irregular coin-sized hole had also been punched through the bodywork some ten centimetres further back towards the cabin.

As he replaced his helmet in the car, the concerned voice of Hiro crackled.

"What happen Kevin? We see almighty spin on monitor. Is car okay?"

"Sure, the car is okay, never mind about me!" he responded sarcastically.

"Sorry Kevin, of course we worry bout you, but we see you okay on TV."

"Not to worry, Hiro, I was just pulling your leg. I'm sure I'll be able to drive back on three wheels."

Some ten minutes later Richardson brought the Honda to a stop on the pit apron. Fortunately with the weight bias towards the back of mid-engined race cars, they are often able to be driven slowly back to the pits on three wheels for attention rather than having to be retired.

The front suspension had emerged unscathed and after fitting a new nose section, checking the brakes and fitting new tyres all around, the Honda was ready to take up the challenge in the hands of his chubby co-driver. Kevin had looked askance at the hole in the side of the car.

"Was there a car ahead of you through Arnage? His rear wheels may well have shot some debris at you from this morning's crash there." Barker suggested.

Pondering, Kevin frowned dubiously but chose not to comment further.

Jerry was unable to set a time within three seconds of Kevin's provisional pole, but during his stint, the leading works Porsches both knocked a second off the South African's best. Richardson climbed back into the Honda determined to put the Japanese –Anglo – South African team back at the front.

On his second circuit after the out lap, Hiro's excited voice crackled in his helmet. "Very good Kevin – you now second place. You better one tenth of second more and you go to pole."

"Thanks Hiro, I'll see what we can do."

After passing the pits two laps later Richardson was in the groove again and feeling quietly confident that the car was feeling good to knock the leading Porsche from pole when a concerned Hiro interrupted his thoughts as he was approaching Tertre Rouge.

"Kevin, please you very careful – there is big rainstorm coming. Mulsanne to Arnage very wet already."

Richardson's heart sank. Dark clouds had been threatening for several hours, but had thus far held off. He had been confident of setting the Porsche team a challenging target. The track surface at Mulsanne Corner was already several centimetres under water by the time he covered half a lap. Before he got back to the pits, reports indicated that at least eighty percent of the extensive area covered by the circuit and its environs was on the receiving end of a heavy downpour.

After fitting "full wet" tyres Kevin circulated for another half an hour before handing over to Hoshi Tanaka. The Japanese driver quickly showed his prowess in the wet – no doubt a legacy of his considerable experience of racing in damp conditions in his homeland.

Kevin hoped that they would have a dry track for the next day's final practice session before they headed back to London and the two month wait until the race in June. He was nevertheless over the moon. His previous drives had been in reliable but non-contenders for overall spoils, unless the "Works" teams had encountered problems.

He had no doubt that their new car and the new team, backed by the maker's reputation for reliability and engineering, not forgetting the pride of the Japanese automaker, was well capable of taking on the established marques and beating them.

Chapter 25
Colombo

Chris Jensen yawned as the anonymous elderly white Toyota drew up under the elegant portal of the Lanka Oberoi Hotel. The doors and opulent reception area beyond, beckoned. It was after 6:30 am and he had hardly slept during the past twenty-four hours. The normally inscrutable face of Inspector Tann sitting beside him in the back seat of the Police car, also showed signs of strain. His eyes seemed to be open rather wider than usual as if he was concentrating on keeping them from closing. They appeared to Chris to be unseeing, although they shone from the reflected energy of the hotel's battery of lights.

They had been met at Colombo's Bandaranaike Airport by a local police officer whose full names would have escaped Jensen even if he had not been dog tired. The genial policeman's second name had sounded as if it consisted of around fifteen to twenty letters, but "Bertie" was easy to remember! Tann, who had sat separately at the back of the plane, had joined them outside the terminal.

A uniformed porter opened the left rear door of the Toyota and welcomed them to Colombo's "best hotel". Jensen reluctantly dragged his weary frame from the confines of the cabin mumbling, "Get me to bed before I collapse right here."

"I agree," Responded the Interpol agent. "I can hardly keep my eyes open." The thought of a comfortable bed and a few hours of shut-eye had obviously given him a brief injection of vigour. He set off for reception before the feeling passed with Jensen close behind. Bertie and the porter remained behind to collect their luggage from the Toyota's boot.

As they were passing through the hotel door, Jensen stopped and turned around surveying the roadway and parking lot beyond.

"I've been so bloody tired that I haven't even thought about our being tailed from the airport or on the plane!"

"Don't worry, Mr Jensen. We thoroughly checked the passenger list before we left Singapore. Nobody suspicious was on board. As you know, the flight was only a quarter full. I certainly did not observe anyone showing an interest in you on the plane. I surveyed the terminal regularly after landing and nobody seemed to be the slightest bit interested in us. In the car I noticed Bertie constantly scanning his rear view mirror on the way here. He also mentioned that another local unmarked car and two detectives have been allocated to serve as back up." The oriental Interpol agent turned and retraced several steps towards the sidewalk.

"That's probably them over there." He inclined his head to indicate another similar pale coloured Toyota that had drawn to a halt a few car lengths behind where Bertie still stood balancing a suitcase on his car's rear bumper.

The Sri Lankan police officer turned as the driver of the car behind switched off its engine. He casually raised his left hand, balled his fist and gave a barely perceptible thumbs up. Jensen noted the other driver's similar response and turned back towards the door.

"Bertie's a very thorough and experienced policeman." Tann continued. "I'm sure he has covered all the bases."

"Well, I have my doubts after my last trip here!" Jensen responded unconvinced. "After Kevin Richardson's previous and recent experiences, I don't know what to think or expect anymore."

"Come on, let's go get some – how do you say – shut eye!

Jensen did not need prompting.

***

Chris awoke with a start. His blurry eyes surveyed the room. Although the curtains were drawn, daylight was streaming rather than filtering through various crevices. His surroundings were unfamiliar and it took him several seconds to realize where he was. He rubbed his sore eyes and stretched his arms upwards and backwards, his knuckles lightly grazing the padded headboard. Then he heard it again – a light tapping at the door.

"Come in." he rasped. He tried to raise his voice, but only a croak emerged from his dry throat. Jensen raised his upper body onto his elbows and coughed to clear his throat. He was about to repeat his invitation when a rustling sound was immediately followed by a white envelope emerging on his side between the carpet and the bottom of the door.

He eased himself off the bed, retrieved the envelope and tore it open. After removing the single sheet of notepaper, he dropped the crumpled remains of the envelope in a bin next to the door. Having second thoughts, he retrieved the sheath and read the scrawled handwriting.

"Dear Mr Jensen, This was received some hours ago, but we did not want to disturb you." An illegible signature was appended above the word "Manager" which was pre-printed on the hotel stationery.

"But you *did* and bloody well woke me up." Jensen muttered, unfolding the single page which had been jaggedly torn from one of several pads he recalled having observed on the reception counter.

It read, "Hi Chris, sorry your flight delayed – I looked forward to breakfast. Regret I'm tied up rest of day. Will 'phone you tonight. If okay, I pick you up tomorrow morning and we drive to Kandy to sign agreement at my attorney office. Yours sincerely, Fernando da Silva."

Jensen looked at himself appraisingly in the large wall mirror. He smiled – the cold shower had done wonders. He felt refreshed and looked forward to setting off on his usual circular walk around Columbo which he had got to know intimately on his regular travels.

Chapter 26

Jensen glanced skywards. The heavens had become even more threatening. The constantly changing mottled patchwork of light and dark grey overhead looked ominous. "Too bad." He thought. "If it rains, I get wet!" The weather was so unpredictable. One never knew in these parts when a downpour would drench you without warning and then stop as suddenly as it had started.

Although he had only covered around half-a-kilometre, Chris Jensen's lightweight cotton shirt was already sopping wet from the smothering humidity. He recalled the first time he had got lost in the Sri Lankan capital some years before. He had always felt rather good that he had managed to find his way to various destinations and back to the hotel, by following the position of the sun in the heavens, without a map. One day however, the sun had been obscured by cloud on his return journey. Anxious to get back for a meeting, he had found himself making three consecutive large time-consuming circles around the Colombo Cricket complex, before he had eventually managed to find the slip road he sought back to the hotel.

He had passed Cinnamon Gardens and decided that he would revisit a particularly ornate Buddhist temple he recalled from a trip several years before. He turned right at the next intersection, stopping mid-corner to familiarise himself with the surroundings. Glancing back along the road he had come, he was surprised to see the Interpol Inspector some fifty metres back on the opposite sidewalk.

"You bloody fool," he thought. The Chinese policeman was stumbling along carrying his jacket under his arm and even from that distance, was clearly suffering from heat exhaustion and the pace Jensen had set. He was about to wave when Tann shook his head, put his finger to his lips before hurriedly jabbing a finger towards the sidewalk behind Chris.

Twenty metres closer to Jensen, a burly, bronzed, but clearly Caucasian figure, dressed in lightweight slacks and a golf shirt, bent down to tie a shoelace. Across the street, Inspector Tann simultaneously stopped to examine a row of colourful shrubs which formed a hedge in front of a newly restored old house.

Jensen expressed a brief interest in the street sign on the corner before continuing on his journey. The temple was located another fifty metres along the street and was set well back from the road. From the outside, the brick building appeared to be nothing out of the ordinary, looking much like a large old house raised several metres above ground level. Around a dozen tiered concrete steps ran the length of the structure which was fronted by a full length veranda. A central doorway was flanked by several square unglazed window apertures set about a metre above the cement floor.

He hesitated at the paved walkway which led to the stairs between two manicured squares of lawn. He was reluctant to look back along the sidewalk. Who was stalking him? What was Tann contemplating? His questions were interrupted by a tall gangly well-dressed Indian with sharp aquiline features who suddenly appeared from across the street. Ignoring Jensen, he almost collided with him before setting off briskly along the pathway for the base of the stairs. Jensen wondered how the man could survive the humidity in such a bulky leather jacket.

Chris followed hesitantly, itching to look around. The Indian stopped on the veranda to remove his sandals before disappearing through the doorway into the gloomy depths beyond.

Two tiers from the top Jensen stopped, turned around clockwise and sat down, reaching for his shoelaces. The burly "stalker" was now abreast of the entrance but after glancing towards the temple and apparently taking no interest in Chris, carried on sauntering slowly past along the sidewalk.

He was still in view when Tann appeared on the opposite side. He continued for several metres before stopping to lean against a perimeter wall. The plain clothes policeman removed a handkerchief from his pocket and started wiping his brow, pointedly looking down the street before hurriedly waving to Jensen to enter the temple. Chris waited for a white Toyota and colourful Tuk-Tuk to cruise past before unobtrusively acknowledging the instruction.

He walked through the large front doorway and found himself in a vestibule from which passages branched off to the left and right. Choosing the left hand one, he passed through an archway and found himself confronted by a two-metre high Buddha statue on a pedestal which dominated the large room. The beam of a floor-mounted spotlight bathed the bronze-hued figure leaving the corners of the room in deep shadow.

Jensen hesitated. Was Tann being over-cautious or had he recognized the man who had walked past? His thoughts were interrupted by a rustling sound. He was about to turn around when his left shoulder was grabbed roughly from behind. His first instinct was to drop to his knees and spin around, but a stinging sensation on the right side of his throat convinced him otherwise.

"You stay still or you bleed more and make very much mess on floor. This knife very much sharp. You better believe." His captor carried on with several guttural threats in a language Jensen did not understand but he presumed were an Indian dialect. The man stopped his tirade, apparently realizing that Chris did not understand his ranting. He removed his hand from Jensen's shoulder, withdrew the knife and continued. "Now you turn around slow or I cut you more." Jensen felt the tip of the knife briefly prick his spine.

He slowly turned to face the man. It was the Indian who had preceded him up the stairs. He winced as the man suddenly jabbed a finger at his throat and displayed a blood red tip, an evil grin creasing his sharp sweating features. The bastard *had* cut him! Jensen's right hand instinctively reached for his neck to inspect the cut.

"You stay still!" The Indian thrust the knife towards him with a chopping motion and he retreated against the wall opposite the Buddha. Jensen recognised it as a Kukri dagger of the type supplied to Gurkha troops and backed even tighter against the wall. The menacing twenty-five cm curved blade glinted in the dim light. The point had also been sharpened for stabbing. The man's grip on the ornate handle tightened and his knuckles whitened through his sallow skin.

"Ahh, Mr Jensen, I presume." Chris started. The well built golf-shirted man from the street had silently appeared behind the Indian startling him as well. "I see you have made the acquaintance of Nawang." Jensen noted the close cropped blond hair and dark moustache. The accent was undoubtedly well-schooled South African. A large calibre pistol was pointed menacingly at Jensen's stomach.

"How do you know my name? What's this about? Let me go, I'm a South African businessman." Jensen's tone was indignant. "How dare you ..."

"Oh shut up Jensen. Spare me the histrionics! You and your friend Richardson ruined our operation. We're going to sort you out for good."

"Who are you?" Then Jensen's brain clicked. This must be ex Major Steve Harvey. His build and confident, or rather, arrogant attitude, fitted Kevin Richardson's description. But how had he managed to get from France to

214

Colombo so quickly, if he had in fact been involved in the attack on Richardson?

The expression on his face must have conveyed Jensen's comprehension, as Harvey's features creased into a cruel smile.

"There you are, no introduction is necessary, so Nawang may as well finish his job."

The Indian took half a step towards Jensen, an evil grin revealing hideous crooked yellow teeth. He raised the chopping dagger and held it at head height thirty cm from his face. Chris was able to examine the sharp blade in close detail and feared it would sever his arm at the shoulder with one blow.

"Drop the gun Mister Harvey and you – drop that knife!" Tann had crept up behind the large South African and stuck his pistol against his spine. Harvey hesitated but clearly did not relish the thought of spending time in jail in a wheelchair. The gun clattered on to the concrete floor.

Nawang hesitated, turning his head half around towards the pair behind, the dagger still poised and gripped tightly in his left hand. Jensen seized his opportunity, aiming a karate chop at the Indian's wrist with his right hand, followed by a left hook to the pit of his stomach. The Indian gasped, dropped the knife and sank to his knees. The handle thudded off Jensen's shoe before rattling on the floor, coming to rest a few centimetres away. Chris side-footed the dagger towards the opposite wall, where it disappeared beneath a wooden cabinet next to the Buddha.

"Well done Mr Jensen. You did not even need me!" A smiling "Bertie" of the long second name appeared from the shadows behind Chris. Another two uniformed Sri Lankan police officers who had hovered in a passage beyond came forward and handcuffed the two prisoners.

"Our Indian colleagues will certainly be very happy to get their hands on Nawang here who is the leader of the Delhi arm of the operation. Your South African force will no doubt also be glad to finally get hold of this mastermind." Tann inclined his head towards Harvey.

Jensen smiled and nodded. He would be relieved once this business was over and he and Jacqui could hopefully get on with their lives.

**

Back in his hotel room, Chris sat on the bed and stared at the telephone for several minutes before rising and walking towards the fridge. He started as the jangling of the phone interrupted his thoughts. He whipped around and was at the pedestal in three giant strides and snatched at the receiver.

"Hello, Chris? I've tried to get you all morning!

"Jacqui! I've been out since eight o'clock. I've been thinking of you all day and was going to phone you."

"Chris, I love you and I'm sorry I have treated you so badly – even before Inspector Themba told me what a scoundrel Graham is. I've wanted to tell you this for weeks, but I've been so ashamed. I never slept with..."

"Please stop darling. I never thought you had. I'm meeting Da Silva this afternoon to dot all the I's and cross the T's and I'll be on tonight's flight." He felt tears welling and hastily continued.

"I can't wait to see you and hold you in my arms. Must Go. Love you."

"Love you too. More than you know."

He gently replaced the receiver.

Chapter 27

Kevin woke with a start and rubbed his eyes. Bright sunshine poured through the window opposite his bed. The curtains had been drawn. He glanced at the clock on the pedestal. 06:05!

"Yes that's right you lazy bugger! You'd better pull out your finger and get up if you want to show the Krauts what a South African driving a Japanese car can do! Well again, maybe I should include a Pom, as the Allies thumped them in the war!" Barker moved towards the bed, but Richardson rolled to the other side and jumped up raising his fists before throwing two punches at the advancing Englishman.

***

The Sarthe circuit was bathed in sunshine by the time they had partaken of a quick continental breakfast and had been escorted by the two motorcyclists and Marc Cheval in his French Blue Alpine-Renault. Richardson's mind was on the car ahead rather than the forthcoming practice session, while Barker played chauffer. How he would love to get his hands on a right-hand drive one!

The two white and red cars were already standing on the pit apron. Four Honda technicians were doing their best to polish the paint off of the gleaming cars, while another four were fiddling around making last minute adjustments.

Chief Engineer cum Team Manager Hiro Yamamoto strode from the lead car's pit to greet them, Hoshi Tanaka in tow. Surprisingly their faces both wore wide grins which took Kevin aback, seeing that their race was rather better known for hiding emotion.

"Today we show German team what Japanese can do! You agree, yes?" His question was directed at Kevin. They both bowed. His smile evaporated almost entirely as his gaze settled on the beaming Englishman. He still did not trust Barker and his ruddy complexion. He had searched the race car but there *was* no place to hide his stock of beer!

"Morning Hiro, Hi Hoshi." Richardson chose to allow the Japanese' omission of his and Barker's nationalities potential capabilities, to ride.

As a result of the late afternoon rain, none of the front-runners had managed to improve upon Wednesday's times after Kevin had packed it in and handed the car over to Hoshi Tanaka.

During the first two hours of qualifying on Thursday morning, the three works Porsches, the lead Honda and two McLarens continually swopped places on the grid.

The Japanese-crewed Honda gradually improved as the drivers got to know the circuit and managed to break into the top six on occasion.

With half an hour of practice to go, Kevin, having set the second fastest lap, left the pits for his "make or break" final stint. After discussing a few minor tweaks with the engineers and pit crew, it was "now or never." He had just completed his out lap and crossed the "Start/Finish" line and was commencing his timed lap when crackling in his headphones startled him.

"Kevin, sorry, but you please come in when finish this lap!" Hiro's voice was imploring and concerned.

"Why, is there a problem with the car? She's handling beautifully, I can't come in now!" Richardson's incredulous frustrated response verged on anger.

"No, no ploblim with car. Car fine, but you please come in. We then tell you what ploblim is! We waiting for you!"

"Well you better have a good reason ..., this session doesn't have long to go if we still have to fiddle with settings..." Kevin stopped when he heard the connection go dead.

He briefly thought about ignoring Hiro's request. But it had been a *command* rather than a request. It struck him that completion of his current timed lap and an "in lap" would involve over twenty-seven kilometres and a further seven minutes. He had also unconsciously slowed down during the exchange and those precious seconds had already negatively impacted on the time he had hoped for. Better he did not incur the wrath of the Chief Engineer!

With nothing at stake, Richardson reduced his speed even further to conserve the tyres and moved off the racing line to allow slower cars to pass so as not to impede their lap times. As he was approaching Arnage, the sharp hairpin, he briefly noted three figures dressed in dark clothing having an apparent difference of opinion right on the verge of the track. He positioned the car to give them a wide berth, but even at three-quarter pace the figures were a blur.

Upon arrival at his pit, he was met by a concerned looking Hiro and several mechanics ready to perform various routine checks to analyse whether the car was performing efficiently. His Japanese co-driver – Hoshi had his helmet on and seemed to be champing at the bit to get his practice stint underway.

Hiro grappled with the lightweight gull wing door before managing to pull it open, the flimsy but resilient hinges protesting as he bent them beyond their intended arc. He jabbered at Kevin in Japanese whilst gesticulating towards Marc Cheval who hovered against the pit wall holding something in a small rectangular transparent plastic bag.

Richardson stared at him quizzically while a mechanic leaned into the car to help him unfasten his seatbelt before he clambered over the wide sill.

"I sorry Kevin, I ..." Hiro stopped mid-sentence.

While Richardson removed his helmet, the French policeman joined them and held up the bag for Kevin to see. It contained what appeared to be a three centimetre long tapered roll of metal.

"Zis bullet zey find in your flat tyre from yesterday. Zee hole behind zee wheel also made by bullet." He withdrew a second bag from his pocket which held another blob of metal. From the latter's flattened nose and general distortion, it had clearly hit something far more solid. From its discolouration it appeared to have been subjected to intense heat.

"Ziss type of how you say – "slug" made for special high powered rifle."

Jerry Barker had in the meantime made an appearance. "That blue/black bullet was lodged between the pipes of the exhaust manifold. One of the mechanics thought it was a bit of rather uncharacteristically poor Japanese welding! It looks like a 7.62mm specially made bronze point."

Kevin stood speechless for several seconds before responding.

"Who do you think it is? Do you think there are a couple of them? Are they after me or are they trying to sabotage the team? Maybe we should speak to the ACO[1] and stop everyone practicing. We can't have these buggers shooting at us and hitting other teams!"

"I am sure zis is zee drug dealers and not involve Honda or other racing teams. I agree zere is danger, but we must not cause worry..." Marc Cheval was interrupted mid-

---

[1] *The Automobile Club de L'Oest was founded in 1906 by car building and racing enthusiasts and is famous for being the organising entity behind the annual Le Mans 24 Hour race.*

sentence by his ringing cell phone. He pocketed the two bullet bags and hastily removed his phone from a clip on his belt.

"Oui?" Cheval listened intently for what seemed at least several minutes, nodding constantly, occasionally responding in monosyllables, all the time edging away from the group. At last he closed the phone and walked back to the curious onlookers.

"Zat was Jean-Pierre. He and George on way here with interesting news. Zey meet us behind pits in ten minute." Turning to Hiro, he continued.

"Mr Hiroshi – I think it is safe for you to continue with practice. Kevin, you please come with me." Without waiting for an answer or providing an explanation, he strode off.

Hiro visibly breathed a sigh of relief. Smiling broadly, he rattled off a staccato of Japanese at Hoshi who donned his helmet with alacrity and hastily clambered through the still open door of the lead Honda. Jerry Barker looked at them, hesitated, and despite not having been invited, hastily set off after Marc Cheval and Kevin who had already covered some fifty metres.

**

The three, including an unwelcome Jerry (from the frowns aimed in his direction by Marc Cheval) were nearing one of the mobile home cum transporter parking areas used by the various teams, when they heard the sound of rapidly approaching motorcycles.

Jean-Pierre's gunmetal grey Kawasaki rounded a distant transporter closely followed by Georges' metallic blue machine. Of considerable interest however, was the burly helmeted third figure – also dressed in black leathers, precariously and uncomfortably perched behind Georges.

Jean-Pierre stopped some distance away and quickly dismounted.

Mark motioned for Kevin and Jerry to remain where they were before he approached the two motorcycles. Jean-Pierre had immediately drawn his pistol and run to Georges who had been fiddling with something around his chest. The intrigued spectators suddenly realized that the third figure's hands had in fact been handcuffed around the rider's mid-section. Jean-Pierre waved his pistol at their prisoner to dismount before leading him to a thin but sturdy steel pole to which he clamped one half of the handcuff. The motorcycle policemen removed and placed their helmets on their bikes' saddles before they and Cheval moved some distance away from their prisoner to confer.

Kevin suddenly remembered the scuffle he had briefly witnessed while cruising back to the pits.

"So that's what was happening, that bugger was being arrested!" He muttered aloud.

"Hey! What? What are you babbling about?" Jerry Barker dug him in the ribs with an elbow to bring him back to reality.

"Oh, um..., sorry Jerry, but on my in-lap, I saw three dark figures having an apparent altercation at Arnage, but I was past them so quickly that I couldn't make out much. It must have been Georges and Jean-Pierre arresting Mister X!"

"Well I'll be blowed!" Jerry's exclamation was interrupted by Marc.

"Kevin, pleeze you come here?"

Richardson set off towards the three Frenchmen with Barker close behind. "Why are you huffing and puffing like that, I thought you had gotten fit to show the Japs a thing or two?"

"Oh, don't you worry about me, I'm feeling good, but am looking forward to lubricating my throat at the pub this evening!"

They joined the three policemen. Marc briefly filled them in on the morning's events. Georges and Jean-Pierre had noted the dark gunmetal grey Suzuki without number plates speeding past their hotel that morning and had decided to follow at a respectful distance. The rider had entered the circuit environs and ridden slowly towards Arnage.

After concealing his bike and helmet in some bushes, he had proceeded on foot towards the Armco barriers around the curve. The two motorized policeman had examined the Suzuki and found a bespoke oval cylindrical container mounted on the side of the bike. Upon unclipping two latches the hinged case had opened lengthways to reveal a specially moulded inner liner containing five parts of a dismantled sniper rifle including a scope and holes for twenty rounds of ammunition. Three of the holes were empty!

Jean-Pierre and Georges had immediately called for backup from the local gendarmerie. After immobilising the bike and unclipping the case, they had hidden the latter in some nearby bushes before setting out to track the would-be sniper. They had found him on his haunches against the Armco on the inside of the track speaking on his cell.

The leather-clad man had heard Jean-Pierre's approach and drawn a pistol but Georges had overpowered him from behind. This scuffle had been witnessed by Richardson.

"I'd love to see that rifle?" Jerry asked hopefully.

"Sorry, zat not possible Mr Barker, zee rifle and pistol have been sent to forensics for checking." Marc responded.

"You mentioned three missing cartridges. We only know of two, don't we?" Richardson opined. Not expecting a response he continued, "How did he know that I was driving, he must have had an accomplice?"

"He say he pay man he don't know with tickets for grandstand and fifty dollars US per day to phone him when you practice. He say he tell man he big fan of you and want to take photographs. We have his cell phone and get our how you say – experts to check calls to trace man. We also ask how he look and where he collect money, so maybe we find him. Maybe he tell truth. Now I introduce you to shooter!" Marc set off towards their captive.

As they approached the burly helmeted rider, Kevin realized for the first time that the two metre leather clad, handcuffed prisoner had giant black hands and was not wearing black leather gloves as he had presumed from a distance. Marc loosened the strap beneath the prisoner's chin and roughly jerked the helmet from his clean shaven skull.

"Do you know zis man?"

Kevin's curious searching stare was met by a sullen glare as the burly ebony-skinned man slowly turned towards him. His heart fluttered as memories of their previous encounter came flooding back. The previous stubble had been replaced by a fuller scruffy salt 'n pepper beard, but there was no mistaking the face and eyes.

"I most certainly do. We haven't been formally introduced, but we definitely got more than acquainted in the ward my wife was being held in at Ondangwa Hospital."

***

Back at the pits Kevin and Jerry were met by a thunderous looking Hiro.

"Why you so long? Practice finish in ten minute. There no time for you to get pole position. Hoshi do good but not better your time. Mr Jerry, he not..." Surprisingly Hiro decided not to finish the sentence and spared the Englishman further embarrassment.

Kevin positioned himself between the pair as Barker's face had turned the shade of beetroot – more likely from anger than anything else. It was clear to everyone that

Jerry's role in the race would be as before – to hold station after Kevin and hopefully Hoshi as well, built up a lead or kept up with the frontrunners.

"I'm sorry Hiro, but it looks like we've broken the last link in the drug chain. Marc Cheval's guys have taken the shooter who I know as 'Kingwill' into custody. With the other members that have been arrested, hopefully their investigations will be concluded soon resulting in the small guys on the ground being rounded up as well and they'll finally leave me alone. So what does the grid look like?"

"Your time still good enough for second place behind Porsche number one car. McLaren number two car third. Porsche fourth. Our other Honda do very good to be fifth before other McLaren."

Richardson looked at his watch. "Hopefully we can hold onto second place for the final ten minutes. My car was really running so smoothly, I think we could..." Kevin's mumbled musings became unintelligible as he pulled himself on to the pit wall.

Chapter 28
Race Day

Saturday 21st June dawned bright and clear, although heavy late afternoon and evening thundershowers were forecast. Sunday's prediction although similar, also indicated the possibility of intermittent drizzle throughout the day. While most teams undoubtedly placed reliability at the top of their list over the forthcoming twenty-four hours, the race was expected to be one of the slower ones in recent years with little possibility of any distance records being set.

Kevin and Jerry had left their hotel early without their usual French motorcycle escort, although all three of the Frenchmen were attending the race and had access to the pit enclosure. Marc had offered to allow Richardson to drive the Alpine to the circuit, but the burly English driver could not be accommodated as well, so the two racing drivers were picked up by Ann and Tracey who had booked in at a nearby hotel.

During the months following the April practice days and pre-qualifying sessions, the Richardson and Jensen families had become good friends and had visited regularly. Chris shared Kevin's passion for cars and the two women found that they also shared a lot of common interests and spare time. The former had been pleased to hear that Chris and Jacqui had booked into the same hotel as Ann and Tracey and the five had arranged to spend a further week in France after the race.

***

3.55 pm arrived. The cars were three-quarters the way around the circuit for the rolling start at exactly four o'clock. Kevin's mind wandered back to his childhood when he had eagerly awaited the overseas magazines reporting on the Le Mans practice weekend as well as the race itself which had taken a month to arrive by "sea mail." These had often carried photographs of what had universally become known as the "Le Mans Start."

In those days, drivers had lined up on the tarmac opposite their cars which were parked parallel to each other at an angle to the pit wall. Waving of the French Tricolor had required them to sprint to the other side, climb in, start their cars and accelerate away before the next car. Fast runners in slow qualifying cars had often found themselves first away. Safety issues had however, arisen when drivers had failed to fasten their safety harnesses properly.

Multiple Formula One World Champion, Jackie Stewart was one of the first drivers to oppose this type of start when he deliberately walked across the track while his competitors ran, nearly being hit by another car in the process. The traditional Le Mans start was changed in 1970 when cars were still lined up against the pit wall with the drivers already strapped in. A year later the Indianapolis type rolling start was adopted.

Kevin was brought back to reality when he rounded Ford Chicane and realized he was seconds away from the Start/Finish line. He checked his mirrors – the second works Porsche was right on his tail. He glanced to the left and accelerated slightly to draw level with the Porsche pole sitter on his inside. Then they were away. He was able to draw away by a full car length, but the German car had the inside line at Dunlop Curve and squeezed him out before the Chicane.

Richardson found his car easily able to stay with the Porsche, but suddenly realized that the second Porsche was all over the back of his car. After negotiating the Esses and Tertre Rouge comfortably, he accelerated and drew away from the silver car down the first part of Mulsanne before having to brake heavily for the first of the two chicanes introduced in 1990 to reduce top speeds of more than 400km/h from being reached. A slight bump to the rear of the Honda reminded him that the Porsche was still there and that the driver was leaving his braking very, very late.

"Crazy bugger, there's twenty-four hours to go!" Kevin stayed ahead through the second straight, Mulsanne and Indianapolis, but realized that the back-up German car had clearly had instructions to be the "hare" with the intention of trying to break the opposition. He negotiated Arnage slightly slower than he normally would have and the second Porsche was through.

"Good, now go and break your car!"

By the end of the first lap, the second Porsche had overtaken its sister car and the Honda was a close third.

Kevin's headphones crackled. "What is ploblim Kevin? Is car okay?" Hiro sounded very concerned.

"No problem at all Hiro. The car's running like a bird. That Porsche driver is mad. He rammed me from behind. He's hoping I'll chase him and over-rev the engine. Who is taking the first stint in that car by the way – is it Werner – I thought I recognized his helmet?"

"Yes." The Japanese sounded very concerned.

"Don't worry, we can out-handle the Porsches and comfortably match their speed. I'll take the other Porsche soon and won't let Werner get too far ahead. If he carries on like this he's going to have to stop sooner for brakes and fuel."

Richardson knew the German ace all too well, having previously had to settle for second best. Today's behaviour however, bordered on desperation. The German team was obviously concerned at the Japanese cars' almost unobtrusive ability to keep pace with the favoured teams in practice. Honda's reputation for reliability was well proven.

"Okay Kevin. You have all experience." The Japanese did not sound convinced.

"Give me another lap and I'll see about taking back second place." The connection went dead.

Although Marc Cheval had initially felt that any danger posed to Kevin and his family had passed following the arrest of Kingwill, he had a change of heart on the morning of race day. They had been unable to verify the Nigerian's allegedly innocent contact man at the track. The presence of Chris Jensen and his wife, the former very much on the gang's hit list as well, had made the French Inspector decidedly uneasy. He had reassigned Jean-Pierre and Georges, and deployed an additional gendarme – Henri, to safeguard the two families for the duration of the race.

Richardson had initially been unhappy, but had quickly realized that the French Inspector had only their well-being in mind. His thoughts had briefly gone back to Ann's ordeal in Namibia and any further thoughts of protestation had evaporated.

***

By early evening, braking and other niggles had begun plaguing the Werner Porsche which had dropped back to a distant third several laps behind the leaders and was having to battle to escape the clutches of a McLaren. Kevin had led for over an hour before handing over to Hoshi Tanaka. The Japanese had risen to the challenge and had kept up with the lead Porsche until the predicted downpour had materialized.

Hiro had for several hours avoided thinking about the fact that Jerry Barker would have to share driving. The necessary stop for full rain tyres had however coincided with the required driving change.

The Japanese Team Leader had however, not bargained on the British driver's wet weather driving skills. Barker had proved more than equal to the occasion swopping the lead with the Porsche several times during the night.

Down the order, the second Honda had circulated steadily in sixth place, several laps ahead of the rest of the field.

Chapter 29
Sunday Morning

Hiro was on hand to help Kevin clamber from the car.

"Velly well done Kev, you holding Japanese flag velly high!" Beamed Hiro. Kevin hurriedly moved out of the way as an enthusiastic Hoshi Tanaka pushed past him. After a wipe of the windscreen, a rapid refuel and quick check of the brakes, the Honda pulled out into the pit lane.

"Oh it helps to have a good car that handles so well and goes like a bird... albeit a noisy one." Richardson responded. The Japanese' expression momentarily changed to quizzical. Not wanting to explain further, Kevin continued.

"The car goes beautifully." Hiro's smile returned.

The rain had stopped, the sky had cleared and a typically June Le Mans sunset had been experienced around Nine pm. The three driver's had maintained the status quo during the night, The lead Honda held a lap advantage over the number two Porsche, although spirited driving by Werner had brought that team's lead car onto the same lap as its team mate.

Kevin looked at his watch. 9.10. He looked forward to a couple of hours shut eye. As he exited the rear of the pits he met Ann, Tracey and the Jensens, the former dancing along the pathway.

"Hi dad, we're off to the big park. I'm going to ride on the big wheel!" The words tumbled out. Tracey was breathless with anticipation.

"Hold on, Trace, surely you want to know how well Dad's doing! Ann interjected.

"Sorry, Dad...are you winning?" his only slightly chastened daughter continued.

"Oh, the guys are doing just great. We're leading, but there's still nearly seven hours to go. I'm on the way to the caravan for some shut-eye." The group turned around to accompany him, their destination lying beyond the team vehicle.

"Dad, look what Uncle Jerry gave me." Tracey produced a slim metallic matt-finished cigarette case. It was obviously of high quality and pricey.

"I'll have to sort Uncle Jerry out, how dare he encourage my daughter to smoke!"

"There are no cigarettes inside, silly! Open it and have a look." Tracey's tone was accusing.

Kevin clicked open the rectangular box, simultaneously sniffing the interior. It had not been used as intended. Inside were two bundles of cigarette cards. They were face up. One had a photo of a youthful, smiling and helmeted Stirling Moss, the other depicted a sombre Juan Manuel Fangio. He knew the series which had become a collector's item.

"That was very nice of him. These are hard to get and individual cards are expensive if a collector needs to fill gaps. I'll thank him when I see him."

"Uncle Jerry said that you may have a card made with your photo on if you race for another thirty years."

"Oh, he did, did he? I'll have to make that a knockout punch instead!" Richardson's tone feigned annoyance.

"Please don't, Dad, I like him and the cards. He promised to give me some more. Will you please keep it for me so that I don't lose it when I go on the roller coaster?"

Kevin smiled. Don't worry, I like him too... sometimes." He pulled the zip of his left breast pocket and slipped the case in.

They reached the Honda Works van cum transporter and said their goodbyes. Kevin turned the handle and entered, unconsciously locking the door behind him. He chose the bottom of the three bunks closest to the door, setting the alarm clock on a built-in side pedestal before slipping off his racing shoes. Too much light streamed in through one of the overhead windows. He reached to close the blind before flopping onto the firm, narrow, but comfortable bed.

One of the crew would wake him in good time for his next stint, but he hated the idea of missing any part of his turn. The car was such a pleasure to drive. He also hated the thought of incurring Hiro's wrath.

***

The silver Porsche loomed large in his mirrors. Richardson's heart sank – he wouldn't be able to hold off the German much longer. His car was just not fast enough. He changed his usual line of approach to the looming corner. It worked, Werner had planned to out-brake him and use the Porsche's superior power to overtake once they had negotiated the hairpin. The German had to rapidly brake, changing his own intended line, allowing the South African to gain precious metres. Werner would have to wait for Mulsanne before he could launch a new challenge.

Kevin glanced in his mirrors. The German had dropped back several car lengths to rethink his strategy. Richardson took a deep breath. He had survived for another lap.

Richardson awoke with a start, taking several seconds to get his bearings. The staccato rapping at the door sounded again. He raised himself on to his elbow and turned the clock towards him. "What the... I've only been here for twenty minutes!"

He slowly sat up and took his time standing up before trudging to the door in his stockings.

He unlocked the door and angrily pulled it open.

"What the h…?" The rest of the intended sentence was cut off in surprise. At the foot of the short retractable staircase stood a well built, blond curly-haired man, wearing dark glasses. The beige slacks and pale blue open-necked shirt were expensive. A cream jacket hung loosely around his shoulders. His right hand was retracted and hidden within the coat.

"Hello *Mr* Richardson, you don't know me, but I have known very much about you for some time and of course, your photograph has appeared many times in the press lately." The accent was guttural and unmistakeably German

"On the contrary, I know exactly who you are. You are Dieter Steinmann, the head of the drug ring that has tried its best to kill me and my family, as well as the Jensens. We did nothing to you or your crooked team. Those inept arseholes drew us into your circle as innocent victims!"

Kevin's reddening face reflected his deepening rage. He took two steps down the staircase, but stopped when the German's right hand emerged from beneath the depths of the jacket and pointed a large calibre pistol at his groin. A silencer added to its menace.

"I wouldn't if I were you." The German waved the gun.

"Now turn around anti-clockwise and slowly climb three steps. Wait for me at the top and do not enter the van until I say so. I *will* shoot you – I won't make the same mistakes those fools you have spoken about have."

Richardson hesitated. Steinmann took a step towards the staircase. The racing driver started turning very slowly and deliberately. He had almost made a quarter-turn when he noticed one of the gendarmes racing towards them. The Frenchman was only twenty metres away.

Steinmann noted Kevin's hesitation and recognition of something or someone to the east. Without looking to see who or what had drawn Richardson's attention, he pulled the trigger.

Kevin felt a hammer blow to his chest. He shuddered, a look of surprise briefly appeared in his eyes. Without comprehending, his eyes closed and he slowly sank to the stairs, settling on his left side, his head awkwardly balanced on a rung

***

"Mr Richardson, Kevin, please wake up, please don't die! Why is zere no blood?" Jean-Pierre's tone was imploring.

Kevin stirred and slowly opened his eyes, struggling to focus. Where was he? Why did his neck feel so stiff? Why couldn't he breathe?

"Oh Kevin, you are alive. Are you okay? Ze doctor is on his way. The Frenchman was so relieved. He bent to help the South African into a sitting position.

"Slowly does it, I'm still trying to get my bearings. What happened?"

"Zat bastard shot you. Pointed towards a sullen Steinmann who was handcuffed to a bench several metres away.

It all came flooding back. Kevin rubbed his neck and stood up gingerly. That step was hard.

"Careful Kevin, you have been shot." Jean-Pierre came forward to help but was waved away.

Hiro, Marc Cheval and an unknown man in a light suit carrying what appeared to be a briefcase, suddenly appeared around the east side of the van. They stopped to catch their breath. They had obviously been running.

Kevin reached to rub his aching left breast, his fingers catching in a horizontal tear in the pocket of his overall. His fingertips explored and touched the hard metal beneath. Tracey's cigarette tin! He reached into the pocket and removed it. A deep elongated dent in the left side continued as a groove almost bisecting the case. "Where's the slug?" He wondered aloud.

"My good friend, I so thankful you alive!" Marc Cheval came forward and hugged Kevin. "Jean-Pierre phone to say you shot and fall down." Richardson pointed to his pocket and held up the mangled tin. Without a word he turned to face the transporter and searched the right hand side of the doorframe. He gestured towards the irregular hole halfway up the van's wall.

"Thank the Lord it hit the tin and ricocheted!"

Cheval walked towards Jean-Pierre conversing in French. Hiro was about to hug the racing driver, but the third man brushed him aside.

"Kevin, I'm Dan Girling, an official doctor appointed by the circuit's authorities. You must be in shock. Please may I examine you? I believe there are bunks inside." He moved to assist him up the stairs, but Richardson climbed them in two steps and pushed open the door which was still ajar.

"Now look, I'm fine and ready to do my next stint. I've waited and been through hell for this. No one is going to stop ..."

Girling, who had already opened the blinds, interjected.

"Now please Mr Richardson, I'm here to help you and make sure you will be okay to enter next year's race. Please unzip your overall to the waist and lie back on the bed." Kevin complied without further argument.

"Wow, that's going to turn all colours of the rainbow! Is it sore when I push here?"

Kevin craned his neck to look at his left breast. "It feels like a bruise!"

The medic removed a stethoscope from his bag and did his normal checks. "Your heartbeat is a bit irregular and your pulse is rather low."

"It's usually around the mid-fifties. Now please give me something for my headache that the authorities won't regard as likely to impair my senses resulting in my and the team's disqualification."

"Look Kevin, after that blow to the chest and taking into account that you were unconscious, you need to rest."

"Ask Jean-Pierre, I was only out for a couple of seconds!"

A worried looking Hiro put his head around the door.

"Kevin, you okay? Other two drivers can finish race – we in second place."

"Over my dead body!" He looked at his watch. "You go and keep them on their toes. I'll be there in two hours." The Japanese beamed and disappeared. He lay back and closed his eyes ignoring Girling.

The exasperated doctor shook his head. "I'm not committing to anything Kevin. I'll have some medication sent here shortly and I'll see you in an hour-and-a-half. Don't go back to the pits before I've seen you. Believe me, I *will* give you a red card if I'm not happy. Now please try to get some sleep!"

"Thanks Doc." He closed his eyes and emitted a snore, a wide grin playing around the corners of his mouth.

Girling wanted to slam the door. Changing his mind at the last moment, he could not stop the heavy thud that echoed in the van.

Chapter 30
Sunday Afternoon

Before the start of the race there had been a loose agreement between Hiro and the drivers that each would do a two hour stint and rest for four. The Team Manager however, reserved the right to swop drivers according to circumstances and dependent upon how the car was placed and performing at a particular stage of the race. Rain during Saturday had resulted in Jerry Barker enjoying an extended stint as he revelled in the conditions.

All parties had agreed that Kevin as the lead driver was likely to do most of the driving, and in particular, when there was time to be made up. He was also scheduled to drive for the last two hours.

As a result of his unfortunate experience Kevin was reluctantly allowed by the track doctor to perform a one hour stint from 12.00 to 13.00 before having to come in for evaluation. If deemed fit, he would drive the last two hours to Four pm.

During his extended and enforced break, much had happened to change the leader board. The second Works Porsche had hit a spinning backmarker resulting in a long pit stop for repairs, which had dropped it to fourth, just ahead of the second Japanese-crewed Honda. Werner in the lead Porsche had made up ground and lay third, two laps adrift of the lead Honda driven by Hoshi. The surprise package had however, been the McLaren which had taken a thirty second lead through sheer reliability.

Kevin had managed to reclaim the lead, but the unscheduled premature stop at the end of the one hour stint allowed him, had let the British car sneak back into first place. Jerry Barker had driven for the next hour, managing to hold on to the McLaren which could not match the pace of the Japanese car on the straights.

The two teams' cars final stops coincided and Richardson left the pits on the lead McLaren's tail. The British machine piloted by their number one driver – Ken Barton, was surprisingly rapid down the straights. Not having been behind the driver/car combination before, he decided to play a waiting game and tailed Barton for two laps, trying to memorise his approach and exit lines through several corners he believed had the most potential for an overtaking manoeuvre.

"What is wrong with car, Kevin?" A concerned Hiro cut into his thoughts. "Why you not overtake?"

"Nothing is wrong with the car Hiro..., Barton is a good driver and the McLaren seems to have found some extra pace. I'll have a go this lap."

"Please do it Kevin!" An annoyed Hiro terminated the conversation.

Richardson pulled off a successful pass during the next lap which was followed by a long congratulatory monologue from Hiro. Kevin came close to terminating the call, but thought better of upsetting the Japanese Team Manager. Once behind, the McLaren driver either lost his spirit, or his car went off song, allowing the Honda to steadily pull ahead, the second placed car continuing to lose several seconds a lap.

Driving well within the car's potential, Richardson's Honda held a one minute and forty second advantage over the McLaren with an hour to go. Werner in the Porsche lay third, just over a lap adrift, with the second Japanese-crewed Honda still fourth, a further lap behind.

Kevin made his final stop for fuel, tyres and a routine brake pad check. Barton in the McLaren followed just as the Honda was leaving the pit lane. The British team had clearly realized that there was no point in trying to make up time by delaying their stop, as they could not match the Honda's pace.

The status quo remained for another twenty minutes when Kevin's headphones suddenly crackled. "McLaren in pit with flat tyre, Werner now second. Please you go faster!" The tremor in Hiro voice relayed his concern. The Japanese was well aware of the German driver's reputation for either breaking his car or reeling in the leaders.

"Don't worry Hiro, my car is going smoothly and I can reduce lap times by a couple of seconds if necessary. Where is Werner?"

"He one lap and eight seconds behind you. Last lap he five seconds faster than you, so you see him in your mirror soon."

"Thanks Hiro. Don't worry... a lap is a lot to make up in forty odd minutes!"

Kevin had noted the distant silver car in his mirrors on the previous lap, but had thought that the second Works Porsche car he had overtaken several laps before had "got a second wind" and was possibly attempting to improve its overall position in the top ten placings. He speeded up.

During the course of the next lap, Richardson saw the silver Porsche more frequently and not only on the straights. As they entered Mulsanne, Werner's car was suddenly all over the back end of the Honda. The Honda's speed down the straight was marginally faster than the Porsche, but under braking Werner appeared suicidal, almost punting the Honda off the circuit at Mulsanne Corner. Kevin managed to hold onto the lead as the Porsche driver ran wide, but by Indianapolis Corner it was the same story. To protect his car, Richardson changed his line and Werner was through. The Porsche disappeared towards Arnage.

Seconds later a huge cloud of dust ahead suggested that a car had left the circuit. Kevin slowed as he entered the corner as visibility through the billowing cloud was poor. The brief silhouette gave no clue as to the identity of the car which appeared to have hit the Armco. He radioed Hiro describing the incident. The Japanese undertook to revert as soon as he could.

Richardson put his foot down. There was no sign of Werner up ahead.

He passed the pits. A board held by one of the Honda pit crew indicated that he was in the lead. There was no indication as to the race number of, or the gap to the second placed car. His headphones crackled a minute later. "You right Kevin, Werner Porsche go off at Arnage with flat tyre, but he going again – very slowly to pits. You will see him this lap."

"Thanks Hiro! Who's second?"

"McLaren just over one lap behind. Japanese Honda next!" He was elated.

A lap later, Kevin passed the German as he limped off the circuit towards the pits. He smiled. "Well that's one lap he'll battle to make up!" he thought looking at his watch."Fifteen minutes to go – two laps after this one."

With a lap and a half to go Richardson was halfway along Mulsanne straight. A hundred metres ahead a Porsche 911 backmarker suddenly braked, swerved and left the circuit after an impact with the car ahead. Kevin braked heavily to crawling speed. A bright red Porsche had run into the back of another slower contender for the G T category.

The stricken cars had ended up on opposite sides of the circuit. The front of the Honda suddenly slewed to the left, but Kevin caught it before it spun and stopped on the shoulder. "Shit, I've hit their debris." He radioed Hoshi, hastily explaining his predicament to the shattered Japanese.

Richardson pulled back on to the track and limped the stricken car towards the finish, keeping off the racing line so as not to impede the rest of the field. The Japanese driven number two car overtook to reduce its deficit by a lap. Not long after, the McLaren roared past, placing itself on the same lap as his car. Kevin looked at his watch. "Five minutes to go." Once the McLaren passed the "Start/Finish" line, Barton would be on his last lap and the same lap! He had to get there first!

He accelerated, but the unhappy car snaked dangerously across the track. He looked in his mirrors. Fortunately nobody had been close enough to have a heart attack!

Kevin called Hoshi. "Where's the McLaren?"

"He pass here sometime ago. Where are you?"

"I'm approaching Ford Chicane, I'll be there soon!"

He glanced at his mirrors as he exited the last curve before the finish line. His heart sank. A gunmetal hued car loomed large and then was past in a flash. He didn't have time to hope it wasn't the McLaren. Kevin crawled the car to his pit, refusing to get out for several minutes as he pondered what might have been. Eventually Jerry Barker dragged him out.

"Not to worry, my mate, it wasn't your fault. We'll come back next year and run rings around them. At least our number two car came third and that Werner arsehole won't be on the podium!"

Chapter 31
London

After a ten day break in France, Ann, Tracey and the Jensen's had flown back home.

Kevin and Jerry had attended a debriefing at the Honda racing factory in London where the Japanese principals had been effusive in their praise for the drivers, mechanics, engineers and management team. Failure to win at their first attempt had been due to sheer bad luck. They had assured all that they would contest the entire World Sports Car Championship and Le Mans the following year.

As preparation, Kevin and Jerry would be entered in several sports car events in Europe and the US later that year where an upgraded engine would be tested. Kevin's input was required in several key areas including improved aerodynamics, suspension and handling so his regular commuting between Johannesburg and London would continue.

Interpol had used the opportunity of Richardson's presence in the city to discuss the forthcoming trial of Steinmann and the other heads of the drug ring. A date was still to be set and Kevin and Chris would be required to testify during the initial stages.

Kevin had resisted the temptation to visit the coachbuilders involved in restoring the Aston again, as several key parts were still awaited and the car was not yet ready for collection. He consoled himself with the thought that he would be visiting the UK again in the very near future.

* * *

His tasks completed, Kevin could not wait to get back home to his family in time for the forthcoming weekend. Jerry had driven him to Heathrow and they had ordered a cup of coffee in one of the lounges while they waited for Kevin's flight to be called. Richardson studied the genial, slightly overweight character across the table.

They had shared so many trials and tribulations as team mates and had grown very close in recent years. He patted the top pocket of his shirt and smiled, his fingers automatically searching for and finding the cigarette case that had warmed from the heat of his body. The groove was however, no longer there!

Tracey had surprisingly forgotten the cards for several days, but in response to her eventual enquiry, Kevin had indicated that they had been packed away and would be returned to her back home. Jerry had come to his rescue with a brand new identical spare box he had retained from the 1980s when he had been a sales representative for an upmarket cigarette company and been driven around in a chauffeured Rolls Royce.

He opened his lips to speak, but swiftly bit his tongue. Any further mention of the case would no doubt result in a gloating Jerry reminding him that he owed him his life and he would never hear the end of it!

Richardson had boarded the plane which had taxied to a runway out of sight of the terminal. Jerry was on the way to his car when he heard a plane take off. Almost immediately a sharp cracking sound split the heavens. He spun around. A bright orange/red glow momentarily lit up the sky, almost immediately being followed by a pall of black smoke.

"That plane has lost an engine!" He exclaimed to no one in particular before setting off at a run for the terminal.

The End